# Three Cold Dishes

## By
## William R Brakes

I have published four sets of short-stories, all of which are available from Amazon as paperbacks or ebooks:

fragments: naked and bright
connections: ragged and precious
catalysts: whispered and strange
wabi-sabi

'Three Cold Dishes' is the first novel I have published (although not the first I have written).

I am always eager to receive the comments of readers, especially if there is something about my work which you'd like to criticise.
email: [bill140347@btinternet.com](mailto:bill140347@btinternet.com)

**November 2023**

# Three Cold Dishes

**A novel about revenge**

# -1-

Afterwards, Richard goes into the ensuite bathroom and I hear the sound of the shower. I picture him naked, eyes closed, face lifted into the spray, long grey hair hanging down his back, his lean body impressively fit for a man of his age. A cock that's not so impressive, but then again, I don't have that many to compare it with.

I take a deep breath, close my eyes. He deserves what's coming, that's for sure. He's a gold-star bastard. I always knew about his past, what he'd done all those years ago, but I've tried to keep an open mind, given him a chance to show that he'd changed. After all, people do change, people grow up; and anyway, he may have had an explanation for his behaviour as a teenager, some excuse that showed it wasn't as bad as I thought. Not likely, but possible. I've given up on that now: he's beyond all redemption. In fact, if there were some sort of record for the number of negative attributes a man could have, Richard would be in line to break it. Sexist, misogynist and chauvinist for starters. Then there's racist and homophobe. He's not a paedophile (as far as I know), because I'm over the age of consent, but come on! He's old enough to be my ... Yes, really! And all the others ... who knows how old they were?

So have I made it clear? I don't like the guy: he's a nasty specimen, a geriatric wanker.

And he was rubbish in bed, despite all that bragging about his sexual prowess. Once he was convinced of my compliance, his love-making became perfunctory at best. I may not have much experience, but even I know the difference between giving and taking: I know what constitutes egocentric sex and how objectionable it is to be on the receiving end.

The truth is, he hasn't changed, he's just got older. He's still the same self-obsessed prat I imagine he must have been forty odd years ago, only now he can't hide behind the excuse of youth.

I get out of bed and extract the knife from my bag. I take another deep breath. My pulse rate has increased, hands are a little moist, the adrenalin's pumping. But I'm in control. I'm doing what is right, this is what I've prepared for. The bastard's days are numbered.

I've done my homework, I know the best access point, the best angle, the correct pressure for maximum effect. For deadly effect. I've checked the bathroom and know he'll have his back to the door. It's easy. I can do this.

Yes, it's true, there's a one-in-three chance that Richard is my grandfather. But so what? It makes no difference. All rapists deserve to die.

# -2-

The first time my mother died, I was still young, ten or eleven. They let me sleep in a bed at the hospital, in the room next to hers. I remember the warmth and comfort of that bed. I hadn't slept in a bed very often, so it was a treat. Mostly, Mum and I used to share a sleeping bag on cold cardboard in the meagre shelter of shop doorways. There was that one time when Dad found us. He told me to call him Joe but I knew he had once been my father. He took us to a hotel and I remember how wonderful that was: a soft, pink bedroom, full of warmth and fluffiness; pretty little jars of soap and shampoo, all smooth and sweet-smelling; bacon and beans and orange juice for breakfast. But the next day Joe disappeared and Mum said we couldn't stay in the hotel, we had to go back to the street.

We were beggars, Mum and me, I suppose that's what you'd call us, although I never heard her use that word. When there was enough money in the bowl, we bought food, usually hamburgers and warm drinks. One time we had cash left over and Mum bought me a book. It was called *The Wind in the Willows.* I read it many times. Mum kept it in the suitcase, with the other things.

I knew Mum was ill when she kept coughing and her body was hot to the touch although she kept shivering and complaining of feeling cold; and there was blood on her hanky. That went on for several days until a man in a yellow jacket – I think he was a street sweeper – said he would call an ambulance.

They told me Mum had caught 'flu and it had turned into pneumonia. When she died, they gave me her suitcase.

Then I was taken to live with Jack and Mary. I had a bed in their house, although it wasn't as soft as the hospital bed or the hotel bed. Still, it was softer than the pavement. They said I had to go to school. They took me, even though I didn't have the proper uniform.

Later they found me reading my book, sitting in the doorway of *Waterstones* in town. I had walked out of school because the girls there weren't very nice. Jack made me go back and I walked out again. This happened many times.

Then I was taken to live with some other people, I don't remember their names, but their house was noisy and smelt of fish. There were other children living there, all sorts of ages, but what they had in common was that none of them liked me and I didn't like them.

I was moved again, to another house, another bed. Then soon afterwards, moved again. I don't remember how many times and I don't remember the different names. There were lots. Usually, they were nice people to begin with, but their niceness never lasted long. In some cases, they made me cry and enjoyed doing that. Some of them made me go to school, but I could never stay there. The nasty girls at school always complained that I hurt them.

When I was thirteen, I went to live with Mum and Dad. That's what they told me to call them. Their real names were Frank and Celia Jackson. They said they knew I'd been shifted from pillar to post, but that was stopping now, I would live with them forever. They were kind to me most of the time and I was pleased for that; I liked their big house and I liked the big bed I got to sleep in. I lived with them until I was seventeen. I think of my time with them as the start of my proper life. The first start.

They didn't make me go to school, but I had lessons with Mrs Archer, who came every day apart from weekends. We did lots of English (which I loved) and Maths (which I hated) and History which was sometimes okay and sometimes not. Mum taught me French and Music and Chess. I don't remember any lessons in Geography or Science or Art. We certainly didn't do any Sport, apart from an hour or so at the swimming baths each week. I was okay with that, because the one thing I'd liked about school was when we had races and I always won; knowing I was fast, Mum let me run round the park on my own so long as it wasn't too dark.

When I wasn't in lessons with Mrs Archer and wasn't out running, I mostly sat on my bed and read. Mum gave me lots of books, some new and some from the library. Mum said if I got better at French, she'd buy me some French novels which she said were even better than English ones. But she never did.

When I wasn't reading, I played with the things in my old mum's suitcase. That case was like a toy box, a treasure chest.

# -3-

When I was living with my new mum and dad (which is how I thought of them), I spent a lot of time with my old mum's suitcase, and became very familiar with the contents. These were:

- In an envelope, several documents, including an out-of-date passport, a driving licence (I never even knew old Mum could drive), birth certificates, a marriage certificate, Mum's GCSE certificate.
- Letters to Mum from Joe (my old dad) before they were married. Not many but I read them so often I knew them by heart.
- Clothes. A few fancy clothes I couldn't ever have imagined Mum wearing, such as frilly underwear, stockings, hot pants.
- A transparent bag with a few baby items: a tag from when I was born, three small teeth, a lock of hair.
- Grandma's diary.
- A medal from a dancing competition, with no date on it.

- A toothbrush, a nail-file, a comb.
- Other miscellaneous items: a spoon, a watch (with a clock-face dial) which didn't work, a ring, a golf ball, an old pair of glasses, well-worn ballet shoes, an afro wig.
- £1240 in £20 notes.
- A few photos – me as a baby, Mum and Joe on their wedding day, other people I didn't recognise.
- My book, *The Wind in the Willows* by Kenneth Grahame.

The first time I found the money, I couldn't believe it. To think that Mum had all that money hoarded away and we were begging on the street. My first thought was to go out and spend it, to buy lots of clothes and make-up and jewellery. Then I thought maybe Mum's plan of saving it wasn't such a bad plan. Presumably, she was making sure we had something to fall back on if a real emergency arose, and although her getting ill and then dying could be said to have been a real emergency, I'd survived; I was okay. I'd been looked after, given food to eat and beds to sleep in, so couldn't really complain, even if I didn't like the ones who hurt me, or the ones who made me go to school. Now, with my new mum and dad, I had it made. They were well off, I could tell by the posh things in the house, by the huge number of channels on the TV, and how they always said 'yes' when I asked for anything. They were both white, but didn't seem to mind that I was brown, in fact hardly ever mentioned it. So I didn't need to spend that money. I could save it. So that's what I did, saved it, put it back in the suitcase and counted it often to make sure it was all still there.

Before she died, old Mum had told me about the most important item in the case, and it wasn't the money, which she didn't mention at all. She said Grandma's diary was precious. She said I must keep it safe. She said I should read it carefully and then when I was older, I should read it again and I'd understand it better. It would tell me who I was. That's what old Mum said.

I didn't really get it. I already knew who I was. I was the daughter of Mum and Joe. Because Joe was black, my skin was browner than most of the other children who lived near us. (At that time I didn't know there were other places where this wasn't so.) Some of the children at school laughed at me for that, joked about my suntan, called me names. What else was there to know about who I was?

I was the brown girl who read and the brown girl who ran in the park and the brown girl who played with her treasure chest. I didn't have any friends, but that was okay, what did I need friends for? My new mum and dad tried to get me to mix with girls my own age and arranged for the children of their friends, or 'cousins' as they called them, to call round. I tried to be polite but they were not very nice girls and most of them only came once.

As I got older, it was Grandma's diary that became my favourite object in the suitcase. It contained important information. That's what my old mum had told me and I began to see what she meant.

# -4-

I never knew my grandmother, she died before I was born. But she'd lived for nearly forty years, so you'd think maybe she had thirty years or so of writing diaries. If so, she threw most of them away, because in the suitcase there was only one diary and even that wasn't full. It was for the year 1966. The entries ended in August.

At the front, Grandma had drawn a colourful picture with flowers and rainbows and suns and stars. She'd made an intricate pattern around the words DIANE (her name) and DIARY, using the fact that they started with the same three letters. It was clever. It was a young person's diary. I worked out she was about fifteen or sixteen when she wrote it.

Most of what she wrote was either about pop music or school, about singers and bands who I'd never heard of (apart from *The Beatles*), about boys she fancied and girls who were nasty to her. Her comments were often mixed with stars and exclamation marks and several underlinings. I suppose that was what they used instead of emojis in those days.

The entry for August 6th was the last one. It was headed PARTY in thick capital letters and five different colours, surrounded by stars and balloons and hearts. Her entry for that day spread over the next four pages, but it didn't make much sense when I first read it. I think she was writing in some sort of code, probably to protect the meaning from prying eyes.

At the end of the entry there were three names written in capital letters:

        RICHARD WRIGHT
        STEPHEN GREENE
        GRAHAME DEFREITAS.

As I got older, I re-read Grandma's diary many times and it gradually made more sense. I realised this was the night when she lost her virginity. I remember the day when that occurred to me, because on the same day I spotted that the rest of the diary wasn't entirely empty. There was an entry in October, with one word. Again in capitals, but no colours: 'PREGNANT', followed by several exclamation marks. Soon after that I connected Mum's birthday (April 22nd) and her age, with Grandma's diary. Then I knew it was at that party, on the 6th of August 1966, that my mother had been conceived.

# -5-

The second time my mother died I was seventeen. Rewriting Oscar Wilde to suit my situation: "To lose one mother might be seen as misfortune, to lose two is downright carelessness". Yes, my new mother died, along with my new father. It was a road traffic accident. Apparently, they drove round a bend to be confronted by a large truck hurtling towards them on the wrong side of the road. They both died instantly (so I was told).

That signalled the second start of my proper life.

A lot of visitors came to call after the Jacksons died. Police, of course, and a reporter from the local newspaper. Then various neighbours and friends and family connected to the Jacksons. They all wanted to check that I was okay.

Why wouldn't I be? I was fine. It wasn't me who'd been in a car crash.

There was a solicitor who told me about the will. After that, he arranged everything, starting with the funeral. I told him to, and said he could send me the bill. I had my eighteenth birthday on the day of the funeral.

The end result was that I owned a house, a large house. The Jacksons had no children of their own, so left everything to me, their one adopted child. That included all their savings, apart from some small amounts given to various charities. What was left was a considerable sum of money. I was rich.

The first thing I did was to take out my old mum's £1240 from the case and give it to charity. I found one that claimed to look after homeless people, an appropriate choice, I thought. A month or so after that I withdrew several thousand pounds from my account and put it away in old Mum's case: I realised I needed the comfort of having cash in the house; it must have been something in the genes.

That year I had taken my A levels in English and History and had recently got the results back – a 'B' grade in both, which was what I needed to go to my first choice of university. But now there seemed no point. I didn't need a career – at least not for several years – I could live comfortably on my inheritance. There was another reason I didn't want to go to uni. When I read about being a student, it seemed to involve lots of fake friendships, getting drunk with people, pretending to like them. That sort of life didn't appeal to me. I knew I'd enjoy the studying – English Literature was going to be my course – but I could still read while staying at home. Avoiding all that phoney socialising seemed a good idea. I was happier on my own.

So I stayed at home, in the house the Jacksons had bequeathed to me.

Although I'd lived at the Jackson's house for five years, now they were no longer there it felt different. Now it was mine, all of it. I could go into rooms I had rarely been into before, such as their bedroom, or Frank's study. I had sole use of the kitchen. I could also come and go as I pleased. The Jacksons hadn't been strict, but they had done the parent thing – they expected me to tell them where I was going when I went out and what time I'd be coming back. Because of that, I hadn't gone out very often.

But I was still a teenager and what was the point of life if you couldn't enjoy it, have fun, try new experiences? Perhaps socialising didn't have to be phoney. It was like being let off the leash, I suppose. I was eager to do the things I hadn't been allowed to, wanted to spread my wings. I went to bars and restaurants. To clubs. To gigs and concerts and festivals. I sampled lots of different drinks, tried various pills, got to recognise the difference between real and fake. I enjoyed meeting boys, some of them were even quite fun and I could handle those who weren't. I avoided getting into any boyfriend/girlfriend type of relationship. I didn't want that, couldn't see the point: why would I want any commitment that stretched beyond the present? I'd read enough stories about independent women whose lives had been ruined by falling into a subservient role with some man. I enjoyed sex, but wasn't keen on the emotional baggage that too often was associated with it. Sex was a pleasure and that was the beginning and end of it as far as I was concerned. From the books I'd read I thought it was girls who were supposed to be the romantic gender, but I found that some boys could be far worse. There were even some who cried real tears when I told them (after sex) that I wasn't interested in anything else. I enjoyed that, seeing them cry and hearing them beg: it made me feel alive, even more than the sex itself, alive and powerful. But all in all, that period eventually confirmed what I'd suspected from the start – that was not the life for me. Staying home and reading was preferable, so, after my six months or so of wild living, that was what I mostly did.

Stayed home.

Read. Literature, good literature, also had the power to make me feel alive.

On the few occasions when I felt the desire to get out of the house, I went to cinemas or museums or art galleries. On my own.

I learned to drive and bought a second-hand car. I could have afforded a new car, but that seemed too flash. My four-year-old, white Ford Focus suited me fine. I didn't use it much.

But in case I caught the travelling bug, I got myself a passport. That wasn't easy. As well as the problem everyone has with getting a photograph accepted, I had more hassle than most because of my lack of a simple narrative around my name, my background, my address. Eventually, after many false starts, I was deemed a legitimate citizen, honest enough to be worthy of a passport. I took a trip to the Canary Islands to celebrate and enjoyed some brief respite from the English winter.

Becoming more settled in my life, having calmed down, I relished luxuriating in the Jackson's big bath – now, my bath – or lazing in front of the wall-mounted TV, or working my way through their wine cellar. And reading. I continued to read avidly. The Jacksons' bookshelves were mostly filled with old-fashioned crime novels intermixed with Victorian classics. When I tired of them, I ordered modern books through *Amazon*, buying e-books which could be read anywhere – in bed, in the bath, in the garden – but also paperbacks and hardbacks: physical books continued to hold a fascination for me.

The garden was getting overgrown. I tried a bit of weeding and pruning and cutting of the grass – the Jackson's had bequeathed me a well-equipped tool-shed. But it all seemed like a tiresome waste of time, a holding back of an inevitable tide. Pointless. So I hired a gardener, on the recommendation of a neighbour. Felix, although that may not have been his real name: I didn't question him too closely.

It was nearly a year after the Jacksons had died, (I usually thought of them as 'The Jacksons' now, rather than new Mum and Dad), a few months after I had rejected the wild life-style, that I found the letter.

## -6-

I had kept the house virtually intact, just as the Jackson's had left it, in the year or so since their joint funeral. It still had all the old furniture: why change what doesn't need changing? But my plans for the future, such as they were, included the idea that at some point I would resume my studies – perhaps I would enrol for an Open University degree? If I did, I'd need a place to work, so I set about re-organising Frank's study, emptying the filing cabinets, clearing the drawers, throwing out assorted debris. Someone from his work had come just after he'd died and taken what were presumably all the important things. What was left was mostly scraps and doodles. That's when I found it: an envelope with my name on. I assumed the Jacksons were waiting to give it to me when I was older.

They thought I was a child, still too young. They were wrong, I was plenty old enough.

The letter was from my old mother. She wrote it when she knew she was dying. It was a long letter, so maybe she'd begun it earlier. The first couple of pages were about how much she loved me and how sorry she was that she hadn't given me a better childhood. Blah, blah, blah. Then there was a lot more boring guff about how she'd loved Joe and had been sure he'd be a good husband and father, but that he'd let her down, let us both down. That he wasn't the man she thought he was, and then there was more about how sorry she was, as if that counted for anything. The interesting part was about her mother, my grandmother.

Grandma's short life had, according to my mother, been dominated by heroin addiction. It had all stemmed from that party in 1966. I'd been right, that was the night when Mum had been conceived. When they found out she was pregnant, Grandma's parents had wanted nothing to do with her, told her she'd brought shame on the family, so she had to leave home and find somewhere else to live at the tender age of sixteen. That shook me. I mean, we're not talking Victorian times here, this was the nineteen sixties. I thought by then society was beginning to grow up, but (apparently) not universally so, not in the provincial town where Grandma lived. Fortunately, the older sister of a friend of Grandma's shared a flat with two others and they took her in. That group of girls helped her through the pregnancy and birth, and she carried on living with them as a single mother, the four young women sharing the care of the child. But they also got her into drugs, and before long she was hooked on heroin. By the time the baby was a toddler, Grandma had turned to prostitution to fund her habit, and that became the pattern of her life. My mum's account skipped over her own experience as a young child, growing up in that household, with the confusion of having four drug-obsessed 'mothers'. She, my mother, moved out of there as soon as she could, as soon as she had a viable alternative. The letter wasn't precise, but she must have been about seventeen years old when she met Joe and they were married soon after. My grandmother died of an overdose in 1987, aged just thirty-seven.

Even this wasn't the most interesting part of Mum's letter. For that, she returned to the 1966 party and the three men Grandma named in her diary. The ones in capital letters: Richard, Stephen and Grahame. According to Mum, any of them could have been the one who made Grandma pregnant, any one of them could have been my mother's father, my grandfather, she never knew which one, had no way of knowing. Apparently, my mother was the spitting image of *her* mother, so there were no give-away signs, such as big ears or curly hair. There was one more fact she revealed about that party, and it was the most significant fact of all: the sex had not been consensual; that night, all three of those men, in turn, had raped my grandmother.

What amazed me was Mum's description of her mother's sense of guilt. She, Grandma, was the victim – three times over – yet still she felt guilty. At the time, she never told anyone she'd been raped, because she felt so ashamed. Her daughter, my mother, was the only one she ever told, and that was, according to my mother, during what was her last, brief 'clean' period, twenty years after the rapes.

Those were different times, of course, even though we were already into what was supposed to be a sexual revolution. From what I've read, I know it was a very one-sided (i.e. male-sided) sort of revolution. In those days, it was nearly always the girl who was said to be to blame if she was raped – she dressed provocatively, she led men on, she was 'asking for it'. I looked back at Grandma's diary. She liked wearing clothes that she described as 'with it' – I guess that meant fashionable. When she left home to go to school, she turned the top of her skirt over several times, to bring the length above the knees. At school she and her friends seemed to have a running battle with teachers who tried to get them to wind their skirts back down. To the party, Grandma had worn a short, pleated skirt, and she loved the way it flared up as she spun around when dancing.  And she wore a tight t-shirt, with no bra underneath. She must have looked quite something, a typical sixties 'bird'. (Grandma's diary taught me a lot of slang from that era!). Very sexy. But that doesn't excuse them doing what they did. It wouldn't be a valid excuse now and it wasn't a valid excuse then. It's all simply wrong, wrong, wrong. Rape is a crime. Never mind what was thought acceptable, or at least excusable, at the time. On that night, there was a victim and three criminals. The victim deserved justice. The criminals should have been made to pay for their crime.

They all got away with it.

## -7-

I enjoyed living in what I still thought of as the Jackson's house. Who wouldn't? With enough money to not have to think about earning a living, I could indulge myself with books and wine, spend hours downloading classic heavy-metal tracks and playing them good and loud, watch old movies on TV. From time to time, I dipped into Grandma's diary and old Mum's letter, focusing on the rapes and those three men Grandma had named. I tried to imagine what it must have been like for Grandma, both at the time and the weeks and months afterwards. When she found she was pregnant. I thought a lot about crime and punishment. Scenes unravelled in my head as though I was living in a novel. Imagined scenes.

I began to enjoy cooking for myself – I bought an 'Eating for One' cookbook and despite a few disasters soon became quite good at it. Any night I didn't fancy cooking, I'd happily go out to a restaurant. I didn't mind eating alone, despite the strange looks I got and the occasional inappropriate comment from waiters. I always took a book with me.

I was entirely self-sufficient. I was content. Life was grand.

For a while.

The need for something more from my life was slow to surface. My plan to study had flickered briefly, but ultimately felt too much of a commitment and I wasn't sure I'd be able to stick at it. In its place, I had nothing. I lacked direction, and that grew into a nagging worry. I found that however enjoyable a way of life might be, it can still become tedious if it lacks progression. I needed a project, a purpose. Something to challenge me and something I could succeed at, but it had to be something worthy, something to hold my attention and reward that attention.

I thought some more about Grandma, about crime and punishment, about my imagined scenarios.

I read again Grandma's account of the 1966 party. She had been cautious in her language, wrote nothing explicit, but now I knew what I knew I could read between the lines. It had been an appalling episode in that young girl's life, and I'm sure the memory haunted her until her death twenty years later.

My scheme began as no more than a shadow of an idea. As a new year gradually unrolled, eighteen months after the funeral, eighteen months into my life alone in the Jackson's house, the idea took shape and in time coalesced into a plan. Three men. Three rapists. Three criminals. Those men had evaded justice. And – assuming they were still alive – those men continued to evade justice over forty years later. That was long enough. It was about time the gang rape of my grandmother was avenged.

My initial thought was to simply give the names to the police, tell them what had happened, with Grandma's diary and Mum's letter as evidence, and let the law take its course. There have been plenty of investigations and prosecutions arising from what they call 'historical abuse', the law finally coming down on the perpetrators of sex-crimes of the past. But I had doubts. Maybe it was only celebrities who were properly investigated – ageing pop singers and DJs, men who would generate extensive press coverage, whose arrest would provide kudos for the constabulary, support the public's faith in the long arm of the law. Would the police pursue crimes as vigorously when the alleged victims were nonentities? I was not convinced they would. Why would they be bothered with my grandmother, a woman who ended up as a drug addict and a prostitute? Would they care that she had been raped three times on one night over forty years ago?

I am not a fan of the police. That comes from living on the street. I have strong memories of how some of them took great delight in repeatedly telling us to 'move along', perfectly well aware that we had nowhere to go, merely enjoying causing us aggravation when we were doing nobody any harm. One particular PC was always searching Mum for drugs, not that he ever found any. Didn't stop him. Wasn't averse to checking me out too, young as I was. An excuse for a quick feel. No, I'm not a fan of the cops.

So I was reluctant to go to the police. Anyway, did I really need to go down that route? There are other forms of revenge, ones that don't need the involvement of official processes. The guilt of those men was beyond doubt. No investigation was necessary. Skip the trial and the verdict, why not move straight on to carrying out the sentences?

Those men should be punished. What would their punishment be and how would it be imposed? That could wait. I would first enjoy the process. I had a project. I'd find these men. I'd hold them to account. Then I'd decide how to punish them. I felt a buzz run through my body as I imagined the scene, imagined confronting them. Just a small matter to come first: I needed to find them.

# -8-

Richard Wright was the easiest to track down. He had a *Facebook* page. Yes, of course there were many users with that name, which confused matters. A former guitarist with *Pink Floyd* who had died recently was the most notable one, and briefly I wondered if he could be my target, but no, the age and background didn't match. In fact, identifying the real Richard Wright, the one I was after, was not as hard as I feared. He was the only one who was the right age and the school he'd attended was the Boys' High School, the counterpart to the Girls' High that Diane named in her diary. Increasingly, I thought of her as Diane rather than Grandma. I'd never known her in person, so had no memory of her as a grandmother. I knew her mostly through her diary, the diary of a sixteen-year-old girl called Diane.

From his image, Richard looked like an ageing hippy. He had long grey hair tied in a ponytail, he had studs in his ears and nose, a heavy chain around his neck, with a locket resting on a hairy chest. He was not ugly, but his face was weather-beaten and crinkly, as though he'd spent too many years in the sun.

His leisure interests included swimming, paddle-boarding and kite-surfing: I was getting the picture. Many of the photos on his page showed scenes of beach and water. I guessed he lived by the sea, and the locations mentioned in his postings narrowed it down further. I soon worked out that he lived in the county of Norfolk in East Anglia and the references to trips to Kings Lynn suggested the north-west of that county. I noticed that another of his interests was running: I filed that away as a potentially useful connection. Locating him had to be the priority. My first instinct was to private message him on *Facebook*, but I couldn't think of any way to explain why I wanted to contact him. I couldn't reveal who I really was, that would make him too defensive. No, I had to be less direct, subtler.

He was a runner. How keen was he?

I booked into a caravan on a site in Hunstanton. I was sure he lived either in Hunstanton itself or in a nearby village.

Like many places around the country, Hunstanton has a *Parkrun* every Saturday morning. Before leaving home, I'd registered with *Parkrun* under an assumed name, and downloaded the necessary barcode. The first Saturday I was in Hunstanton, I put on my track-suit and running shoes and jogged down to the race start outside the Boat

Club, enjoying the crisp but sunny March morning. These events, at various locations all over the country, are all the same, and yet each has its distinctive characteristics. This was the first one I'd been to that provided such a scenic view: we'd be running alongside The Wash. Also, the ground underfoot would be the concrete of the promenade rather than the grass I was more used to: I wasn't sure I'd like that. As people gathered, I could tell this event was on the small side, barely a hundred runners. So much the better for spotting a sixtyish man with long grey hair. How many could there be?

    The race director gave us the usual spiel: she invited visitors to make themselves known (I kept quiet); advised about controlling dogs and children; described the course – up and back twice, couldn't be much simpler. There was the usual small bunch of youngsters in running vests, looking like serious athletes and jostling together at the front. There was a similarly familiar-looking group of less athletic, elderly walkers, who steered themselves to the back. I took a place around the middle and settled into a gentle pace, not aiming for a time. I kept looking out for my target, among runners near me, and those we passed coming the other way, further ahead or lagging behind. I finished in a modest twenty-five minutes or so. I hadn't seen anyone who looked like my Richard Wright: I was disappointed.

When I got back to the caravan, I took off my glasses and afro wig, showered and dressed, and waited for my phone to 'ping' with the results from the run.

A little later, I felt like punching the air. Yes, there was a Richard Wright listed in the results. So he *had* been there. How had I not spotted him? His finishing time was over thirty-one minutes, so he'd been behind me all the way. Still, I was surprised I hadn't seen him. I'd waited around at the finish, hadn't left until the tail-walker had passed the finish line. Never mind. I was getting closer, and there was always next week.

# -9-

I spent the week exploring the town. Not that I needed the whole week, there not being much to discover in Hunstanton: a few specialist shops, lots of cafés, take-aways and charity outlets, a modest library. I sampled a couple of the pubs, found them to be less smart than I was expecting, with rather tired décor and customers to match. The beer was okay. I took a regular morning jog along the promenade in that chill-but-warm mixture that comes with an English spring. There was a fairground which was closed for the off-season. I relished the sea air: a refreshing improvement on the exhaust-soaked atmosphere of the city.

The next Saturday there was a strong north-easterly wind, apparently not unusual for this part of the country. I started the run at the back of the pack, among the push-chairs and dog walkers. I gradually moved up the field, trying to pace myself at a gentle six-minutes-and-bits-per-kilometre. I finished in thirty-two minutes, scarcely out of breath, but still hadn't spotted Richard. Perhaps he'd given this week a miss, put off by the wind.

But no, back in the caravan I checked the results on my phone. He had completed the run and finished just two places ahead of me. Yet somehow, I'd missed him again. *How?*

The third week I finally saw him. Despite again finishing in what appeared to be Richard's normal time, I first saw no sign of him and felt exasperation bubbling to the surface. Then a tallish man walking away from the finish took off his red bobble hat and shook out a mane of long silver-grey hair. *Stupid!* I'd been so focused on the hair that I never thought he might wear a hat! Never mind. Now, I'd finally seen Richard Wright in the flesh: there was no mistaking that hair.

He was close enough to talk to. 'Nearly had you there,' I called out.

His head turned sharply, 'Some of us oldies have still got it.'

'Yeah,' I said. 'Well run.'

He walked away and I stood for a while, clapping in some of the later finishers. When Richard was nearly out of sight, I followed him. I expected him to be heading for one of the car parks, but in fact he climbed the slope up to the cliff top. By the time I got there, there was no sign and I thought I'd lost him. All I could see were a couple of dog walkers. Then I spotted him crossing the coast road and heading into a residential area. I ran across, and again saw the black shirt and grey hair as he turned into a side road. Two houses in, he opened a gate and walked up a path. I ducked out of sight in case he looked back. Another step completed: now I knew where Richard Wright lived.

I grabbed a tuna sandwich from the corner café on the way back, and sat in the caravan planning my next steps. This had been a good day, although it was only the start. I needed to get closer to him. If I was too direct it would look suspicious, he'd smell a rat, so I needed to be careful. Ideally, I needed him to think he was taking the lead.

It would help move things forward if I could find out his habits, his daily routine, find places where I might be able to get him to notice me and indulge in some innocent chat.

The area where he lived was quiet and peaceful, so as I wandered those streets over the next few days, waiting to catch sight of him while trying to remain inconspicuous, I rarely saw anyone. It didn't stop me being cautious. Anyone I did see would probably remember me: Hunstanton's not overflowing with people of a brown complexion. Still, walking was safer than driving – I didn't want my car connected with this part of town. I proceeded with care. Even so, it didn't take me long to find out a few useful pieces of information: he usually went out for a morning run at around 8.30; his shopping trips into town often ended up at *Costa* in the high street; and he was a regular visitor to the library.

It was on the Thursday that I managed to time my run on the prom correctly and spotted the red bobble hat ahead, passing the blue-roofed ski café. I soon caught up with him and ran alongside.

'Hello again,' I said.

He turned to look at me, but showed no sign of recognition.

'At the *Parkrun*?'

'Right,' he said, and then added: 'Nice morning for it.'

'Sure is. Are you going far?'

'Heacham.'

'Too far for me. This is my turning point. Here, at the grey house. Have a good one.'

As I turned and started running back, he called out after me: 'See you Saturday. Summer root.'

I waved over my shoulder, with no idea what he meant.

I wondered if I'd misheard. Perhaps he'd said 'Summer Fruit'? That could be some traditional Norfolk greeting? But no, what he'd actually said was 'Summer *route*,' as I realised come Saturday. The race director explained that during the summer months, the prom gets too busy and too congested with the clutter of kiosks, so they use a different course. This time, we ran up a zig-zag slope to the cliff top, then along to the lighthouse. Two full laps on the grass and one shorter, before returning to the prom. Same distance, of course, five kilometres.

I easily spotted Richard, now I knew it was a red bobble hat I needed to look out for, but I deliberately ran a few places behind him, and kept my head down when we turned, avoiding eye contact. I suppose I was 'playing hard to get' if you want to give a name to the strategy.

When I crossed the finish line, he was still there, doing some stretching but that may have been an excuse. I hoped it was an excuse.

'Beat you again,' he said. 'You should try running faster.'

'Ho, ho,' I said, making a show of breathing heavily. 'That start was a killer. I never really got going after that.'

'Excuses, excuses. At your age you should be slaughtering me. Include some hill runs in your training. Build up those thigh muscles.'

Had he given undue emphasis to the word 'thigh'? 'Right,' I said. 'Thanks.'

Our first proper conversation. It didn't matter how inane the exchange had been, contact had been established. I wanted to tell him I could take ten minutes off my time if I could be bothered to try. That would wipe the smile off his face. But I wanted to keep up the pretence that I was of a similar standard to him, it connected us. Him a worn-out oldie, me a struggling beginner.

## -10-

I was enjoying living in a caravan. It was several steps down from the luxury, the space and the soft furnishings of home, but it had all I needed, and its compactness had its own charm. The cooker needed a little persuading in order to grant its cooperation; there were some hazardous nails on the patio as I discovered when I wandered out barefooted; and the Wi-Fi was unreliable. The first morning, being awakened by elephants in hobnailed boots galloping across the roof had been a bit of a shock. Now I knew they were simply seagulls: who knew they could be so heavy-footed? A few hitches, but overall fine. Having a purpose, my project as I thought of it, may have contributed to my sense of well-being. It was good to have a focus.

I needed more information about Richard Wright. I checked his *Facebook* page again. I found a link to a website, his website. It looked professionally produced, slick and stylish. It was proclaiming Richard Wright as an 'upcoming author'. There was a picture of him that made him look younger and more serious. The central message was an invitation to 'watch this space' for exciting news, coming soon. There were icons for links to other sections, including background, interests, book-signings, but they were all inactive. I was guessing the site was under construction.

But it had been useful: I now had an idea for how I could get closer to my target. I metaphorically rubbed my hands.

The next time I spoke to Richard was in the library, a few days later. I'd watched him go in and decided to give him fifteen minutes to get settled so as to make my arrival seem less planned. It was another cool and windy day, a jeans, jumper and jacket day: my summer clothes remained in the wardrobe. I wandered across to what they call The Green, admiring the view down to the pier, such as it was: it's the only pier I know that doesn't actually jut out into the sea! There were a few other hardy wanderers around, dog-walkers, elderly couples out shopping. After a suitable interval, including a moment of panic as the wind nearly got under the wig, I walked back to the library and went in. I saw Richard sitting behind a table, facing into the room, turning the pages of a sturdy tome, probably an encyclopaedia. He seemed to be taking notes.

I ignored him and shuffled along the fiction aisle.

'The coaching manuals are over by the wall.'

I turned and gave him a look.

'Just a suggestion. You could pick up some training tips.'

'You're okay,' I said and went back to my pretence of scanning the romance section. A few minutes later, I stepped across to his table. 'That looks like serious stuff.'

'Research,' he said. 'Getting details right, it's so important.'

'What's wrong with the internet?'

'That's you youngsters all over. Any question, simply Google the answer. It must be right, my phone says so. Well, let me tell you darling, it's not to be trusted. Fake news abounds.' He closed the fat volume and patted the cover. 'For reliability, go to the oracle.'

I wasn't happy about that 'darling', and I would normally have walked away at that point, but now I had a way in and didn't want to waste it. 'So what are you researching so diligently? Something to do with your work?'

'Background. For my next novel.'

'You're a writer?'

'Yup.'

'Gosh. I've never met an author before. Have I heard of you? Should I ask for your autograph?' I thought I simpered rather well.

He stood up and reached his hand across the table. 'Richard Wright. You won't have heard of me. Not yet. My first novel is coming out in September. After that, autographs cost two hundred quid.'

I shook his hand. 'How do you do? Emma. Emma Woodhouse. Autographs free.' I smiled in what I hoped was an endearing way.

I didn't prolong the conversation: whet their appetite and leave them wanting more, a sound strategy. The book I'd randomly chosen I passed through the check-out machine – I'd registered the previous day as a temporary member – and left him to his research.

For the next few days, I made sure I took my training runs away from the promenade and the cliff-top, so as to avoid any chance of bumping into him. I gave the next two *Parkruns* a miss, although I checked the results and was pleased to see the name of Richard Wright among the finishers, indeed with a pb to his name.

I was hoping his curiosity might have been aroused, that having seen me about the place a few times, he'd now be aware I'd gone missing. Might make him more conducive to a closer relationship.

So it was about a fortnight after the library meeting that I spoke to Richard again. It was cold and rainy, more like October than May, and I'd seen him enter *Costa* and sit at a table near the window. I waited a few minutes and then went in myself, deliberately not looking in his direction, but making quite a performance of closing my umbrella and giving it a good shake.

'Emma,' he called as I stood at the counter.

I turned towards him. 'Oh, hi. Raymond, isn't it?'

'Richard.'

'Right.'

'Yes, Wright.' I looked blank. 'Richard Wright. My name,'

I gave him my brightest smile. 'Oh yes. I remember.'

He invited me to join him and I carried my skinny latte and piece of carrot cake to his table.

'Not seen you for a while. You missed the *Parkrun*.' Was he relying on not having seen me or had he checked the results? I hoped it was the latter.

'I've been a bit under the weather.'

'Sorry to hear that. Hope you're recovered now. You're looking as fine as ever.'

I puffed my cheeks. 'No-one's looking great in this weather.'

'Apart from you, the fragrant Emma.'

I was pleased he was making these feeble attempts to flirt with me, but I tried to steer the conversation into a more appropriate format for two strangers from different generations finding out things about each other. Slowly, slowly.

I adopted the persona of a shy and nervous young girl. 'I like it here,' I said. 'Good coffee, good cake.'

I asked him how long he'd lived in Hunstanton. He said ten years or so, and went on to tell me miscellaneous facts about his Hunstanton life, his days on the water, his running, the places he liked to eat, friends he drank with.

He told me he lived in a small semi behind the coast road, up on the cliff. I said I'd never been up that way. Sometimes, lying feels so natural.

'I'm guessing, Emma, that you've not lived in Hunstanton long.'

I shook my head. 'No, not at all. I'm just visiting.'

He raised his eyebrows. 'A bit early for the tourist season. Not much chance of topping up your tan.' He gestured to the window. It was still pouring.

'No, not a tourist either.'

'A woman of mystery,' he said. 'Intriguing. I need to see if I can get the truth out of you. Would you like another coffee? Doesn't look like the rain's stopping any time soon.'

We had more drinks. I let him prise 'the truth' out of me.

'The truth is. I feel a bit foolish saying this. Especially seeing as you're ... You know.'

'Come on, Emma. Out with it. You've got me on tenterhooks.'

'I want to be a writer.'

'So you thought you'd visit Norfolk to get advice from that famous writer Richard Wright.'

'Oh no. I never even knew ...'

'Okay, darling,' he said, and patted my knee. 'Just kidding.'

I hope I blushed, but it's hard to do that on demand. I smiled weakly. 'Part of the action of my novel.' I grinned inanely. 'Takes place at a seaside resort. So I thought I'd come here to get a feel for what it's like.'

'Good plan, Emma. Like I told you the other day, getting details right is the most important thing. One slip and some reader will pounce on it with glee, and hammer you mercilessly.'

I wondered how he knew that, since he hadn't yet had a book in the public domain. But I thanked him and before long I left, claiming I needed to get some shopping and was willing to take my chances with the spring showers.

That evening I had my first taste of Hunstanton fish and chips, giving in to the pull of tradition, even though it's not my favourite meal. The fish was tasty enough – caught locally, I guessed – but the chips were limp and greasy. I decided I wouldn't be repeating the experiment. I opened a can of lager and settled down for some serious reading, but found it hard to concentrate. For once, reality in the shape of project-Richard-Wright was winning out over fiction. I mulled over the possible continuations of our relationship, then opted for an early night. As I lay awake, I counted the unpleasant characteristics I'd observed in that man: there were many.

# -11-

The next morning, woken too early by the now-predictable stampede on the roof, my first task was to get rid of the debris from last night's dinner: the caravan smelt like a chip shop, the air heavy with cheap vinegar.

After breakfast, I decided the key to determining my next steps was to appraise my progress so far. Not exactly rocket science. I thought about Richard Wright. I looked back at Diane's diary, which I'd brought with me. There was a boy she referred to as 'R'. He seemed to be the class nerd, and he came in for a fair amount of ridicule, including from Diane herself. Somehow this didn't seem to fit with Richard Wright. Can a person change that much? There were lots of words I'd use to describe him, but 'nerd' wasn't one of them. No, I was fairly sure that wasn't Richard. On the other hand, there was a boy termed 'DW' that seemed a better fit. Could the 'D' of DW stand for Dick or Dickie? The phrases 'full of himself' and 'thinks he's God's gift' seemed much more appropriate, much more likely precursors to the personality of the Richard I'd met.

Diane wasn't much given to physical descriptions, but she referred to DW's thick, dark wavy hair and his sparkling blue eyes. The eyes had gone the same way as the hair. I would describe them now as grey-green rather than blue, and decidedly non-sparkly.

Was I being too hasty in ascribing the adjective 'unpleasant' to this twenty-first century Richard? Were there redeeming features? He was an old man, and that led to some inevitable consequences in terms of attitudes and behaviour. He liked the sound of his own voice. Perhaps that was also inevitable, him being a writer. He was definitely old-fashioned. I'd not seen him use a mobile phone. Perhaps he didn't even own one; now, that *would* be old-fashioned.

I needed to get to know him better. Forty-five years ago, he'd been a rapist. He was still a rapist, the passage of years made no difference to that, it's not an attribute that can be discarded along with last season's coat. But had he evolved at all? Had he repented? Those were important questions; at least, some might think so, although I was less sure. Anyway, was there any regret, any remorse? Repentance wouldn't help Diane any, but it would maybe help me, help me come to a decision as to what to do next.

There was a loud rap at the door. On a caravan site, visitors are rare – there is no post, no deliveries, and neighbours are transient strangers, barely nodded to, easily forgotten and not likely to come calling. After the initial surprise of the knock, I decided it must be a member of the site-staff, with some administrative information they needed to impart.

Fortunately, I sneaked a look through the crack in the curtains before opening the door: it was Richard. I hastily put on the wig and glasses and then half-opened the door.

'Richard.' I hoped I sounded surprised.

'Good morning, Emma.'

'This is a surprise. Not sure I'm ready to receive visitors.' I clasped the neck of my housecoat.

Richard was in his familiar black running gear and his red bobble hat. 'I was running past. Saw you put the rubbish out. Thought you might like to join me.'

'Nice thought. But sorry, not this morning. You know.' I placed my hand on my stomach. 'Women's problems.'

He held up a hand. 'Too much information. Say no more.' He turned away. 'Hope you're better by Saturday,' he called over his shoulder as he jogged off.

Success! No way had he been simply 'running past'. He'd taken the trouble to seek me out (goodness only knows how), then chosen to lie about it. So it seemed I had made an impression on him. And he believed he was doing the chasing. If it hadn't been for the age difference, I might have actually enjoyed the moves in this game, this dance of romance. I was enjoying it anyway, but not for the romantic element: he was very old.

When I got to the *Parkrun* start on the following Saturday, Richard was already there, warming up.

'Looking good,' he said. Was that me or the weather? 'The wind seems to have dropped.' Probably the weather, then. *Shame!*

'Thank goodness. I hate the wind.' I lifted each knee in turn to my chest, jogged on the spot, circled my arms.

'Shall we run together?' he suggested.

'Okay.' Now that he was hooked, or rather now that he thought he'd hooked me, I felt more relaxed. I could have some fun.

By the time we reached the top of the slope, he was breathing heavily. 'This feels good,' I said. 'I think I'm getting the hang of it.'

He didn't have the breath to answer.

I kept up a rattle of frivolous chat as we ran across the cliff-top, commenting on the other runners around us, on the improved weather, relaying information on time and distance from the tracker on my phone. He responded with nothing more than the odd grunt. We were running at a faster pace than his usual and as we passed the lighthouse for the second time, I could tell he was flagging. I accelerated through the final kilometre, and by the time I was back at the Boat Club, he was way behind, still languishing on top of the cliff.

A couple of minutes later, he stumbled across the finish line, well-flushed and exhausted. I waited while he recovered. Eventually he had enough breath, although he was still red in the face: 'Where the hell did that pace come from?'

I shrugged. 'I added some hill sessions to my training.' I patted my thigh.

'Funny.' He bent over, hands on his knees. 'I'm whacked.'

'Poor old thing.'

He wandered around the finish area, sipping at a water bottle, eventually recovering his more normal complexion.

'Right,' I said. 'Now I can see you won't be needing CPR, I'm off,' and I turned away to head for home.

'Hang on,' he said. 'What are your plans for later?'

I turned back, raised my eyebrows, said nothing.

'Only. If you wanted to join me for a drink. We could talk about your writing.'

'Are you sure? I mean, I wouldn't want to … you know … take advantage.'

'It would be my pleasure. And sharing a drink with a pretty girl will do my reputation no harm at all.'

I smiled.

'So. *The Waterside*? Around twelvish?'

# -12-

It turns out that writing fiction is not as easy as you might think. In the couple of hours I had at the caravan before meeting Richard, I decided I should make a start on my supposed 'novel'. I managed to come up with one germ of an idea and then wrote a paragraph and a half expanding that theme. Reading it back, I realised it made little sense: in a word, it was rubbish. So I'd have to wing it. I found a white, roll-neck jumper in the wardrobe and threw that on with chocolate-brown slacks – that would do. I headed for the pub.

As its name suggests, *The Waterside* is a pub on Hunstanton front, looking out across The Wash. I walked through the narrow door into the main bar, pinching my eyes to adjust to the dim interior. I spotted Richard at the bar, his grey hair tied in a ponytail, his pale blue shirt open at the neck, his dark jeans hugging his sturdy legs. He had a pint glass in front of him, already half-empty. 'What are you drinking?' he asked.

I opted for a dry white wine and we took our drinks beyond the gloom, out into the bright, sunlit conservatory. Richard was obviously well-known here. He'd been joking with the barman when I walked in, and as we passed through the bar he waved to various other customers, several of whom gave me a good stare. One came up to him and whispered in his ear. They shared a laugh.

We went out onto the small veranda which had views of the promenade, the beach and the calm sea beyond, and although it was busy, we managed to find a vacant table. There was some genuine warmth in the sun.

'Good choice,' I said, indicating the view.

'Not been here before?'

'No. First time. May not be my last.'

'Cheers,' he said, holding his beer towards me. We chinked glasses.

'So how goes the novel?'

'Oh, early days,' I replied, getting ready to waffle. 'You know.'

'Sure do. And early days can last an awfully long time.'

I smiled and shrugged. I hoped he wouldn't grill me too closely.

'Fill me in on the outline. What you have so far.'

*Oh dear*! I couldn't remember what I'd written earlier, so spouted words off the top of my head. There was one event that came easily to mind. 'So.' I took a deep breath. 'There's a party. Back in the day. A group of youngsters, teenagers. All quite drunk. It gets late, it's dark, and some of them decide to go down to the beach.'

'Is this how the novel starts?'

'Oh, probably not. I was thinking I'd maybe need some early chapters about who these kids are, a bit of background on each, the relationships between them. You know.'

'Don't.'

I raised my eyebrows.

'No preamble. Start with the party. Or even start with the group running down to the beach in the moonlight. Starting with action is good. Starting with description is bad. You can always fill in details later, as needed, use conversation between the characters to tell the reader who they are.'

He took a healthy gulp of his drink. I sipped the wine. 'Tasty,' I said. 'Another good choice.' Probably he'd let the barman choose: it was no more than palatable.

'What about character?' he asked. 'Who's your main protagonist?'

'Diane,' I said, without thinking. 'A young girl.'

He frowned. 'Old-fashioned name. You might want to change that. What's she like?'

'Er ... Young. Female. That's about all I've got so far.'

'Character is so important. It's what draws the reader in, so concentrate on getting it right. What I do –

for my main characters and sometimes also for the minor ones – I draw up a fact sheet, a sort of profile. The obvious physical characteristics – hair colour, size, shape, etc – but also personality. What makes them laugh? What are they afraid of? What's their greatest ambition? Things like that. I can give you a list.' He took another swig of his beer. 'That provides you with a framework, it informs how your character reacts to whatever's going on in your story. In fact, I find the process of constructing the profile is valuable in its own right and once it's done, I feel I understand my character. And once you know your characters, they come alive through your writing, so your readers readily connect with them. The battle's half won.'

'Wow. This is so helpful. Thank you, Richard, so much.' I drained my glass.

'Another?'

'It's my turn.' I reached for my bag.

'Nonsense. My invite, my treat.'

I'd normally have held my ground, insisted on paying my whack, but I could tell that in his mind Richard still inhabited an era in which the dominance of the male, as leader, as provider, was a given. Not disturbing this pre-historic view seemed wise, strategically. 'Okay,' I said. 'A small one.'

He returned with another pint for himself, another large glass of wine for me and a packet of dry-roasted peanuts, which he ripped open and scattered onto the table.

A tall, middle-aged man with a beard stood up from a nearby table and sauntered towards us. He slapped Richard on the shoulder. 'Thought I heard your dulcet tones, Dicky. Are you going out this afternoon? The forecast says the wind will pick up later.'

'Hi Mick. This is Emma.'

'Hello Emma,' said Mick, grinning. 'Nice one Dicky. Perhaps you'll be too busy.'

'I'll catch you later.'

'That was Mick,' he said, rather unnecessarily, as the beard returned to his table. 'One of the kitesurfing crowd.'

'Okay,' I said, nodding. 'I've seen them out there. Looks impressive.'

'Have you ever given it a go?'

'A bit too energetic for me. And cold and wet, surely. I mean, you need the wind and then …'

'Wet suit. That's the secret. Keeps everything well wrapped up. But it is pretty tough on the arms.' He held his fists out, displaying some impressive muscles.

'Rather you than me.'

The intervention of Mick had disrupted Richard's seminar, and the conversation veered away from writing. He asked me about my home-life, my childhood, jobs, boyfriends. I was non-committal, and when I couldn't get away with stalling, I merely lied. The last thing I wanted was him getting to know the real me. That was not what this was about. I needed to get him talking about himself.

'So have you always been a writer?'

'Like I told you, first novel out in four months' time. New to the game.'

'But unpublished stories? Writing for fun? Making up things for your kids? Authors always seem to say they've spent their lives telling stories.'

'No children. That's the first error in your little fantasy. Oh, I suppose I wrote at school, donkeys' years ago. Won a few prizes. But mostly back then it was drumming I was into. After that, it was painting.'

'Gosh. Painting? Drumming? It sounds like you've had an exciting life.'

I hoped that would spur him into revealing more, seeing as talking about himself was something he clearly enjoyed. But rather than the painting and the drumming, it was his writing he concentrated on. How he'd started, where he got his ideas from, how he approached the editing process. I asked him if he'd ever suffered from writers' block. 'There's no such thing, writer's block. Pure invention.'

'Really?'

'Yup. A writer can always write. No reason not to. It may not be any good, mind you, but you can always do it, get words on the page. And afterwards you have something to work with, something you can shape into something better.'

'Fascinating.' I grabbed a handful of nuts.

'You must let me read what you've written,' he said.

'Oh, no,' I said. 'Well, not yet. It's not fit for human consumption.'

'Be brave. Stick your head above the parapet. Let people criticise you. It's the only way to learn.'

'Right. But I'd like to, you know, tidy it up a bit first. Like I said, early days.'

'And like *I* said, early days can last a long time if you let them.' He drained the last of his drink. 'I think, young Emma, I'm going to make you my project. I'm going to drag you, kicking and screaming, from embryo to fully-fledged writer.'

'Gosh. You're being so kind. Not sure what I've done to deserve it.'

'Being young and pretty helps.'

I smiled and finished my drink.

'I've been meaning to congratulate you,' he continued, after a pause. 'Your run this morning. Most impressive. My legs are still stiff as boards.' He rubbed them.

I shrugged.

'Shouldn't have been surprised. Must be in the genes.'

'How do you mean?'

'You know. Usain Bolt. Linford Christie. Natural speed.'

'Don't forget Mo Farrah.'

'Right. All those Ethiopians, Kenyans. As well as the Jamaicans.'

'That wouldn't be a tiny bit racist, would it?'

'No, no.' He waved his hand, emphasising. 'Don't get me wrong. I haven't got a racist bone in my body. Back in the day, I used to mix with all sorts in the music business. Blacks, Asians, queers, Irish. All the same to me. But you have to admit. You know. The data can't be wrong. And like you saying you're not into water sports. That's another thing. Blacks can't swim, can they? Well known.'

# -13-

Back in the caravan, I sat on the sofa and closed my eyes, took some deep breaths. I was proud of myself. I hadn't thrown anything at him, I hadn't yelled abuse at him, I hadn't even stormed out of the bar, at least, not in a way that anyone had noticed. I consider myself to be a tolerant person, but the most difficult thing to be tolerant of is the intolerance of others. Richard's blatant racism and sexism, made worse by his being unaware of his own bigotry, was hugely insulting. But I don't believe he noticed that I'd felt insulted. That's what I was proud of. I swallowed my instinctive reaction, smiled sweetly, and changed the subject. There were a couple of dogs on the beach, barking and spoiling for a fight, while their inept owners pulled on leashes and pleaded ineffectively. I pointed out this scenario to Richard and we watched it play out, laughed at the antics of the dogs and their owners, especially when the smaller dog, a poodle I believe, was picked up by its owner and marched off the beach to safety.

I went to the ladies, and when I got back told Richard I had to leave, I'd had a message on my phone about some domestic emergency in the caravan that needed my attention. No, it was nothing he could help with. Someone from the maintenance team was coming to fix it.

In fact, all that needed fixing in my caravan were two fried eggs, to accompany a beans-on-toast lunch, but I couldn't have stayed in his presence any longer. I opened a bottle of wine. The two glasses at the pub needed supplementing.

Well, I'd got my wish, at least partially. I now knew Richard Wright somewhat better. One thing I knew for sure: he was never going to be my favourite person. I was able to come up with excuses for him, the generation he came from and all that. But really there was no excuse. He was not a pleasant man, locked as he was into a world-view from a bygone era. But that still wasn't enough. I still needed to know about his past, to build a picture of who he really was and who he'd been in the past. How deep did this unpleasantness run? What I really needed was to get him to talk about the party, to hear his side of the story, as it were. I wasn't sure whether he'd reacted to my using the name Diane. Especially in the context of a party and a night-time beach escapade, even if it was purporting to be fiction, perhaps it had rung bells with him. He had no reason to connect me to that time, clearly way before I was born. So even if he remembered the party and Diane's part in it, he might have thought my use of the name was no more than a coincidence.

Yes, I had to find out more.

Did that mean I had to put up with more of his bigotry? If so, then so be it. I'd heard worse. What I had never done is heard worse and done nothing about it, let it roll over me as though it didn't matter. Swallowing the bile was the hardest thing.

Although I'd left the pub in a rush, Richard had managed to slip a card into my bag as I walked past him. 'Send me something,' he'd said, 'whatever you've got.'

I studied the card. I was guessing that, like his website, it was produced by his publisher: it had that similar professional feel. His name was in large fancy writing, with 'TIME ON MY SIDE' underneath. I presumed that was the title of his novel. The only other thing on the card was an email address. No phone number, I noticed: perhaps he really didn't own a mobile.

Sending him some pages masquerading as the beginning of a novel seemed the best way to keep the contact going. He would be able to continue his pretence that his interest in me was to help me as a writer, while it was in fact *my* project that was proceeding nicely. Of course, I could see him regularly at the Saturday *Parkruns*, but they didn't afford much opportunity for conversation.

No, I needed a more private meeting. The writing connection was the key.

A few days later, I wrote Richard an email, with an attachment. The wind must have been in the right direction, because it sent almost immediately.

> *It's not much, and I know it's not great. But it's a start. I look forward to getting your feedback. Don't spare my feelings!*
> 
> *Emma*

When I described it as 'not great', I wasn't being modest. I knew I'd never make a writer. I'd taken the party scenario and developed it a bit, adding in plenty of drinking and dancing and a bit of flirting. No names, apart from Diane. No mention of any rape, although the possibility of sex occurring was hinted at.

Within an hour, Richard had replied.

> *Thanks Emma. There's a lot to talk about. Why not come over for dinner? R x*

# -14-

'You found me.' Richard opened the door almost before the bell had finished ringing. He had on the same jeans as at the pub, now topped with a white, open-necked shirt, not tucked in; his hair was still in a ponytail; he was barefooted.

I held out the carrier. 'Six Buds, as promised.' I'd first offered to bring wine, but he'd insisted that beer was more appropriate.

'I knew you were my sort of girl.'

I followed him along the hall, into a living area. There were other doors – what looked like the kitchen at the far end, before that a bathroom, I guessed, and perhaps a study. The house felt bigger than it looked from outside. 'Something smells good,' I said. You have to say it. He'd offered to cook a curry and that's what it smelt like, nothing special.

'Hope it tastes as good as it smells,' he said. 'Settle yourself down. I'll put the rice on.'

The large room had a dining table at one end, already laid with mats and cutlery. But it was the rest of the room that grabbed my attention. I've been in a few homes occupied by single men. The ones that aren't pigsties are generally minimalist, with bare surfaces and a large wall-mounted TV as the focus of attention. If there are photos, they're of football teams with cups, or maybe a family party. Richard's room had photos galore, hanging on walls, crammed against each other on the sideboard and mantelpiece, filling up what would otherwise have been four rather bare bookshelves.

I checked out the books first. I spotted a couple of Alistair Macleans, at least one Le Carré, others of similar ilk: nothing that appealed to me.

The photos were an intriguing mix, but no celebrating football teams and no grinning families. There were plenty with Richard himself taking centre stage, posing with a surfboard or action shots of him paddle-boarding, kitesurfing, other water-based frolicking. I'd seen many similar photos on his *Facebook* page. Then there was a different sort, when he was younger, playing drums, sitting behind drums, or posing with others, presumably members of a band. They all had beards, long, straggly hair and mouths contorted into snarls; they were dressed in leather and chains, with plentiful conspicuous tattoos

But the most interesting, and the most numerous of the photos, were black-and-white pictures of women. Young women. Young, naked women. Naked women in provocative poses. If you were being generous, you'd call it erotica, but a better description would be pornography. It was the youthfulness of the faces that struck me, the poses exhibiting a strange combination of youthful naivety and knowing lust. I know there are some men who like that mixture. Presumably Richard was one of them.

He came back from the kitchen clutching two opened bottles of Bud and gave one to me. 'Cheers,' he said. We chinked bottles. 'Look at you,' he said, spreading his arms and standing back as though admiring the scenery. 'A few steps up from the running gear.'

After much internal debate, I'd plumped for a knee-length, sleeveless denim dress, button-through. I'm not one for make-up but thought a little eyeliner and some pale lipstick might be appropriate. 'What do you mean? I'll have you know my tracksuit is the height of fashion.'

'But it's not so successful at revealing your shapely curves.'

I sipped the beer, cringing inside. 'I've been admiring your collection of photos. Interesting.'

'Do you like them? Quite distinctive, I feel, they give the place a special vibe. When pals come round, they always provoke interest.'

'And when women come?'

He looked at me, trying to figure me out, I guess. 'Yes. They like them too.'

'What does your wife think?'

By now, we were sitting opposite each other, on the two sofas. Had he been standing up, I think he'd have staggered back: that was certainly what the look on his face conveyed. He soon recovered. 'What makes you think I'm married?'

'One: your status on *Facebook*; two: a light untanned band around the ring finger of your left hand; three: a letter on the hall-stand addressed to Mrs Wright.'

He held up his hands in surrender. 'Guilty as charged, Monsieur Poirot. Except Lisa left last year and I haven't seen her since. Haven't bothered to update my status yet. But we're well separated, and soon to be divorced, so we're free to do our own thing, go our own ways.'

# -15-

I sipped the beer. My eyes drifted back to the photos. I could sense Richard watching me, perhaps trying to judge the effect of his announcement, about his marriage, about his separation. I tried to keep my features passive, to not give anything away.

I wanted to ask about the women in the photos, but decided to bide my time on that, wait for a more suitable moment. 'What was the band called? Should I have heard of you? Were you successful?'

'Lots of questions. We had several names. 'Pink Fluffy Unicorn' was one. That was supposed to be ironic, but not sure anyone got it. 'Death Wish' was another, that worked better. But you might have heard of 'Twisted Barbed Wire,' TBW as they called us. Our single made the top hundred.'

I shook my head. 'Not really my scene. I'm guessing heavy metal. And when you say 'top hundred' I presume that means ninety-something. Like, not top fifty.'

'Okay, it's easy to scoff. It's a tough business.'

I smiled. 'Just kidding. In fact, I'm impressed. Top hundred. Wow.'

'Don't go over the top. So, I suppose you'd be more into boy bands? One Direction? Or is it Justin Bieber?'

I pulled a face.

'Ed Sheeran?'

'Better, but I'm not that into any pop. Prefer classical.' I knew I was safe in my lie. Richard was not going to be an expert on classical music. 'Piano concertos are my particular favourite. You know, Beethoven, Rachmaninov, that sort of thing.'

'Interesting.' The blank look on his face confirmed my suspicion.

A buzzer sounded from the kitchen. 'Grub's up. Hope you're hungry.'

# -16-

I presumed the dinner was supposed to be some sort of chicken korma, although if I'd cooked it myself it would have been creamier and spicier and there would have been more nuts and raisins. His version was distinctly bland, relying, I presumed, on supermarket curry sauce for most of its flavouring. 'Tastes good,' I said.

Richard's mind was still wandering about in the past, back when he was a pop star. He had a string of stories, most of them rude, some mildly amusing, tales of wacky antics, boys at play. It sounded like a well-practised routine and I guessed I was far from the first to hear it. When he told tales involving famous people (which he did a lot), I had to be careful not to react to the names of the rock band legends. I was safe with Ozzy Osbourne - everyone's heard of him - but I claimed not to have heard of Robert Plant, Ian Paice or John Bonham. Apparently TBW had been warm-up act to some famous bands, back in the day.

'It was a great time. Met some wonderful people. Saw plenty of action.'

'How do you mean?'

'Action. You know.'

'You mean sex.'

'Yup, sex.'

I munched on a piece of chicken. It could have done with another ten minutes or so. I wondered how to frame my next question. 'So, you're talking about casual sex with fans. Groupies? Didn't they tend to be very young, in those days?'

'We had all sorts. They came for the big names, you see, but because we'd shared the stage with them, that brought us into the frame. Stardust by association. There was plenty to go round.' He saw I was still waiting for some response to my implied question. 'We never asked for birth certificates, if that's what you mean. They were plenty old enough.'

'Aren't you worried? There have been those cases where men have been prosecuted years later. Women have claimed they were abused when they were young, underage, and the culprits have been convicted, labelled paedophiles. Rapists.' I watched him as I said the word but there was no reaction.

'Oh, don't get me started on all that nonsense.' He waved his fork in the air. 'Yes, okay, I guess Jimmy Savile probably crossed the line. But most everyone else was just having fun. You had to be there. The idea that the girls were blushing virgins, taken advantage of by rich popstars, that's so much crap. It was the girls taking advantage of us, if anything. They'd try anything to get backstage, to get into changing rooms. If there were bouncers on the doors, the girls knew exactly what sort of persuasion to employ, which buttons to press, access guaranteed. They weren't after autographs, you know. And it was way before the selfie generation. Notches on their bedposts, that's what they wanted. And okay, we played along. Who wouldn't? Everyone had fun. No-one got hurt.'

He had more tales to tell and as he told them I nodded and smiled in all the right places and tried not to let my judgment show.

I mopped up the last bit of sauce with some naan bread. 'Well, that was very tasty. Congratulations on your culinary skills. I hope your wife appreciated it. Your former wife.'

'Glad it met with your approval. Now, I'm not much of a one for desserts, so it's cheesecake or ice cream.'

'Cheesecake sounds fine.'

We finished our third beer as we gave the cheesecake a bit longer to defrost. My eyes wandered again to the walls and the photos of naked women. I stared at one in particular. Then I realised. This was not a photo of a woman, but the photo of a painting of a woman. And the same was surely true of the others. I checked with Richard.

'Yup,' he said. 'All my own work. Once I'd finished the paintings, I took photos. Gave one to the model and kept one for myself.'

'And what happened to the originals? The paintings themselves?'

'What do you think? I sold them, of course. That was the point.'

'How did you get hold of the models? And persuade them to pose like that?'

'Now, now, Miss Woodhouse. I'm beginning to see your game.'

I raised my eyebrows.

'Keep turning the conversation onto me, my pop career, my painting. We're supposed to be talking about you. Your writing.'

'You've seen right through me.' I wiped my mouth on the serviette. 'Yes, trying to put off the evil moment.'

# -17-

I poured cream on the cheesecake. Tesco's finest, I was guessing. It tasted okay. 'I'll leave you in peace while you eat,' he said. 'But the verdict's on its way.'

Once we'd finished dessert, Richard pointed to the sofa. 'Take a comfy seat, Miss Woodhouse. I'll fetch us some post-prandial Glenfiddich. Okay for you?'

'Sounds fine.' I sat down. The girls in the photos – and mostly the models *were* girls, not yet women – continued to fascinate me. I wondered how many of them Richard had slept with?

He brought our drinks and sat down opposite me.

'Right. Stand well clear, Miss Woodhouse, here it comes. First off, your spelling is atrocious and your grammar not much better.

'I used the spell-check.'

'Why doesn't that surprise me? Your generation.' He gave some sort of snort. 'The computer says *yes*, but what you don't get is that the computer may be mistaken. Those devices are blunt instruments, far from infallible. You need to take control of your technical skill, not rely solely on the machine. Do you read?'

'Hardly at all,' I lied. 'Magazine articles, you know.'

'Not enough. Get stuck into some good quality literature. That way you'll begin to develop a better feel for words, for sentences, how the written medium works. And your spelling will improve.'

'But the story?'

'If. And it really is a big if. If one can ignore the clumsiness of the prose, I *suppose* there is the beginnings of a tale there.'

'You know, when I said don't spare my feelings ...' I gave a weak smile and took a sip of the whisky.

'Well, there's no point in sugar-coating. You need to face the truth. Having said that, there is some promise. It's all a bit slow. Needs sharpening. Presumably this Diane is going to choose one of her suitors. So far, she's virtually offered herself to each of them in turn. One thing I didn't get. There's no indication of a date for this party, no year, not even a decade. When is it supposed to be happening?'

'Well, I hadn't really thought.'

'You need to. It matters, Miss Woodhouse. Character, location and period. All crucial.'

'I suppose, middle of last century, the sixties, say? I quite like the sound of that decade. You know, flower power, ban-the-bomb, sit-ins?'

'Yes, years of change. Revolution in the air. Exciting times.' He was remembering.

'Do you remember them? The sixties? I was thinking, say 1966?'

'Now you're talking. Russian linesman, extra time. Alan Ball covering every blade of grass, Nobby Stiles without his teeth. Some people are on the pitch, they think it's all over – it is now.'

It wasn't until the end of this recitation that I realised what he was talking about. 'Oh, football. The World Cup, wasn't it?'

'We were over the moon. Glory days. Hurst's hat-trick. Dancing on the pitch. Then we had a party to celebrate. Best night of my life. First time I got properly pissed.'

This had to be Diane's party. How far could I push him? 'So you boys all got together, a lads' gathering. Chanting, reliving the goals. Drinking the health of the players.'

'Oh no, there were girls as well. Andrew had organised it. He had a girlfriend and she invited a bunch of her friends. We had a record-player. Records.'

'So there was dancing. What did you dance to?'

'You're being very nosy, Miss Woodhouse.'

'No, I was just thinking. I could borrow from your experiences for my party. You know, my novel. Bring some details of your party into mine.'

'The Rollings Stones. Hits album. We were all into the Stones in a big way, proper rock-and-roll, not like those pansy-boy Beatles.'

'High Tide and Green Grass.'

'You're right. What a pretentious title! And how come your classical education stretches that far?'

'You pick things up. Some things seem to stick.' In fact, Diane had mentioned that title in her diary. I tried to remember what else she'd written about. There was a Bob Dylan LP. But the moment had passed.

'So, how's the whisky? You're supposed to have brandy after a meal, but I always prefer scotch.'

'Tasty,' I said. Did I not know any other word?

'It has that combination of bite and smoothness. Not like your Bells' rubbish; other high street brands are available. It has to be single malt.' He held his glass up to the light, then took a sip and licked his lips. My eyes were wandering again. 'I see you're still checking out my photos.'

I nodded. I had to admit they were drawing me to them. 'I'd like to have seen the original paintings.'

'Well, you're in luck. Like I said, I sold most of them, but there are a couple I kept back, for my own pleasure.' He poured more whisky into our empty glasses. Trebles, was my estimate.

'Really?'

'Yup. Do you want to see them? They're upstairs.'

# -18-

I knew it was coming, of course I did. Even at the pub there had been that look in his eye, and over dinner his intentions had become obvious. Whatever their age, lechers are easy to spot.

Now was my moment to make my excuses and leave. But I wasn't prepared to waste this opportunity. I might not be able to get this close to him again. If I rejected him now, he might call it a day, cut his losses and keep his distance, no longer be within my reach. I'd come with a plan and I would see it through, whatever it took. Anyway, I really did want to see those paintings.

I grabbed my bag and followed him upstairs. I told him I needed the loo and he took my glass and directed me to the ensuite. It was a luxurious, modern bathroom, large bath and separate shower, all high-quality spec. On the shelf behind the wash basin were the expected items: razors, deodorant, after-shave. I sneaked a look in the cabinet and that told a different story: it was crammed with feminine toiletries. Hmm. I checked my bag. I'd come well-prepared, but it was comforting to check again. I splashed water over my face, flushed the toilet and walked back into the bedroom.

Richard was sitting at the foot of the king-sized bed that dominated the room. I noticed an extra couple of buttons of his shirt were undone. He passed me my drink and patted the space by his side. I sat down and took a healthy swig of whisky. On the wall in front of us were two large paintings of naked women.

I tried not to gasp, but the poses were eye-watering in their explicitness. One woman was lying back, legs spread, intimately touching herself and looking directly out of the canvas, straight at the artist. The other was standing, her bare bottom the most prominent feature. She was looking over her shoulder, one hand cupping her breast, the fingers of the other hand between her lips.

Both women were black as ebony.

# -19-

'Wow,' I said. 'These are good.'

'Thank you. I probably could have sold them. At the time my work was selling well. But I held them back. They were my favourites.'

'How on earth did you persuade the women to pose like that?'

'You'd be surprised. What girls will do if you only ask them. And I paid them of course, they were professional models.'

I was conscious that Richard had somehow managed to edge closer to me. His leg was now touching mine. My instinct told me to move away, but I didn't want to give him the satisfaction of having provoked a response. Also, I didn't want to break the mood. There definitely was a mood.

'You like my pictures, then? Do they turn you on?' He drained his glass and placed it on the dressing table.

'Oh no. I'm not that way inclined. In fact, when I see a woman's naked body it stirs something catty in me. I'm drawn to all the spots and scars, the blemishes.'

'Not many blemishes on those two black beauties.'

'True. Such perfect skin. Flawless, you might say. Is that artistic licence, or were they like that for real.'

'Oh, they were both beautiful girls. Sisters as it happens. Sonya and Patience.'

'I can see the family resemblance. Did you sleep with them?'

'You do ask some very personal questions, Miss Woodhouse.'

He looked at me and waited until I turned to him.

'I think it's about time I began to ask you some personal questions. And you should consider giving me some truthful answers.' His voice had changed. There was a threatening edge to it, as though there was anger bubbling up.

'Really? I'm so not interesting. I've done nothing, I'm nobody, a blank sheet.' I shrugged and smiled, aiming for coyness.

'Hmm. Maybe. And then again, maybe not. I think you're a bit of a pretender, a player. A girl who hides and deceives, adopts disguises. A mystery girl.'

'What on earth makes you say that?'

'Okay. Cards on the table time.' He brushed his hands against each other. 'Let's start with your hair. It's not your own, is it?'

I wondered how he knew. But it was no longer important. I took off the wig and slipped it into my bag. I scratched my head with both hands. My dark straight hair fell into a long version of a Pixie cut. It needed a trim, and I knew that the blue tint had begun to fade. I turned back to him, eyes open wide.

'That's better.' He lifted his hand and looped a strand of my hair around his finger. 'Natural. And I'm guessing those glasses aren't strictly necessary.' He took them off, rather clumsily catching my right ear, and stared through them. 'Plain glass, methinks.'

Again I looked at him. Where was this going? I had a good idea, and hoped I was right: it would make my task much easier.

'Next question. What's your real name? I may be gullible, but even I know that no-one in the twenty-first century is actually called Emma Woodhouse.'

I didn't argue. 'Frankie,' I said. 'Frankie Jackson.' Any reason for pretence had vanished. And each reveal made it more certain how this evening would end.

## -20-

'And what is your game, Frankie Jackson.' His tone had softened again, despite the challenge of his words. It occurred to me that it was he who was the bigger pretender here, the fake, the one masquerading as something he was not. He had one thought in mind and everything else was plain flim-flam. 'What are you about? What are you actually doing in Hunstanton? Why are you in my bedroom?'

'The last question is easy: you invited me. If you want me to go, you only have to say.' I stood up, placing my half-empty glass next to his on the dressing table.

'No, no. Don't do that, Frankie. Sit down. We're just getting to know each other. And I'm not complaining. I like that you're here. I like you. Please.'

I picked up my glass again and sat down.

'So tell me. Who are you? My dusky maiden. And what goes on in that pretty little head of yours?'

I cringed again, trying hard not to show it. 'Sorry Richard.' I sipped the whisky. Thinking time. 'Sorry to disappoint you. There's really no great mystery. I actually do want to be a writer. I know I'm rubbish at the moment, but I know I can get better. I thought I'd get some inspiration from being at the seaside, like I told you. Away from the distractions of the city. And I have to admit I'd seen your web page. Such a kind face. Not aloof like some of those famous authors. I didn't dare ask you direct, you being a published author and all. So I decided to sort of creep up on you.' A good balance I thought. Enough truth, enough flattery. Yes, I'd got it about right. I sniffed, suggesting tears weren't far away.

Richard put his arm around me, comforting, paternal. *Yeah, right*.

'Like I said, Frankie. I want you to be my project. I'll give you all the help you need. With me in your corner, I'm sure you'll make it.'

I turned to him. 'Thank you, Richard. You're a kind man.'

Then he kissed me.

And that was my second and final opportunity to cut and run. But I didn't. Why would I? I'd prepared for this, guessing that this was a likely outcome of dinner at Richard's place. And now I had to go through with it. This might be my only chance.

So I kissed him back.

Then, reaching into my bag, I pulled out the pack of condoms. 'Best be safe,' I said, and smiled my sweetest smile.

# -21-

Afterwards, Richard goes into the ensuite bathroom and I hear the sound of the shower. I picture him naked, eyes closed, face lifted into the spray, long grey hair hanging down his back, his lean body impressively fit for a man of his age. A cock that's not so impressive, but then again, I don't have that many to compare it with.

I take a deep breath, close my eyes. He deserves what's coming, that's for sure. He's a gold-star bastard. I always knew about his past, what he'd done all those years ago, but I've tried to keep an open mind, given him a chance to show that he'd changed. After all, people do change, people grow up; and anyway, he may have had an explanation for his behaviour as a teenager, some excuse that showed it wasn't as bad as I thought. Not likely, but possible. I've given up on that now: he's beyond all redemption. In fact, if there were some sort of record for the number of negative attributes a man could have, Richard would be in line to break it. Sexist, misogynist and chauvinist for starters. Then there's racist and homophobe. He's not a paedophile (as far as I know), because I'm over the age of consent, but come on! He's old enough to be my ... Yes, really! And all the others ... who knows how old they were?

So have I made it clear? I don't like the guy: he's a nasty specimen, a geriatric wanker.

And he was rubbish in bed, despite all that bragging about his sexual prowess. Once he was convinced of my compliance, his love-making became perfunctory at best. I may not have much experience, but even I know the difference between giving and taking: I know what constitutes egocentric sex and how objectionable it is to be on the receiving end.

The truth is, he hasn't changed, he's just got older. He's still the same self-obsessed prat I imagine he must have been forty odd years ago, only now he can't hide behind the excuse of youth.

I get out of bed and extract the knife from my bag. I take another deep breath. My pulse rate has increased, hands are a little moist, the adrenalin's pumping. But I'm in control. I'm doing what is right, this is what I've prepared for. The bastard's days are numbered.

I've done my homework, I know the best access point, the best angle, the correct pressure for maximum effect. For deadly effect. I've checked the bathroom and know he'll have his back to the door. It's easy. I can do this.

Yes, it's true, there's a one-in-three chance that Richard is my grandfather. But so what? It makes no difference. All rapists deserve to die.

# -22-

As a child, the word 'holiday' was never part of my vocabulary, I didn't have that sort of childhood. But I'm guessing that how I felt on getting back from Hunstanton was similar to how most people feel at the end of a holiday: some disorientation, some disappointment, but mostly a feeling of contentment, a return to familiarity and security. I was beginning to understand the meaning of the word 'home'. There's a lot of guff written about how home is about people, 'home is where the heart is' and all that, but really it's plain bricks and mortar. A good solid home waits to welcome you back with warmth, ready to wrap you in its domestic blanket, to comfort and re-assure you. It's where you feel safe.

Yes, it felt good to be back home, back in the Jackson's house. I reintroduced myself to the simple pleasures that space provides: a full-length bath, a well-equipped kitchen, TV with an abundance of channels. Plenty of room, room to breathe, room to think.

The priority, though, before allowing myself to indulge in all this luxurious space, was to smarten the place up. Having sat empty for three months, the house had acquired a layer of dust, a few cobwebs, and an overall odour of musty staleness. I opened all the windows to let in the early June sunshine and busied myself with Hoover and duster and spray-polish. I don't mind housework: it's not hard labour and has a therapeutic dimension. You don't need to think about what you're doing, you can let your brain wander freely to other things. When the chores began to get tedious, I treated myself to a run, and it was good to get back onto familiar routes, nodding to fellow joggers and dog-walkers, working up a sweat. I missed the clean clarity of the seascape, probably the high spot of my Hunstanton adventure, as the air around my home, by contrast, was steeped in pollution. Also, the backdrop to my running was now, once again, chiefly grey walls and grey buildings, no more bright sky, sea and sand. What I didn't miss was the relentless wind that seemed to dominate the weather of the Norfolk coastline.

A visit to the hairdresser enabled me to get my hair smartened up and the colour renewed. I was pleased to be done with the wig. I treated myself to a day in the local spa, enjoying some gentle massage and other pointless pampering, before relaxing in the pool. Yes, I'm a strong swimmer: I didn't tell Richard that.

Other treats included a new tattoo on my left shoulder and another piercing in my nose. I thought about the tattoo at some length and eventually plumped for a curly letter 'D' (for Diane) and inside it the numeral '1'. I told the tattooist to leave space for two more numbers.

One third of my project was now complete, but I had mixed feelings about how the first part of my mission had panned out. The practicalities couldn't have gone better. That was no surprise, and also no accident: I'd prepared thoroughly, tackled the event with full attention to detail, adopted what might even be termed a professional approach. As I anticipated, when naked in a shower a man is at his most vulnerable, most easily dispatched. Once I was sure Richard was dead, I'd cleaned myself thoroughly, then set about tidying the place, making the bed, washing up and putting away crockery, cutlery and glasses. My fingerprints and DNA would be all over the place, but that didn't matter. There would be plenty of other people's as well, as Richard was hardly living in monk-like seclusion: his *Facebook* page revealed that he had many friends who came and went on a regular basis, enjoying his company and his hospitality. I suspected there would be evidence of his wife's presence, rather more recent than the 'last year' he'd mentioned. If there was close scrutiny of the traces in his house, the crime scene, there would be many visitors whose identification would take precedence before they began to consider my tracks. In any case, my DNA did not feature on any data-base, so the police would have to find me first to establish a match. There was little likelihood of that: I had no connection with Hunstanton, never mind any connection with Richard Wright. Anyone who saw us together would remember him as being accompanied by a young woman called Emma, a woman with a wild African hairstyle and red-rimmed glasses, and there would be no discernible link to me, Frankie Jackson, who looked quite different and was living quietly in the city, over a hundred miles away.

I had taken his computer, the easiest way of removing evidence of our email exchange. It also might lead the police to consider robbery as a motive. I checked to see if he'd printed off my fake novel, but found no sign of it: in fact he didn't even seem to possess a printer. I wanted to take the paintings, but dared not: anyone seeing me leave with those large canvases tucked under my arm would have raised an alarm. I did slip two of the black-and-white prints into my bag. I left in darkness, saw no-one and no-one saw me.

The caravan site had posed the biggest problem. I'd taken plenty of cash with me to Norfolk, to make sure I wouldn't need to use ATMs, nor make purchases on my credit card: the electronic world creates the most visible foot-prints, so for anyone attempting to stay under the radar it's best avoided entirely. But paying cash for hire of a caravan turned out to be no easy matter. I had to make up a sob story for the receptionist, all about an abusive husband who I was running away from, how he never allowed me the use of bank cards, and no, not a cheque book either. In the end she accepted my bundle of £20 notes as the lesser evil: I'd threatened to walk away, and she figured she'd get into more trouble with her superiors for leaving an unpaid bill to be chased than for accepting payment in cash.

The internet is a wonderful resource and it provided an invaluable guide for all my preparatory work. Among other things, I had found a site that supplied fake number-plates. Oh, it was dressed up as something less illegal, but the main point was that they facilitated the customer making their own, so the plates created were untraceable, there was no record. If the police ever got around to tracking the car with that registration number, as identified by CCTV at the campsite, the roadside cameras would confirm that after leaving Hunstanton it headed for Peterborough and the A1, then travelled north before turning off after fifty miles or so. After that (as far as the cameras were concerned) it vanished. I had navigated my way south, through a network of minor roads (hence avoiding prying cameras), before taking off the plates in a quiet lay-by. From then on, my car no longer exhibited any connection with Hunstanton and I could take a leisurely drive home.

As an extra precaution, I had the car re-sprayed. I chose a particularly vibrant shade of red.

So I'd left no trace. Richard's computer, together with the knife, the wig, the glasses, two arty photos and the number plates, I put into old Mum's suitcase. I decided it was the safest place. Any attempt to dispose of them would have carried more risk. They'd never be discovered in that case, because nobody would ever look there. Why would anyone come into *my* house looking for evidence to link with the murder in sleepy Hunstanton of some old former rock star and would-be author, with whom I had absolutely no connection?

# -23-

So yes, as far as the practicalities were concerned, I considered part one of my project to have been a success. But in other ways, I was not as satisfied as I thought I would be. I didn't regret killing the man. *No way*! It was justice for Diane. On top of that, there being one less fascist bastard in the world could only be a good thing. I'd enjoyed dispatching him. And yet, there was something missing. The problem was, I never confronted Richard Wright with his crime, never made him face up to what he did in 1966. I never had the satisfaction of seeing the look on his face when he discovered who I was and realised what I knew. That would have been the icing on the cake.

Probably it would have not been possible, because in actual fact, I don't think he had any memory of Diane. I'd mentioned the name on more than one occasion and never saw a flicker in his eyes, no hesitation in his actions, no hint of a suspicion that I might be referring to someone who was at that party all those years ago, a girl he'd raped. He remembered the party, that much was clear. He remembered the football match, the World Cup Final, he remembered getting drunk at the party afterwards, but I suspect that was it. I believe the rape of Diane, in his mind, in his memory, had blurred together with the various other sexual adventures of those and later years, with groupies, with models, some of them legal, some not, some consensual, some not. Many of the fans were underage I was sure, and I could see from the photos how young the models looked, the models who posed for him. And there was another thing. Once I was in bed with him, I could tell there would have been no turning back. You get that feeling, sometimes. If I'd resisted, if I'd changed my mind, told him, 'No,' I'm sure he'd have ignored me, persisted with his endeavours. I'd gone to his house, gone to his bedroom, I'd kissed him, and as far as he was concerned that amounted to a non-contestable green light. Of course, my feeling does not amount to evidence, but I'm sure he would have had no qualms about raping me, all the while telling himself that he wasn't, that it was my choice, that my 'No' was simply my provocative way of saying 'Yes.'

So, for raping Diane, and for an attitude that hadn't changed, he deserved to die. It was still a shame I hadn't got him to face up to his crime. All I'd managed, as he collapsed in the shower, was to whisper in his ear: 'This is for Diane.' So if he did remember her, he knew she had finally got her revenge.

It hadn't been perfect. I could get better. I'd need to get better, for my own satisfaction. But for now I needed to relax, to settle back home, making the most of my leisure, free from the compulsive drive that had occupied my few months in Norfolk. I needed a break.

I indulged myself with some excursions to my favourite restaurants.

I bought some weighty tomes, fantasy sagas running into multiple volumes.

I found some box-sets on Netflix to submerge myself in for a few weeks of back-to-back gorging.

Night-time was best. I put freshly-ironed sheets on the bed – I hate duvets – and now the weather was warmer I could sleep naked. I slept long hours of dream-free sleep.

I treated myself to one afternoon of particular extravagance. I am not a 'shopaholic', a term I fail to understand. I normally avoid shopping at all costs. I rarely seem to get on with shop assistants (nor them with me), and changing rooms are either impossibly cramped or embarrassingly open-plan, added to which I dislike rubbing shoulders with other shoppers. So I buy most of my clothes online. But when you've spent your early life having to make do with second-hand clothes, with worn and ill-fitting trousers and jumpers, shoes with soles flapping off, there is something special about an excursion to posh shops. So I treated myself to an afternoon of extravagance, not looking at price-tags, buying on a whim and the more outrageous the better. I wouldn't want to do it every week, but it was near enough my birthday and I'd earned a reward, a treat. Then I bought several bunches of flowers to distribute around the various rooms of the house, a couple of bottles of decent champagne and three boxes of quality chocolates. I had the wherewithal for a party, a birthday party.

Even for me, a party for one would have had limited appeal. I needed some male company, not least because having Richard Wright as my most recent sexual partner left an unpleasant taste that needed washing away.

The King's Head is a suitable pub for what I had in mind. I dressed smartly, but not tarty. Scarlet lipstick works from a distance. Closer up, a combination of mascara, eye shadow and eyeliner pushes the buttons I wanted to push. I sat at the end of the bar sipping my dry white wine. The pub was busy, but not over-crowded. There were three likely lads at the other end of the bar, heads together, seemingly in debate. I was guessing that some sort of drawing of lots was going on. Eventually, one of them sauntered across to me.

'Would you like a drink?'

I held up my near-enough full glass. 'I seem to have one. Even given my alcoholic tendencies, two drinks at once would be overdoing it.'

'Sure,' he said. 'Yes.' He didn't seem to have any more chat-up lines.

I helped him out. 'But you can stay and talk to me, if you like.' I indicated the stool next to me. 'I could do with the company.' I looked him full in the face. The eye make-up did its job.

He sat down. 'It's Mrs Jackson, isn't it?'

'Good memory, but it's Ms, not Mrs.'

'Sorry. I'm Danny,'

'Frankie,' I said, and we shook hands, very formal. His hands were rough. I'd met Danny before. He worked at the garage where I'd had my car resprayed. He'd made it obvious that he fancied me, but I had been cool with him, given him no encouragement. But now was the time to be more encouraging. He had soft brown eyes and long eyelashes, unusual in a man. I liked the sound of his voice, soft like his eyes, rich with a touch of humour, as though his voice was older than his years. Rough and soft. Yes, he'd do.

The chatting-up-stroke-pick-up game is complicated these days, with the influence of women's lib along with the spread of gender flexibility, binary-identifiers, trans-sexuality, and so on. But in the traditional male-dominated heterosexual encounter, it's still the case that the man thinks he's charming the woman with his wit and erudition, his compliments and his well-practised routine. But it is in fact the woman, even though she might appear the passive participant, who's doing the choosing, as it always has been. If she doesn't want to know, it doesn't matter what he says, he'll get nowhere; on the other hand, if she does want him, he can get away with any amount of nonsense. I'd chosen Danny and he was still thinking he'd chosen me.

Not that it made much difference. He came back to my place. (I persuaded him? He persuaded me?). I gave him champagne, which, so he said, he'd never drunk before. We had sex. It was okay, sort of medium, perhaps six out of ten, six-and-a-half? Not bad, given his evident lack of experience. It washed away the two out of ten that had been Richard Wright's geriatric effort. As a touch of irony (of which Danny was totally unaware), the musical background to our lovemaking was a loop of rock music that included TBW's one hit single, 'Take me, make me, break me.' Danny wanted to stay the night, but I made it clear that wasn't an option. I gave him a parting gift of a box of chocolates and an exchange of mobile numbers, although I had no intention of phoning or texting him. He was good, but not that good.

I slept well, enjoying the cool sheets and the double bed, and slept late, making the most of the lack of stampeding animals on the roof. Life was fine.

Since I'd been back, I'd been checking the news from time to time, but never found any mention of the murder of an old man in Hunstanton. I'm sure if the victim had been a young and attractive female, the media would have swarmed all over it. But that morning I logged on to the online feed from the Eastern Daily Press and found the item I'd been looking out for. It gave the name of the victim, but no other details. Unexplained death, it said, probably a burglary gone wrong, it hinted.

I shook my head. If only the headline had been: 'Death of a Rapist.'

# -24-

Over the weeks of that summer, my mind continued its post mortem (so to speak) of the Richard Wright chapter of my life, before drawing the curtains closed, slowing down its reruns of the key episodes, eventually ceasing the meticulous checking of details. It was over, done and dusted; one rapist had been duly dispatched. (*Hurrah!*) And as that phase ended, so I scrolled forward towards the next name on Diane's list: Stephen Greene. I already knew uncovering him was not going to be easy, not as easy as it had been with Richard: a quick trawl of *Facebook* and *Instagram* had yielded nothing relevant, and the thought of further searching did not appeal. Yet.

There was no rush. Diane had waited over forty years for her revenge and could wait a few more weeks, even months. I could take the time to recharge my batteries, regain some energy. Get plenty of sleep. I could read, I could listen to music, I could watch trashy TV. Danny from the garage was texting me on a regular basis, suggesting we should meet up again. I ignored him: eventually he'd give up. When I fancied another two-person party, I'd find someone more interesting to take to bed.

Meanwhile, in quiet moments, my thoughts turned to the future. I resolved to think through the next stage of my project more thoroughly. Once I uncovered Stephen Greene, I would get it right. I would make sure he faced up to his crime, admitted his guilt. Once it was over, I wanted to feel I'd done justice to Diane's memory.

# -25-

Visitors to a town house are more frequent than visitors to a caravan. When the bell rang, I was not surprised. I assumed it was Danny (in which case I'd send him packing with some choice words ringing in his ears), or the morning post, or possibly my Amazon delivery - I'd sent for a couple of newly-published hardbacks. It was none of those things.

'Hello, babe.'

I was not expecting a tall and broad, middle-aged black man, with a wispy beard and straggly dreadlocks. He was dressed in faded jeans and a grubby denim jacket. He was not carrying post or parcel. Some random stranger, then, but no, there was something about him that looked familiar. He was a man from my past, from long, long ago.

'Aren't you going to invite me in?'

It was Joe. My father. My former father, grown older.

'Hey,' I said. I couldn't bring myself to say the word "Dad". 'What do you want? How did you know where to find me?'

'That's a bit rude, girl. Aren't you pleased to see me?' He held his arms wide. If he was expecting me to move forward for a hug, he'd have a long wait. I wasn't pleased to see him, and that was the truth. I didn't know what to say, so I said nothing.

He placed his palms together, as though he were praying. 'Aren't you gonna invite your old man into your lovely home?'

*Of course not,* was my immediate thought, but my intuition told me such a response would lead to an ugly doorstep confrontation. I stepped aside, let him walk past me into the hallway. He smelled of sweat and booze. I closed the door. When I turned, he had already walked through into the living room. I followed closely behind. He didn't sit down. He stood in the middle of the room and managed to fill it. That's crazy because it's a big room and he's only one man, but once inside he seemed to grow taller, broader. It felt like there was an alien presence in the room, something that didn't belong, like a cancer. I wanted the room to swallow him up, wrap him up, not allow him to contaminate my world. But it didn't. It was he who grew, dominating the space. Some men can do that and I hate them for it.

He turned around, three-sixty degrees, studying the walls, the furniture, looking out towards the conservatory and the garden. 'Wow, babe. One mighty pot of gold has landed plum in your lap for sure. Hasn't it just.'

'What do you want?' I asked, again.

'Hey, girl. What a thing to be asking me.' He frowned, and a slow harshness crept into his voice. 'Can't a father come calling on his little baby, now? You're too good for me, is that it? All grown up and turned grand, turned posh. Turned white.' He spat out the last word, like a curse, staring me full in the face, eyes wide with menace.

After a few electric moments of silence, he sat down on the sofa, spreading himself, stroking his hands across the material, showing his rotten teeth, but not properly smiling. 'Fine, fine,' he said, adopting a softer tone.

I stood looking at him, looking at this worm that had crawled into my life. Wishing so much that he hadn't.

'Have you got a beer, girl? I could really use a beer right now.'

'No,' I lied. 'I don't keep alcohol in the house.'

'That don't sound like no daughter of mine.' He laughed, an empty derisive sort of laugh. *That's because I'm no daughter of yours*, I thought.

I wanted this man out of my house. Supposedly he was my father, but that meant nothing to me. I had no family feelings towards him, no feelings at all, apart from negative ones. He had a small part that he played in my distant memory, a memory which was dominated by the sound of my mother shouting and screaming and sobbing. Then he had come back, maybe three times, four? Once he took us to a hotel. Once he took us on a bus, I don't remember where to. But always he left again. That's what I remembered: he never stayed. And he always lied, because every time he entered our lives, he was full of how this was going to be different but it never was. He was always full of shit. I don't know how many times he broke my mother's heart. But he never broke mine. By the time I was old enough to have a heart, it was locked away in a steel box where he couldn't get near it. He came. He lied. I didn't believe him. He left. That was all. That was it.

Until now. Now he was here and I was scared. I wanted him gone.

He tried to engage me in conversation. Said he was sorry my mother had died. He meant my old mother, his supposed wife, who had been dead for nine years. A bit late to be showing sympathy. He asked what I'd been up to in the intervening years. He asked about the owners of the house, he didn't know their names and I didn't tell him. How had I come by it? He asked about boyfriends.

I told him nothing. I didn't even bother to lie. I kept asking him why he had come, how he had found me, what he was doing here. What did he expect to get from me? He only smiled, with that threat in his eyes.

Eventually he told me how he'd got a job at *KwikFit* and that he'd talked to Dave there, someone who knew me. He meant Danny. Oh, Danny. I knew he'd become a bit fixated on me, his texts revealed that much. I must have given him more personal information than I should have. So when he talked about me to Joe, Joe guessed who I was. It's not Danny's fault. After all, there aren't that many brown girls living around here, brown girls on their own with no apparent family.

I registered the lesson: it was already the case that I rarely told anyone the truth about my background, but in future I'd be even more careful. I resolved to invent a history, a safe history I could stick to, that would give nothing away, and that I could use whenever anyone probed too deeply into my past.

But that was for the future. I first had to deal with the present.

# -26-

Still Joe was sprawled across my furniture, still oozing his poison into the air.

'Any food going, girl? I could just manage a slice of leftover pizza.'

*Just a guess? Or did he know I'd ordered a takeaway the previous night? Had he been watching the house?* 'No. Fridge is empty.' I could see him looking towards the kitchen door, as though considering checking. 'I want you to leave,' I said. 'You have no business here. Get out.'

He stood up, but I knew it wouldn't be that easy. He sauntered towards me, arms hanging loose. He was a good head taller than me. He came close enough so I had to lift my head in order to look him in the eye. 'It's been real nice renewing your acquaintance, Frankie girl. I'm sure we're gonna get along just fine from here on. You're just a little shy of your old man, that'll be it. Understandable.'

'No. That's not how it is. You and me playing happy families? Never. That's not going to happen, no way. I don't want you coming anywhere near me again, this is the last time you set foot in this house.'

'No? No, girl? Wrong answer.' He pointed a finger at me. 'You've got a good thing going here. And I'm going to be sharing it. I'm your father and I'm owed.'

'You have no rights here. You're not my father. Not in any meaning of the word that counts. You're owed nothing.'

He smiled again, that empty smile. 'You've got spirit girl, I'll give you that. But you're not giving me the right answers. You're not being welcoming to your old man. That needs to change.' He took another step towards me. Now we were within touching distance. My nose was filled with the smell of his body, the smell of his sweat, the smell of his sour breath. But I didn't turn away. I stood my ground. This was my house, my territory.

He seemed to come to a decision, and the next time he spoke it was gentler, he had lost the snarl. 'Since you have no beer in the house and no food, I'm guessing you don't have no cash neither. In which case, I'll be taking my leave of you, lovely daughter of mine. But let's make another date, for... What shall we say? Seven days' time? I'll come back.' He pointed again. 'And I'm expecting you to be a bit more hospitable, next time.'

I shook my head. Didn't trust myself to speak without crying. I folded my arms across my chest.

'In particular, you'll have a little gift waiting for your old man. Shall we say five hundred pounds? To tide me over.'

'No way,' I said. 'You're getting nothing from me. Get out of here and stay away.'

Then he left.

And once he'd gone, that's when I cried.

# -27-

I sank down onto the floor, my back to the door, my head in my hands and cried. I cried a lot and I cried loudly. But then I stopped, came back into the real world. I am not normally the crying sort, I have never been able to see the point of it, can't see what good it does, what it achieves. So on the rare occasions the tears come, they never last long.

I went to the fridge and took out the bottle of *sauvignon blanc* that I'd opened the previous night; I poured a large glass and took a gulp. I am the drinking sort: alcohol I can see the point of. I carried the glass back into the living room and sat down on the sofa. The sofa where my father had been sitting, the sofa that now felt soiled, sullied, contaminated.

Father. The word meant nothing to me. He was an old man called Joe. A nasty old man, a bully and a thug. Probably worse. At one point, when we were standing close, I was sure he'd been on the point of hitting me. His fists had been clenched and there was a red rage in his eyes. It wouldn't have taken much to tip him over the edge.

I tried to remember what old Mum had told me about him. She did talk about him from time to time. I usually switched off, I'd heard it all before and it was boring. He'd hit her, I knew that. More than once. There had been cuts and bruises and even broken bones. And then there was the way he disappeared for months on end, she often talked about that. And how he'd keep coming back. He sometimes turned up when we were living on the street. There was that night in the hotel with the lovely bed. Other times as well. He took us to a posh café one time, fed us up. I ate too much, I was full to bursting and then I was sick, which made him angry. And he took us on a trip, I remember a bus ride, can't remember where we went.

But those gaps in between, big gaps. Where did he disappear to and why? Now I realised: he'd been in prison, hadn't he? Mum used plenty of mealy-mouthed phrases, but now I was older and wiser and could read between the lines. Yes, it made sense: he was a habitual criminal, a regular convict. Now he'd come back, into my house, slouching on this sofa. I felt like screaming.

I got the Hoover out, swept what I imagined was his debris from the sofa and the carpet, although there was nothing to see. I sprayed plenty of air-freshener in all directions. Anything to erase evidence of his presence from my world. I wished the memory was as easily erased.

He would never set foot in this house again: that was my resolution. I wouldn't let him. But then, when he came back next week, how would I stop him? The front door I could lock and bolt. But around the back? The conservatory door wouldn't stop a persistent mouse, never mind an angry thug like him, and from there access to the rest of the house opened up. Maybe I could get an alarm, a whole system, with cameras and motion detectors, buzzers and bells and flashing lights. I'd been thinking of doing that anyway. But would it help protect me against Joe?

I imagined it, me barricaded in my own home while he laid siege, paced around, battering at the doors and windows: no, I couldn't face that.

I should contact the police.

I thought about what Tricia had said. Tricia was someone I chatted with on the internet, a virtual friend, not a real friend, we'd never met face-to-face. She had a stalker and contacted the police, but – in her words – they didn't want to know. They did nothing and then later she ended up in A&E when her stalker caught her and beat her up. She hadn't been online for a while.

How much less likely were the police to act if the so-called stalker was the complainant's own father? No, the police were not the answer.

I tried to imagine letting Joe in and talking to him, negotiating. I could give him five hundred pounds, not a great sum after all, and tell him that was all he was getting. But as soon as I pictured that face, that vacuous grin and those furious eyes, I knew it would never work. He'd be like a tiger who'd tasted blood. He'd come back again and again, demanding more and more. And if I didn't give him what he wanted, he'd threaten me, and then he'd hit me, I was sure of that. Maybe worse. I'd seen it in that face: his fists were his weapons of choice and he was accustomed to using them to get his own way. That's what his face told me, and the scars on his knuckles were evidence enough. Me being his daughter would only give him more justification, not less. 'I'm owed,' that's what he'd said. No idea what he meant, but he believed it, so I had to believe it too.

Could I lock the house up, like I had when I left to track down Richard, lock it up and run away? Hole up somewhere safe until the dust settled, wait for Joe to give up? No, I couldn't see that working either. As soon as I came back, so would he, hungrier and angrier than ever. Or else he'd break in when I wasn't here, take everything he could get through the door, and wreck what was left.

I was running out of options.

I was running out of time.

I was running out of wine.

A quick trip to the corner shop and I had soon replenished the wine, and had grabbed some miscellaneous food items from which a dinner might emerge. That was the solvable problems sorted.

Meanwhile, I thought again about the scenario where I invited the man into my house, feigning conciliation. Could I persuade him to take a shower? A man is at his most vulnerable when he is naked in the shower, and I still had the knife. But what then? The body would be in *my* shower, oozing blood onto *my* bathroom floor. A lot of mess to clear up, including a body to dispose of. The police aren't that inept. I'd end up as chief suspect, with means and motive and Joe's DNA everywhere to seal the deal. No, the buzz I'd feel as I slid the knife in would be wonderful, but it wouldn't compensate for the inevitable years in prison that were sure to follow.

# -28-

I needed some distraction, so threw myself into preparing a meal.

Onion, peeled and chopped, sizzling in the pan.

A pack of mince.

Followed by some red peppers, mushrooms, garlic peeled and crushed, tin of chopped tomatoes.

A couple of red chillies, finely chopped.

Not sure what I was making. I found some leftover veg in the fridge and added that. Sprinkled on some random herbs and spices.

Boiled water in a pan for pasta.

Loud music and a concerted attack on the wine. My sort of meal.

# -29-

When the bell rang a week later, I had two plans. Plan A was worth a shot, but to be honest I had little confidence in it. It was Plan B that was the real deal and, once I got the ingredients in place, that wouldn't fail. I wouldn't allow it to fail.

When Joe arrived, I was welcoming, although the word 'Dad' still wouldn't pass my lips. I brought him a cold beer from the fridge, and one for me, and sat opposite him. He looked round the room as he had on his previous visit. 'This is a right nice place you've got here. Some of this would fetch a price, no mistake.'

'Nothing's for sale,' I said, my friendliness already beginning to wear off. I drank from the bottle in my fist and looked at him, trying to find some emotion other than hate. I failed.

I went to the drawer in the sideboard, pulled out the envelope with the money, and handed it to the man on the sofa, that invader, that predator, that alien claiming to be my father. He looked in the envelope, rippled through the notes. 'Good,' he said. 'Good girl.' He raised his bottle.

'Now,' I said, in my firmest voice. 'That's it. You've got what you came for. You take the money and go. You don't come back.'

He didn't rush to leave: I can't say I was much surprised, but I clung to a faint hope.

'And if you ever do come back, if you ever so much as set foot in this road again, you'll regret it. I'll set the police on you.'

'You can't get rid of me that easy. I live here.' He saw the look on my face. 'Yeah, surprise, eh? I live right in this road, near as dammit. My landlady, Mrs Arnold, lets me use that parking spot on the corner. So you'd better get used to seeing me around. Anyhow, why would the police be interested in me? What have I done? I'm your father, come visiting. You've given me a present. Where's the crime?'

'Oh, I'm good at making up stories. I'll tell them how you've bullied me, beat me up. Even raped me. That'll make them pay attention.'

'What a pile of crap,' he said, giving me that fake smile. 'You'd never go through with it, and if you did, they'd never believe you. No bruises, no blood. No evidence of any fight. And me clearly so innocent.' He spread his arms wide.

'You've got a criminal record. Not so innocent.'

'Petty thieving. Handling stolen goods. Alleged breaking and entering. Never anything violent.' I didn't believe him.

I stood up. Gestured with the bottle. 'Get out,' I said. 'Get out of my house. Now.' He didn't move. He took another swig from his bottle.

'The thing is, Frankie. It seems to me, you've come up with this little package, five hundred quid, without even breaking sweat. Like it's nothing to you. In which case, I'm guessing you could find some more. So let's give it two weeks this time, give you a chance to gather a bit more cash together. And next time, you'll have another envelope waiting for me. With a warm five grand nestling inside. How would that be?'

I shook my head. 'No way. You must be crazy. To think you can just waltz in here, demanding money from me, expecting me to do your bidding, meek as a lamb. No, that's it. You've got all I'm giving you. This ends here.'

He held up the envelope and flapped it at me. He shrugged. 'I'm owed,' he said. 'You owe me.'

'You said that before. How do you make that out? I hardly know you. How can I owe you anything?'

'Strictly it was your mother. But she's not with us, God rest her soul. And you're the one with surplus funds. So you're the one that'll have to pay the debt.'

'You're talking gibberish. I owe you nothing. Mum owed you nothing. If anything, it's you who owes us, for all the stinking shit you poured over us.'

He stood up, brought his face close to mine, full of vicious threat. I could see him clenching his fists, see the wheals on his knuckles: oh yes, those fists had been much used. Then came the smile. 'Nice try, girl. Trying to wind me up, get me to give you a belting. So's you've got some evidence. Nice try, but no fucking cigar.' He sat down again.

Then he told me his tale, his reason for feeling he was due. No idea why he told me, it was hardly a story that was going to generate a whole lot of sympathy from me. Quite the opposite.

# -30-

When he and Mum were first married, they rented a grotty flat in Hounslow, above an estate agents. They wanted to save up for a deposit, to buy a house, or at least a flat of their own. Joe and a friend of his set up what he called a 'freelance company', doing small domestic building jobs: roof repairs, putting up fences, laying drives, that sort of thing. They were so successful that within a year or so he presented Mum with a wad of cash, several thousand pounds, enough for the deposit. But rather than being delighted at the news, according to Joe, Mum 'went off on one'. And before he knew it, she'd grassed him up to the police.

'All I was guilty of was making too much profit,' he said. 'What more did that woman want? Of course, once the cops were involved, I was banged up and the money went into their Christmas party fund.'

'Ah,' I said, nodding. 'I think I'm getting the picture. The truth is you were going house-to-house, finding vulnerable old women and conning them out of their life savings.'

'No, no, girl. It weren't nothing like that. We were straight up. Performing a service. Doing essential repairs, for a fair price. If you don't catch those things early, they'll cost you far more in the long run.'

'Yeah, right. I'm sure that's what you told them. Two con men. You deserved what you got.'

He ranted some more. About losing his hard-won cash, and how it was all Mum's fault. Apparently, I'd come along by then, so (according to Joe) she had even more reason to need his cash. If she'd kept her trap shut, they'd have had a life of Riley. As it was, he'd had to scrape and scrounge ever since, in and out of nick. Not his fault. He was the victim.

'Once you've got a record, no-one will give you a job. Cops are on your back for the slightest thing. It's a vicious circle.' Only now he was here to put things right. He was giving me the chance to make it right by giving him what was his due. What would get him back on his feet.

I let him rant away. The more he moaned the more pathetic he seemed. Pathetic, but still dangerous. 'I think we're done here,' I said. 'Just go.'

And soon after that he did leave. But not before we'd had one more predictable exchange. I'd told him to leave and not come back, and if he did, he'd be sorry. Even to me, it seemed a pretty empty threat. He responded by saying again that he'd return in two weeks and I'd better have five grand in cash waiting for him. Or else. His threat felt more believable.

So just a sample of your normal father/daughter banter.

At least he hadn't hit me, I thought, as I sat down after he'd gone, with a large glass of wine. I'd imagined he might. But otherwise, it had proceeded as expected. He was a pathetic wimp of a man, no backbone, weak and worthless, despite his stature and his aggression. I cared nothing for him. He thought I was an easy touch, which made me despise him more. I'd known he wouldn't be content with five hundred pounds, but I thought it was worth one more try before I put my real plan into operation. Under my real plan, I wouldn't be giving him any more money. In fact, I wouldn't be seeing that miserable man, my so-called father, ever again.

He underestimated me. Richard Wright had underestimated me, thought I was easy meat, another in his long line of victims. I was beginning to understand the way my life was developing: men underestimating me was going to be a pattern and I was going to use it to the max.

As far as Joe was concerned, the important fact I'd discovered from the meeting with him was where he parked his car.

## -31-

I waited four days. I needed to calm down after the stress of Joe's visit; I needed to get my thoughts in order; I needed to make preparations. I needed to convince myself that the plan would work. To be as sure as I could be. I checked out his car, where it was parked. Made sure he didn't see me looking. I drew out the cash I'd need.

Then I texted Danny:

*I've got a beef casserole on the go, too much for one. Do you want to share it? x*

Danny turned up with a cheap bottle of rosé and an even cheaper bunch of flowers, smelling of cheap aftershave and looking rather sheepish. The poor chap hadn't had much experience with women, certainly not with someone like me: very confusing for him. He'd bombarded me with texts, pledging undying devotion: I'd ignored them all. Now, out of the blue, I'd invited him for dinner. I'd even put on a suitably revealing dress in his honour, together with a welcoming smile and powerful perfume. *Poor chap indeed!*

The conversation at the dinner table was amusingly stilted: I didn't help him out too much, it was fun watching him squirm. He asked me about family, about where I'd been to school, favourite subjects, even asked whether I'd ever had any pets. I invented answers. The only thing he said that would have been interesting if I hadn't already guessed it, was that he lived at home with his mum and he hated that, but couldn't afford to move out. I asked if he had any ambitions and he said he wanted to be a businessman. When I asked him to explain, it became clear he had no idea what that career actually entailed, apart from some spurious guff gleaned from watching *The Apprentice*. After one of the many lulls in the conversation, he admitted he'd been surprised to get my text, that he'd begun to think I wasn't – you know – interested in – you know.

'Don't get any ideas, Danny boy. This isn't going to be the start of a five-star romance. Look, you've heard of one-night stands, haven't you?' He nodded. 'Well, think of this as a two-night stand. Second half coming up.' I raised my glass to him and took a swig. 'But first, there's a little favour I need to ask of you.'

'Anything,' he said. 'Just say the word.'

I went to the drawer in the sideboard and took out an envelope, rather fatter than the one I'd given Joe. The moment when Danny looked inside the envelope was precious, I wished I could have captured it in a photo.

'Wow,' he said, eventually, yet predictably. 'How much is this? What's it for?'

'It's for you, Danny. All of it. You can count it when you get home. You just need to agree to do me a small favour.'

His face beamed, as though it were bathed in sunlight shining out from the envelope. I hadn't been sure whether five thousand pounds would be enough. Now I knew it was. He took out a few of the notes. It looked rather like he'd never even seen £50 notes before.

'You know a man called Joe?'

He looked blank.

'Joe Peterson. Old, tall. Black.'

'Got you. He worked at our place for a while.'

'Doesn't anymore?'

'Oh no. He was only with us... what? Two weeks? Something like that. The boss sacked him. He was on the fiddle. Nicking stuff and selling customers direct, not putting sales through the books. That sort of thing.'

'Figures. But before he left, you and he had some cosy chats I believe?'

'We worked together on a couple of cars. Nothing special, just normal. Passing the time.'

'You talked about me?'

'Oh no. I wouldn't do that.'

'Are you sure?'

The way I said it shook him. He looked at me. Shrugged. 'Okay. But nothing, you know, personal. Just normal stuff. He talked about the girls he'd had, you know, and I, well, I might have mentioned you.'

'You see, Danny, there's a problem. Because after your little conversation, this Joe started taking an interest in me. Didn't listen when I told him to get lost. He's been stalking me.'

'No. Oh God. I'm sorry. I never meant. You know. He must be old enough to be your ... you know.'

'He's been stalking me and getting persistent, rather too persistent. Won't take no for an answer. The other day he got in here. Pushed me around. Grabbed me by the throat.' I paused for effect. 'Tried to rape me.'

'Oh God.' Danny put his head in his hands. 'I never thought. If I had, I'd never have, you know. What a bastard!'

'So here's the thing. He told me he'd be back, and I believe him. I don't want him coming back. I want him to stop bothering me. And seeing as you are the cause of the problem, I thought you could maybe help me out. This little gift is a thankyou for doing that. The money's all yours, if you stop him molesting me. A simple request Danny: make Joe Peterson go away.'

# -32-

I took Danny to bed. He said he loved me. *How sweet*! He probably thought that was the polite thing to say when you had sex with someone, especially when you had sex twice. He was improving, definitely a seven this time. If he got the impression there were more episodes of that nature to come, provided he did what I wanted, so much the better. Although that's not what I said. What I said was that if he got rid of Joe, there'd be another five thousand pounds coming his way. Not sure what was the bigger incentive for him, more sex with me or another 5K. Either way, by the end of the evening he had agreed to do what was necessary.

It had taken him a while to cotton on, a sign (I guess) of his law-abiding nature. He complained that Joe was a big man and that he, Danny, didn't have the muscle to put the frighteners on him. 'But I know some lads,' he said. 'They're big and I know they'd quite fancy bashing a black guy.'

'No, Danny. Forget that. No mates. We have to keep this private, clean and simple. Our secret.'

He lowered his head, like a schoolboy being disciplined by a strict teacher. I put my finger under his chin and lifted his face to mine. 'You and me. That's all. This is between us. And Joe disappears. You make Joe disappear.'

The rather bewildered look on his face told me I needed to be more explicit. 'You see, Danny. You're a mechanic.'

He nodded.

'You know about brakes, brakes on cars. You know what might cause brakes on cars to fail.'

That's when it clicked. His eyes opened wide, he swallowed hard and licked his lips. To be fair to him, beyond that, he didn't flinch. Once he'd got it, he just nodded slowly.

'Remember. There's another five grand waiting for you.' I patted his breast pocket where he'd put the first envelope. I put my finger to his lips. 'And not a word to anyone. Our secret.' I kissed him lightly, pulling away when he tried to kiss me back: *always leave them wanting more.* 'Now go and make it happen.'

I wasn't sure if it would work. Danny was young, unworldly, and what little I knew of him told me he was a good, decent lad, not given to criminal tendencies. But he was infatuated with me and I was banking on that, and then there was the inducement of more money coming his way than he'd ever had before. Together, those factors ought to be enough to override his conscience. Would they though? I didn't know.

I also didn't know for sure that he had the wit and the technical expertise to do what was necessary. To tamper appropriately with Joe's car, so the driver wouldn't notice anything until the brakes failed when he was driving at speed. I'd told him the make and colour of the car and where it was parked. Would Danny even be smart enough to make sure he didn't get caught doing the tampering?

A lot of uncertainty. Many questions, many doubts. I'd done my bit. Now I could only wait to see whether Danny would deliver the goods.

# -33-

Those were painful days. I like being in control of my affairs, the manager of my own destiny. I hate having to rely on others. Fortunately, I didn't have to wait long.

Three days after I'd delivered my instructions to Danny, the local TV news carried a shot of a crumpled blue *Toyota* wrapped around a tree. I recognised it immediately as Joe's car. The cause of the crash was unknown (the reporter said), but no other vehicles appeared to be involved. The driver had been taken to hospital in critical condition. Police gave the estimated time and place of the accident and were asking for witnesses to come forward. They were particularly keen to hear from anyone with dashcam footage of the road around the time of the incident.

I was more than relieved, delighted you might say, although this was both good news and bad news. Danny had ensured the car had crashed: tick. And Joe had been injured: tick. But not killed: cross. Oh well, you can't have everything. Perhaps he had suffered excruciating pain in the accident and would continue to suffer in hospital: there's always a bright side if you look hard enough.

Our little section of north London is much like a village. There's a row of shops and cafés between the two tube stations, there's the garage, three pubs, side roads with a mixture of residences, including two blocks of flats, and a small park on the other side, bordered by some ancient woodland. That's about the extent of it. And like a village, there's always chatting on corners and in bars, plenty of gossip. I try not to get drawn into it. Even with my next-door neighbours, the conversations rarely stretch beyond the weather or the traffic or the days of collection for the bins after a Bank Holiday.

I often shop at Hassam's on the High Street. It has an off-licence section with a surprisingly interesting selection of wines, but mainly I use it for staples: eggs, milk, bread. It's probably more expensive, but it's handier than making the trek to Tesco's.

After the initial report of the accident, up-dates were never going to figure large in the local press or TV, it hardly being the news item of the year. But because the crash had happened on the by-pass, on the outskirts of our 'village', I knew there'd be information going the rounds in the neighbourhood, and Mo at Hassam's was usually the hub for such data-transfer. I lingered in the side aisle as I heard the discussion at the till between Mo and two elderly ladies. Apparently, the driver had been drinking before the crash and was two-and-a-half times over the limit. He was in hospital and unconscious: 'serves him right,' according to one of the ladies; 'lucky he didn't kill someone,' according to the other one. Mo informed them that if the driver ever became conscious again, he'd suffer from permanent brain damage. So he'd heard.

I keep away from the gossip circuit because it can't be trusted. I assumed these details about Joe were unlikely to be 100% accurate, having arrived at Mo via several exaggerating steps. Even so, the gist was probably correct.

By the time I took my basket to the counter, the ladies had left the shop. Mo continued the conversation as if I'd been a party to the earlier exchange. 'They say he was drinking hard at the King's Head, old Freddie saw him there. Several hours, drinking on his own. No-one knows who he is. Freddie said he'd been in a few times, but only recently. He's not local, he was renting a room from Phyllis Arnold on the corner. He worked at *Kwik-Fit*, you know, the garage. Jane said he gave her a good deal on two tyres.'

'Did he? I get my car serviced there.' I felt I should contribute something.

'Twelve pounds thirty-eight. Did you know him?'

I shook my head and handed over a £20 note. I'd never heard of any of the people Mo had mentioned. He assumes everyone knows everyone. He gave me my change. 'He was black, you know. That's why I thought ...'

Endemic racism they call it. It's never more than a whisker's width away. Mo's complexion was hardly whiter than white, so you'd think he'd know better. But that's what 'endemic' means. It's inbuilt, automatic, outside all logical thought but at the forefront of emotional reactions. Always. It's nasty but you tell yourself you're used to it, even though you never are.

Back home, I checked my phone. There was a text from Danny.

*I need to see you. Can I come round? x*

I replied: *No, not here. I'll meet you in the park.*

We agreed time and place, and half an hour later I walked through the park gates and climbed the path to the crest of the small hill. Danny was already sitting on the bench in blue overalls with a logo on his chest, his work-clothes. I sat next to him. We didn't look at each other. It felt like an episode in some spy drama, the cold war, secrets and intrigue, that sort of thing. We needed grey drizzle to be thoroughly authentic; instead we had bright summer sunshine.

After checking there was no-one within earshot I spoke: 'Well done, Danny. I don't think that bastard will be troubling me anymore.'

He didn't look at me. Out of the corner of my eye I could see him shake his head, fiddle with the button on his sleeve, scratch his nose.

'You okay?' I asked.

'Sure. Yes. Okay.'

I slid the envelope along the bench. He didn't touch it. 'As promised,' I said.

'No,' he said. 'No. I didn't do nothing.'

I looked at him. 'What?'

'I didn't do a fucking thing. I couldn't.' He was still looking straight ahead, not at me. It was the first time I'd heard him swear.

'I thought you knew how to ...'

'Oh, I know how. But when it came to it, I couldn't. Bottled it. And then he crashed. No idea why. Except it's like I wished it, ain't it? It's my fault. My fucking fault.'

'Wait, Danny. Let's rewind here. To be clear. You didn't mess with Joe's car? Didn't fiddle with the brake cable?'

Danny shook his head.

I let out a puff of air, lifted my face to the warmth of the sun. 'So.' It was taking me a while to process this. 'So it was an accident. A real accident. Simple as. Nothing to do with you. Nothing to do with me. Well. Who'd have thought?'

'But don't you get it?' Now Danny did turn to me. 'I wanted it to happen. So much. So he wouldn't mess with you no more. Then it happened. So I'm still to blame. It happened because I wanted it.'

'Don't be silly. I wanted it too. And probably there are others. Plenty of others. I doubt he was the most popular guy around, plenty of enemies. But it's not their fault, it's not our fault. It's not your fault. The prat got pissed and drove into a tree. Fact. Accident.'

'Still. I can't stop thinking. You know.'

We sat in silence for a while. 'Take the money,' I said.

'No, really. I don't deserve it. I didn't do nothing.'

'You've earned it, Danny. You've earned it.'

He took some persuading, but eventually he slipped the envelope into his pocket. I felt sorry for him. That was a strange feeling. I don't usually feel sorry for people, weakness not being something I admire much. But Danny was trying to be strong. He just wasn't very good at it.

I made it clear when he took the money that this was to be the end of all contact between us. He wasn't to call me again, or text. He nodded. I think the events of the previous few days had cooled his ardour. He would be pleased to be rid of me, rid of the reminder of what he'd nearly done, and what he still believed he had caused. He'd be able to concentrate on growing up.

# -34-

When the day arrived, the day Joe had said he'd call back, I was on edge, trying to keep busy. I pulled up some weeds Felix had missed from the patio area. I rearranged the furniture in my bedroom, moving the bed against the other wall, to give a better view over the park. I played music loud. I went to the computer and tried to get interested in a live news feed, but it was something political, didn't hold my interest. I threw out Danny's wilting flowers. I washed the kitchen floor.

I wasn't really expecting Joe to appear, yet I still feared that he might. The word on the street – or at least, the word in Hassam's - was that he was still in hospital, in a coma and barely alive. But I didn't trust it. Didn't trust that man not to find a way. Perhaps he hadn't been injured at all. Perhaps it hadn't even been him driving the car, he'd lent it to a friend.

Then the day came to an end, and Joe had not come calling. I felt I could relax.

The next day I flew to Lanzarote. Yes, it was peak season, but I couldn't wait. I could consider it a late birthday present to myself: my twentieth birthday had recently come and gone.

I needed to get away from the environment which had been contaminated by Joe, by Danny, by my memories of Richard Wright, memories of sex and death.

At the *Hotel Lava Beach*, I swam in the pool, read under the sunshades, sipped cocktails in the evening.

I ran on the prom in the early morning, while it was still empty and cool; later I wandered along the sand towards Puerto del Carmen and watched people relaxing, swimming, sunbathing.

I avoided the clubs, I had no wish for any social contact, certainly not the mock-intense emotion associated with those cattle-markets.

I allowed the hotel waiters to flirt a little, as they do, and I flirted back, all the while making it clear there was nothing on the agenda beyond flirtation. Then I gave in and let one of them, a well-muscled young Greek, called Ramos, take me to bed. Not my wisest decision: he earned no more than a five, and that was me being generous.

I ate well and drank well and slept well. I particularly enjoyed the freedom that comes with spending all day in a brief bikini, bare skin plastered in high-factor sunscreen. Yes, even people of colour need protection from sunburn.

I returned home a week later, to the evident signs of early autumn, and it felt like returning home after a holiday, some disorientation, some disappointment, but mostly a feeling of contentment.

*The heart is where the home is.*

# -35-

When I flew to Lanzarote, I'd left my phone at home. Most people couldn't do that, they see their phone as a lifeline, a vital connection to a world that gives their existence legitimacy. I don't think like that. My phone is a tool, an add-on, not an essential ingredient of real life. You might call me old-fashioned. In Lanzarote, I had no need of that tool: I left it behind.

Once I was back, I recharged it and checked for missed calls. There were several voicemails and texts from Danny. I didn't bother to read them or listen to them, I could guess what they contained. There were other texts from names I didn't recognise. In the email inbox there were dozens of messages: advertisements, scams and other irrelevancies. None of this interested me. I took the simcard out of the phone and cut it into several pieces. I found a stiletto heel to drive through the phone itself. I slid the remnants into an envelope and placed the envelope in old Mum's suitcase.

I bought another phone, pay-as-you-go, with a new number. There were no contacts I wanted to enter. I would mostly use the phone to download books or surf the web when I was away from my laptop.

I called a security firm to install a top-of-the-range system. Joe may have no longer been a threat, but I couldn't be certain of that, and anyway, who knew when the next slimeball would crawl out of the swamp The guys who fitted the alarms pointed out the inadequacy of the locks on my windows and doors: I upgraded them.

I ordered two cases of wine.

I ordered hard-back copies of the books on that year's Booker Prize short-list.

I down-loaded a selection of movies that I'd not yet watched, from a list of the previous decade's 'top films', according to some survey I found online.

My life was beginning again.

With my private world in order, I could turn my attention to the outward-looking theme of my life, my project, my mission. I read Mum's last letter again. I read Grandma's diary again, especially concentrating on the entry about the party. The wrongness of it all hit me afresh. So much damage caused, so many ramifications. Yet for those who caused the damage, no consequences at all. Not then, anyway. Maybe now chickens were coming home to roost, first for Richard Wright, next for Stephen Greene.

Stephen Greene. Who was he? Where was he? It was time for me to go hunting.

# -36-

The only lead I had on Stephen Greene was the school he attended over forty years previously, the same school as Richard Wright. I looked it up online. There was quite a history. It had moved to new premises in 1973 and converted to a Vith Form College in 1978. In 1990 it had moved again, and was now a College of Further Education. None of that was interesting, except that it made it very unlikely the present establishment would have any record of pupils who attended the old school in 1966, and certainly no forwarding addresses. I didn't even bother to contact them to check.

Presumably Richard Wright and Stephen Greene had been friends. It was possible they'd stayed in contact, at least for a few years after they'd left school, even if not beyond that. It was a bit late now, but I wondered whether there had been any opportunity to ask Richard. It hadn't occurred to me at the time, because it was Richard himself who was the centre of my attention, my only target. I couldn't remember him saying anything that suggested he was still in touch with old school-friends, but we had never really had that sort of conversation. For all I knew, he might have been.

That's when it hit me: I had Richard's computer. That could well contain the link I needed, the link to Stephen. Assuming the two of them had kept in touch. It was a long shot, but worth a try.

When you use a computer, sitting at a desk, in a room on your own, focused on the screen, it feels as though you're indulging in a private activity. There's no-one looking over your shoulder, monitoring what you're doing, checking you, coming to judgments. Except, in fact, there is, there always is. Oh, maybe not a real person, a physical, breathing, carbon-based life-form, but that observer is there for sure, right by your side. Every key pressed, every icon clicked, every page scrolled through, it all registers somewhere 'out there' (or should that be 'in there'?). Big AI is watching you. Always.

This reasoning went through my head in the time it took me to get out old Mum's suitcase and extract Richard's laptop. Fortunately, I'd reached the conclusion before I sparked the computer into life. Nearly a blunder. Of course, I couldn't use Richard's computer: to do so would be utter foolishness. Even if the police were not actively monitoring any e-activity that they could link to the demise of Richard Wright, as soon as I accessed that computer, I'd begin leaving a cyber-trail across the electronic universe, and that evidence could return to bite me further down the line. No, I must not use Richard's computer: I put it back in the case and put the case back under the bed, and recorded in my mind a mistake nearly made, a mistake to steer clear of in the future. I was still learning lessons.

The thoughts of Richard and Stephen being in contact provoked another idea. Perhaps there existed some sort of old boys' club, for former pupils of that old school. A forum for alumni to get in contact with each other, to chat about the old days.

I searched for it and soon found it. The Old Rubicunds it was called. The name derived from the colour of their uniform, which had been predominately red. It was a closed group, access only granted to former students of the school. I considered inventing a name, to see how robust their monitoring system was, but then I opted for a less provocative path. The only other former pupil's name I knew was the third name on Diane's list, Grahame DeFreitas: I used that. I only had to enter name and years of attendance. One day later, I received the email acceptance.

*Hello Grahame, Welcome to the group. We don't have many from as long ago as that, but there are a few of you still around. Post a short introduction about yourself and see what happens. Good luck!*

# -37-

Browsing through the comments on the Old Rubicunds message-board, I felt like a detective garnering clues – perhaps that Vera from the TV programme, I quite fancied the floppy hat and the overcoat!

I'd kept my initial post deliberately vague, simply asking if anyone remembered back as far as the 1960s. There were a few responses, but no-one claimed to know 'me', Grahame DeFreitas. Then scrolling back through the history on the site, I eventually found what I was looking for, a post from Stephen Greene. There had been a thread a couple of years previously, complaining about how bad the teachers had been, and Stephen had chipped in defending the staff and claiming that teaching was a tough profession. A few months earlier, there was another discussion Stephen had contributed to. A couple were recalling a particularly horrendous algebra lesson they'd shared; it had made no sense to them at all, and they claimed it put them off maths for life. Again Stephen put the opposing view, saying that mathematics was easy if it was properly taught.

I deduced that Stephen was himself a teacher, probably a teacher of maths.

I found one more pertinent clue. There were several posts in which Stephen and someone called Andy compared recollections, about the school and mutual friends and various news items from the 1960s: Radio Caroline (which was a pirate radio station), the death of JFK, and something called TW3 (I couldn't figure out what that was). Then Andy had said he was about to go off on holiday, and Stephen suggested that when he returned, via Heathrow, Andy should 'drop in' and see him.

So, one more deduction: Stephen lived in West London, probably in the vicinity of Hounslow. Just a coincidence, but that's where Joe had said he lived. Funny how you don't hear about a place for ages and then it crops up wherever you look.

I withdrew from the group with some relief. No-one had challenged me, claiming that for some reason I couldn't possibly be Grahame DeFreitas. Also, DeFreitas himself hadn't appeared: I assumed he couldn't have been a participant in the group. So all-in-all, I felt I'd had a success: plenty of info on Stephen acquired and my true identity not revealed, no suspicions aroused.

Although once a teacher, Stephen G may have retired by now. Then again, some teachers seem to go on forever. It was all I had to go on, so I kept my fingers crossed and hit the search engines.

I checked through schools in the Hounslow area. It took me most of the afternoon. Many of the websites didn't list the names of staff members, so I had to record them as 'maybe's, and leave it until later to figure a way to find out who taught there. For those that did give a list, I could check the names and put a cross against the school. Then I struck gold. I guess even Vera needs a bit of luck sometimes! Listed among the staff members of Heathcote Academy was a teacher by the name of Stephen Greene. I couldn't be sure it was 'my' Stephen Greene, of course, but he was in the mathematics department, which made me hopeful. They didn't list contact details for individual teachers, so I sent an email to the School Administrator, saying I was looking for private maths tuition and someone had recommended Stephen Greene. Could he be asked to contact me? I gave my name as Anne Elliot. Perhaps I should have learned my lesson, after Richard had seen through my Emma Woodhouse disguise, but I'm a fan of Jane Austen and anyway this Stephen was a mathematician: the name would mean nothing to him.

# -38-

'Hello. Is that Miss Elliot?'

'Yes. That's me.'

'Right. My name is Dr Stephen Greene.'

Him using the 'doctor' rather threw me. But I'd got him. He was on the line, I mustn't lose him now. 'Hello Dr Greene.'

'I understand you're looking for someone to provide you with private tuition in mathematics.'

'Yes. That's right.'

'Janet didn't give me much information. I don't know exactly what you're after, so I may not be the best person for you. I've not done any coaching for quite a while.'

'Oh, I'm sure you're exactly what I need. I've been told you're the best around. You were a student at the old boys' high school, weren't you, an old Rubicund?

There was hesitancy. He hadn't expected that. But he didn't deny it, so I was sure I'd got my man. Then: 'Who told you that?'

'Oh, she was very definite. She didn't want me to tell you it was her.'

There was another pause, more prolonged this time. I wondered if he'd hung up, assuming I was someone wasting his time. But no. The hesitation was because he liked to think his words through before vocalising them. 'You're not a Heathcote girl, are you? I checked our lists. So which school are you attending?'

'Oh no. I'm not at school. A bit past all that.'

Another prolonged pause. 'Perhaps you'd better tell me exactly what you want.'

I hadn't thought this through properly. I was conscious I was waffling as I tried to tell him what I presumed he needed to hear. The main point was to convince him to agree to giving me lessons.

I think, in the end, he gave me the benefit of the doubt, put my mumblings down to nervousness. 'Perhaps we should meet up. To talk about it?'

*Yes, yes, yes,* I said in my mind. I took a breath. 'Yes, that sounds like a plan.'

'What's the best time for you?'

'Oh, any time. I'm flexible. To suit you.'

'How about Friday this week, after school?'

'Sure. Fine.'

He explained that meeting in school would be complicated, security being so tight these days, he'd need to get clearance for a visitor. He suggested meeting at a public house near the school. We agreed on six o'clock.

So I now knew what Stephen Greene, *Doctor* Stephen Greene, sounded like. Thoughtful, quietly spoken, careful in his word choices. He had rather an odd accent, not London, but not conspicuously regional either. I've watched old TV clips, and announcers in bowties used to speak like the queen, in what they called BBC English or Received Punctuation. Stephen's voice had a hint of that, but it was as though he'd spent years trying to cover it up. That's what it sounded like to me.

# -39-

When I walked into The Crown, I had no difficulty spotting him. He was the only person there, sitting at a table by the window. He stood up as I approached and held out his hand.

'Dr Greene?' We shook hands.

'Can I get you a drink?' he asked.

'Oh no. I'll get it.'

I bought myself a glass of lemonade and lime and sat down opposite him.

'Sorry for this rather sordid setting,' he said, gesturing at the surroundings. I'd seen worse. 'Only, these days, security at school. Forms to fill in, checks to be made. Crazy.' He shrugged and sipped from his half-pint glass.

He was a small man, with thinning grey hair, half-frame glasses. The age was about right. He must have been past retirement age, so why was he still teaching? If I hadn't known his profession, I'd have guessed teacher, he had that look about him. He should have been dressed in a fair-isle cardigan, and a jacket with patches on the sleeves. In fact he wore a rather shiny grey suit and a blue open-necked shirt. I was guessing he had a striped tie that he'd worn all day, now tucked into a pocket. Another thought came unbidden: he did not look like a rapist.

He came straight to the point: 'So you want some mathematics tuition, is that right?'

I nodded.

'What sort of level are we talking?'

'A-level,' I said, without giving it much thought.

'Are you taking a course? At college?'

'Oh no, self-teaching. Self-teaching but not self-learning, if you get my drift. It doesn't seem to stick. That's why I need some help.'

He took a sip from his glass. I followed suit. He gave his next words careful consideration. Like all his words, to be honest.

'Coaching works best when it's just topping up. Helping you over obstacles, clarifying misconceptions. It's not a course in its own right. I wouldn't be able to give you enough time for that. As your tutor, I can't provide an organised course, there's no systematic structure, no scheme of work.'

'Okay. I get that. But I am working my way through an online course. You said: *Helping get over obstacles* – yes, that sounds exactly what I need.'

He asked me when I'd taken my GCSE and what grade I'd got. I made up what I hoped were plausible answers. He asked some maths questions, to check what I remembered. It was algebra, which I'd always found confusing. I tried to bluff my way through but knew I wasn't very convincing. In response to his close questioning I had to admit that in fact there was no proper online course, and that I was only dropping in on some random pages I found through internet searches. (Of course, the truth was not even that, but I had to somehow convince him I was serious.) I could sense it wasn't working. Having been caught out in a lie, however minor, wasn't helping my cause. He asked me where I lived, and when I told him he said that surely there was someone closer to home I could go to. He was trying to get out of it.

I drained my glass and took a deep breath, and then replayed the one ace I seemed to hold: I told him how strongly he'd been recommended.

'And who was it who recommended me? You didn't say before.'

'I'm sorry Dr Greene, I really can't say. But she was most definite. *That Dr Greene is the business*, she told me. *He'll get you through*. You're the only teacher I'd consider.'

He was the same as most people in one regard: flattery was a powerful inducement. Whatever his doubts about coaching me, I'm sure it was my lies about the recommendation that swung it.

All that was left was to discuss some practicalities, the fee he'd charge, how often we'd meet, those sort of details. I'd clinched it. Dr Stephen Greene was going to teach me A-level mathematics. *Good luck with that*, I thought, as I made my way back to the tube.

Of course, I had no desire to learn any maths. What I wanted was to develop some sort of relationship with Stephen Greene, so I could find out about him, especially find out what he remembered about 1966. About the party, about Diane. Any relationship would do: if student/ tutor was the only relationship on offer, then I'd take that. I'd somehow make it work.

# -40-

Stephen Greene's house was smaller than I was expecting, semi-detached, neat front garden, opposite a park. Lots of trees in the vicinity, and the front garden and surrounding area were layered with auburn leaves: autumn had arrived early. It was a nice area. He opened the door as soon as I rang the bell and led me through to what I took to be a dining room. One wall had cabinets displaying various items of patterned crockery; the wall opposite was covered in bookshelves. I tried to check out the titles, but the only ones I could identify were either maths text books, popular science volumes, or books about trains; there was no fiction as far as I could see, apart from a complete box set of *Thomas the Tank Engine*. In the middle of the room was a dark wood table and four matching high-backed chairs. On the table were a couple of pads of paper, some pens and a pile of text books.

'Take a seat, Ms Elliot.'

'Anne, please.' He didn't invite me to use his first name. He was smartly dressed, hair combed flat with a side parting, every inch a school teacher, peering through the thick lenses of his spectacles.

He had set me the task of brushing up my algebra, via a website with graded practice questions. I'd put in the time, and brought the evidence with me. There was no introductory small-talk: he checked out my work and seemed satisfied.

'What I thought we might try, since you're not following a formal course, is for me to introduce a topic, and for you to follow it up on the website. I can give you the link. How does that sound?'

'You're the boss.'

'But you're paying the piper: I play whatever tune you request.' Was that a smile? I couldn't be sure and whatever it was, it faded fast. Dr Greene was nothing if not professional in his manner. 'But if you are wanting to make progress, you must practise. Practise regularly and practise a lot. Are you prepared to do that?'

'Oh yes.'

He introduced me to differentiation. He spoke slowly and carefully, gave me plenty of opportunities to ask questions, but it was very confusing. If he was a good teacher, then I'd hate to discover how mystifying that topic would be in the hands of a poor teacher.

Back home that evening, I tried some of the questions from the website. I got the first half-dozen right and was beginning to grow in confidence, but then they got harder. I gave up: it was boring as well as impenetrable.

What was I trying to achieve? Essentially, it was to get to know Dr Stephen Greene. I needed to know him well enough to ask him about the past, his past, check out what he remembered. Did he remember that party in 1966, did he remember Diane? How did he feel at the time and how did he feel now, about the events of that evening?

And then what? Good question. All the while I'd been chasing Richard Wright, the ultimate aim was never far from my thoughts, I always knew where the association was headed. Richard's past as a rapist was only part of the picture and, as I began to know him better, I was soon building towards the scenario in which I'd extract revenge for Diane, make him pay with no qualms, knowing what an all-round prick he was. But with Stephen Greene, it already felt quite different. It wasn't that I particularly liked the man. To be honest, he was something of a nonentity. Take away his maths and his teaching and there was nothing left. Yet although it was hard to like him, it was equally hard to hate him. I couldn't imagine stabbing him. Well, I could, but it would be a non-event, like slicing open a pineapple, something that would be neither horrifying nor pleasurable. But yes, I suppose I could imagine it. When I thought about what he'd done to Diane, then I could imagine it. I licked my lips and swallowed hard, feeling my blood pulse.

Perhaps my feelings would change if I got to know him better. Perhaps I'd find a reason for excusing his behaviour as a teenager, maybe even be prepared to forgive him, although I wasn't sure I could give myself permission to do that, it was not really part of the remit I'd set for myself. Alternatively, I might become surer in my condemnation of his behaviour, more certain in my condemnation of the man himself.

This was a complicated business.

I resolved to stick with the lessons for a while, to use this contact to try and draw him out as we got more used to each other. Perhaps he'd relax and allow for some sort of friendship to develop, closer than that of teacher/student. I needed to find something in him to stir my emotions.

I opened a bottle of wine. That usually helps.

I ordered a delivery of Chinese food – three dishes, prawn crackers and two sorts of rice: much of it would end up wasted, but I like to have a choice.

While waiting for the meal to arrive, I had another crack at the differentiation. Bewilderment persisted.

# -41-

It was on my fourth or fifth visit to Stephen that I met his wife, Caroline. The sessions had fallen into a repeat pattern, Stephen checking my progress at the week's tasks, correcting my misunderstandings (or trying to), and introducing a new topic. We'd moved on to trigonometry, which made more sense than calculus, although that wasn't saying much.

Caroline answered the door, 'Miss Elliot, I presume.'

'Yes. Sorry. I was expecting ...'

'Robbo's not here, I'm afraid. Should be back by half past. Do you want to come in and wait?'

*Robbo?* I followed her through to a living room I'd not been in before. 'Robbo said he'd understand if you wanted to cancel today. Or you could wait. You'll still get the full hour.'

'Sorry, Mrs Greene, but ...'

'Caroline, please. Call me Caroline.'

'Okay, Caroline. But who's Robbo?'

She smiled and held up her hands in surrender. 'No, it's me who should apologise. Robbo's what I've always called him, a nickname from when he was a boy. You'll know him by his professional name, Dr Greene. Stephen.'

'Had me confused for a minute there. I'm Anne. Only name I've got.' We shook hands.

She offered me a seat. 'Would you like some tea? I'm sure Robbo ... Stephen ... won't be long.'

Straight away I felt more relaxed, and within five minutes I was getting a more hospitable welcome from the wife than I'd got from the husband in five weeks. I needed to make use of this opportunity. It could be a way in, a means of getting closer to my target.

Caroline, I decided, was best summed up by the term 'smart-casual.' That's how she was dressed, in contrast to her husband's inevitable formal wear (the suit and tie were presumably his working clothes). The same adjective described her manner, her tone of voice, her choice of conversation topics. She seemed to be a naturally friendly woman, but she wasn't about to lose sight of my position in her household – a paying customer, her husband's pupil, not a social equal. Her stylish elegance was rather marred by ugly fingernails, well-chewed.

We drank tea and Caroline provided slices of cake, some sort of sponge which may have been home-made, quite tasty. 'Lovely,' I said, judging it to be the correct response. 'This is such a nice house. Have you lived here long?'

'Oh, donkeys' years. Thirty? Maybe more.'

I looked at the photos on the mantelpiece. 'Are those your children?'

'Yes. Christine and Charlotte. Of course, they don't look much like that now. Both married, with children of their own.'

'How wonderful.' I think that's what you're supposed to say to grandparents.

'What do you do?' she asked. 'You're older than Robbo's usual tutees. You're not still at school, I'm guessing.'

'Oh no. Well past all that. I rather wasted my final years, you know how it is, teenage angst took over, messed me up. I'm hoping to get to Uni as a mature student. I rather fancy accountancy.'

'It's never too late.' She sipped her tea. 'Not these days. Even women can have a career, whatever their background, wherever they come from. Accountancy's a good choice. Companies always need accountants. And they pay them well.'

*What did she mean by 'background'?* 'Are you in business?'

'Used to be. Not anymore. A life of leisurely retirement. A bit of gardening and cooking. Lace-making.' She gestured to a pillow on a stand in the corner, with bobbins and threads hanging from it. Then she stared out of the window, a frown on her face, some thoughts clouding her mind.

'I'm surprised your husband still works, still teaches. He must be of retirement age.

She turned to me, shook her head as if shaking off her contemplation. 'What else would he do? It's his life, mathematics. He has nothing else. Apart from the trains.'

'Trains?'

'Hasn't he mentioned his trains?'

'We only ever talk about maths.'

She stood up and walked across to the window, gesturing for me to follow. This room was at the back of the house, and looked out on a smallish garden, mostly lawn, bordered by a few shrubs. But the space was dominated by a large shed. I suppose 'outhouse' would be a better word, because it was significantly more substantial than your average garden tool-shed. 'That's where he keeps his trains,' she said. 'Ask him and he'll tell you all about them. He loves to show them off.'

# -42-

Soon after Caroline told me about the trains in the shed, Stephen came home and, full of apologies, took me through to the dining room. We had our usual class. He said I was progressing well, but he was lying: I had learned hardly anything, or rather nothing that had stuck. A few snippets of knowledge had come and gone. I suppose it's a standard device, praising your student so as to ensure they stay interested and therefore keep paying for more lessons. For me, learning maths felt like wading through treacle, every step an effort; like wandering through a maze blindfolded, or climbing a semolina-soaked pole while weighed down by a suit of armour. Similes and metaphors, I was good at those; maths less so. My summary verdict on maths was that it was both hard and pointless. Yet I needed to keep going, or at least give my tutor the impression I was keeping going. It was proving tougher than I expected.

At the end of the class I wanted to ask about his trains. Perhaps that would be a way of breaking down the barrier that was separating us, allow some link to develop. But, as usual, Stephen Greene was entirely professional, assigned me my homework and bade me farewell, leaving no room for small-talk.

On the tube heading home, I sat where I always sat, in the relative peace of the end carriage. But on this occasion a family with young children joined me, and the children were mobile and noisy. The parents seemed to adopt a non-interventionist policy. I had my book out, but couldn't concentrate. I realised, not for the first time, how much I hated children. Perhaps 'hate' is the wrong word: I simply wished to have nothing to do with them, to avoid them at all costs, and hoped they'd subscribe to a reciprocal arrangement. Did Caroline hate children? Was that the reason for the rather odd moments in our conversation? When she'd mentioned grandchildren, I was prepared for a roll-call of names and ages, identification of their features of wonderfulness, all that pride that seems to flow so readily. Older people are so much prouder of their grandchildren than they ever were of their children, or that's how it seems to me. They love to talk about them at great length: I have two near neighbours who are prime examples. But no, Caroline gave me none of that. And also, there were no photos of the children on display. The only photograph was the one of her two girls when they were teenagers, presumably ten or fifteen years ago. No pictures of the grandchildren at all, not as babies, not as toddlers. Strange.

And another strangeness. She'd spoken about her husband's 'usual students,' and how they were younger than me. Yet he'd told me, in that first meeting, that he hadn't done any coaching for many years. It was all rather odd. They appeared to be a perfectly normal couple, happily married, comfortably off. Straightforward. One retired, the other content to still be working. And yet there were these oddities. Was I reading too much into them? Maybe, but something about them didn't feel right.

After dinner, I sat on the sofa with the remains of a glass of wine, *Aerosmith* blasting from the speakers. I looked out across the lawn. The garden had that air of closure that comes when the warm colours of autumn have begun to fade, and the signs of the inevitability of winter hibernation are everywhere to see.

Diane's diary was on the coffee table. Something Caroline said had rang a bell and I flicked through the pages of the diary, looking for the relevant entry. Yes, there it was. Diane had mentioned a boy with the initial 'R' a couple of times in the lead up to the party entry. When I'd read the diary before I'd briefly thought that was Richard Wright, before quickly realising I was wrong. Still, I hadn't connected this 'R' with the party. Diane didn't rate him highly: a 'four-eyed creep' was one of the many disparaging remarks she'd written. Also, 'R for rank and revolting.' She seemed to regard him as a nuisance, a persistent fly that needed swatting away, the class nerd and worse. I was curious about the nickname, but a google search was all it took to solve the mystery. There was a TV programme in the 1960s about Robin Hood, and the title character was played by an actor called Richard Greene. That's how nicknames arise – Greene, Robin, Robbo.

I read those earlier entries more carefully, now I knew that Robbo and Stephen were one and the same. Diane really didn't like him, but was actually quite dismissive, as though he didn't matter. I don't think she mentioned him being at the party, although her codified writing meant I couldn't be sure. But he was clearly present in her list of rapists, given his full name. What Caroline termed his professional name.

With Caroline's words still rattling round my brain, and the memory of that tube journey still disappointingly fresh, I thought again about children. I couldn't imagine ever having children of my own, never mind grandchildren. Winding back from that thought, I had to first imagine a relationship with a man – or, I suppose, it could be a woman – that I was committed to making permanent, or at least stable for a while. It had to be strong and secure enough so that the two of us could be prepared to take on the responsibility for new life. Sounded crazily impossible. If I couldn't manage that, the only way I'd have children would be as a single-mum, and that was even more unimaginable, a horrific thought. So how did such a close relationship arise, a partnership ready for parenthood? And why, given that most children are so unpleasant? In stories, it was always love that was the fundamental premise, the driving force. That mysterious emotion overrides everything else (if you believe what you read in novels). It's not that mysterious. I know about love: it's fantastic and electric and flames fiercely for a while, before exploding and dying, leaving cooling embers of fragrant memories. Fun: yes. But permanent? No. Love is always fleeting, always transient. It could not be a reason to subsume your existence into someone else's. Never mind the further progression, the twist of the spiral, that took us into the catastrophic minefield encapsulated by the word 'family'. What a gruesome word! No. Wife, mother, grandmother: these were not terms that would ever apply to me. I refused to be defined by my relationship to someone else. Daughter was bad enough: I thought of Joe, still presumably lying unconscious in hospital. Or dead, I had heard nothing for a while. And granddaughter: I rejected that term also. My reason for going after these evil men had nothing to do with the fact that Diane was my grandmother. This was not a family's revenge. It was simply a woman's revenge. Not even that, there was no feminist agenda, no appeal to the solidarity of the sisterhood. This was *my* revenge, or *society*'s revenge. In raping Diane, those three men had not only sinned against Diane, they had sinned against society, against humanity.

I drained my glass. Not sure any of that line of thinking would make sense to anyone else. It made sense to me, and that's all that mattered. If Stephen and Caroline's extended family was less than ideal, they had my sympathy. Families suck.

It was time for an hour or so of maths homework before rewarding myself by taking a novel to bed. The printed word never lets you down.

# -43-

During my Hunstanton adventure, inertia had carried me forward. I knew what I was planning to do and everything unfolded according to that plan. I suppose it helped that Richard Wright was such an obnoxious bastard. I didn't need confirmation that he was guilty of rape in order to hate him. It was different with Stephen: I felt I was getting nowhere, merely marking time, and I wasn't even sure what I wanted, how I was expecting matters to develop as the days and weeks rolled by. All I knew was that I needed to get closer to him, to get to know him better. But how? This tutor/tutee relationship was telling me nothing about him, he never swerved away from the maths agenda. Did I need to fake an interest in trains? Not sure I could manage that.

Perhaps I needed to be subtler. He had two daughters and who knew how many grandchildren. Could I get to him via them?

There was a third idea. That autumn the English football team had been winning some matches. Accordingly, there was a growth in large red-and-white St Georges' flags being hung from bedroom windows, smaller versions sticking out from car wing-mirrors. The UK news feeds, as usual on such occasions, were making repeated reference to 1966 when England beat West Germany in a football match. Perhaps that would give me an opportunity to ask Stephen what he remembered about that year.

These thoughts buoyed me on my next tube journey towards Hounslow. As it happened, all three ideas bore fruit, although none of them quite as I had expected them to.

That day I had another brief conversation with Caroline which gave me an opportunity to make progress on the trains front. The encounter was not long enough for tea and cake, but I still found time to mention how keen I was to see her husband's trains. 'They sound interesting,' I said, aiming to appear curious but not unrealistically enthusiastic.

'You should tell him,' she said, just as we heard the front door. 'Robbo,' she called. 'Anne says she'd like to see your trains.' She gestured for me to go through to the dining room.

Stephen (I still thought of him as Stephen, rather than Robbo), gave me an odd look, then said: 'Work before pleasure.' We sat down for the normal lesson. I think it was the binomial theorem. *No, me neither.* Once we'd finished and he'd given me my tasks for the week, he stood up. 'Right,' he said. 'It's trains time.'

I followed him into the garden. The shed, or shack, looked even bigger close up. He unlocked the door and led me inside, flicking a light switch.

There's no sense in which I'm 'into' trains: not real ones, not toy ones, neither old ones nor new ones; I don't even enjoy reading about them except when they're used to transport interesting characters to interesting places. But it was hard not to be impressed by the set-up in Stephen's shed. There was a complex network of track in a raised display that filled most of the extensive space. There were tunnels and crossovers and sidings, and plenty of other intricacies that I didn't know the names of. When he pushed the buttons on the control panel, several engines went into motion, pulling coaches and trucks of various descriptions in various directions. Their paths seemed to interlink, to cross over in places, but there were no crashes. There was also an extensive range of plastic scenery, not particularly realistic, but representing a plausible attempt at verisimilitude: signals, stations, trees, farm animals, various figures depicting railwaymen, passengers, onlookers.

Stephen spoke at great length about all of it, adding extensive detail on how it came to be as it was, when and where he'd acquired the various components, which parts of real-life networks were being recreated in miniature. He let me take control of one of the trains. *Yay, exciting, eh?* He closely monitored my movement of the lever, continually correcting my clumsiness.

In that shed, Stephen came alive, I saw a different man. I already knew he had a passion for mathematics, I'd seen that, but I could tell that his engagement with the subject had become jaded over the years, the light had faded and he was a shadow of the undoubtedly energetic researcher he'd been in his youth. But his passion for trains was of a different order, and in that shed he was still vigorously youthful. His face grew in animation as he identified each subtle feature of his lay-out, eager to share the information with me, as though he was showing off a favourite child, proud of his creation. The smoke from the funnels, the chuntering sound of engines in motion, the horn that sounded on entry to a tunnel: every such aspect was an excuse for yet more lively exposition and his face positively beamed as he told me all about it. I tried to pay attention.

'It's wonderful to see you appreciating this, Miss Elliot.' It was a rarity for him to express any emotion. 'Especially with you being a girl. It's normally the boys who get excited.' He smiled with genuine pleasure. I was pleased with myself for having faked my reaction so effectively.

I don't remember much of the detail of Dr Greene's wonderful toy. As I've said, trains leave me cold, so I concentrated on trying to conceal my boredom. What I remember from that visit was the man's evident delight in his train-set, so much more than a toy in his eyes, and his simple pleasure at sharing his obsession with another, even if it was only me, with my feigned enthusiasm and my stifled yawns.

I noticed one other thing in Stephen's shed. The vast instillation filled most of the space, but there was a corner which the track avoided. This corner was decked out as a miniature living room. There was a two-seater sofa, a scrap of carpet on the floor, a coffee table with an angle-poise lamp. Under the table I spotted a bottle of brandy and two tumblers, which surprised me: I hadn't had Stephen down as a drinker. Against the wall was a small book case, with a selection of books on trains and related topics. Did he, Stephen/Robbo, sometimes come and hide away in this shed? Escape from his wife? And when he tired of playing trains, did he settle himself in that corner, sipping brandy and reading about trains? It was possible, but despite his infatuation, something about it didn't ring quite true.

# -44-

The trip to the shed was a one-off. Our meetings returned to being focused maths tutorials, at the end of which I was dismissed as though a school-bell had chimed: he left no space for chit-chat, for non-mathematical small talk, there was no mention of trains. Perhaps if I could have come up with some inciteful question concerning his wonderful hobby, that might have broken down the barrier; but such was beyond me.

All I'd learned from my visit to the shed was that Stephen had an obsessive interest in toy trains. As far as getting close to him was concerned, that was as much a dead-end as his passion for mathematics.

It was a couple of weeks after the train episode that I made progress with another of my ideas. I'd got into the habit of taking a break mid-way through each lesson to use the toilet. The route back from the toilet took me past what I took to be a small study, and I grabbed the opportunity each week to explore that room. I suspected the Greenes were the sort of couple who would keep an address book, an old-fashioned paper copy, and the drawers in the study seemed a likely location. There was an antique telephone land-line in there which reinforced my hunch. I never took too long exploring so as not to arouse suspicion, and therefore it took me several excursions, but eventually I found precisely what I had been expecting: a book containing addresses and phone numbers. The next week, knowing where it was, I went straight to it, flicked through the pages and took photos of the relevant entries with my phone.

I was now in possession of the address and phone number of the two daughters, Christine and Charlotte, as well as the names of their children: they had two each. Thinking about them set me off again, wondering about families. My family consisted of a father, Joe. That was it. I'd heard no news of him since the immediate aftermath of the accident. Despite his invalid status, every ring of the doorbell caused my heart to lurch. I feared his return. I decided to visit him in hospital.

I couldn't bring myself to use the word daughter, nor the word father. I claimed I was just a friend. It was a risk: they may have had a 'family-only' policy, or some other procedural requirement through which I would be excluded. But they didn't. They said Joe had had no visitors, so they were probably pleased one had arrived, that at least there was one person who cared. *Little did they know.*

They showed me where his bed was, near the window in a ward with three other men. To my inexpert eyes, all four of them seemed barely alive.

Joe was wired up to several beeping monitors. He was attached to tubes and needles, there was a mask over his face, with tubes in his nose. His eyes were closed and his face, outside of the beard which it seemed someone had trimmed, was ghostly pale.

I asked a passing nurse how he was. 'He's rather poorly,' was the unhelpful response.

'Are you expecting him to wake up soon?'

'We never lose hope. Once you've seen what I've seen ...' She looked out of the window, temporarily in another place. Then she was back, cloaked again in her professional demeanour. 'If you want more information, you should ask a doctor. I could arrange for someone to talk to you. Are you family?'

I didn't answer the question, or follow up on the offer. I'd sat next to Joe for about ten minutes, listening to the beeps, staring at the zig-zags on the monitors, watching his chest rise and fall. Waiting and waiting. For something. I didn't know what I was waiting for. For some sort of feeling to emerge, I suppose. Here was my father, lying in a hospital bed, probably dying. Wasn't I supposed to feel something?

As I examined my feelings, one thought emerged: the pleasure I could get from placing a pillow over his face and holding it down until the monitors flat-lined.

And there was more to it than that, more than the simple pleasure in securing his demise. Afterwards I would know that he would never leave hospital, and therefore would never visit me again, never speak to me again, never threaten me again. There was only one way I could be sure of that.

I left the hospital feeling a lot happier than I'd entered it.

# -45-

One of Stephen's daughters, Charlotte, lived in Sunderland, not exactly within easy reach. The other, Christine, was more accessible. She lived in the Upminster area, out east, but as her address was quite a distance from the tube station, I drove there.

The road was easy to find: *thank you sat-nav*. Number twenty-three. I sat in my car and watched the leisurely afternoon activity in this quiet neighbourhood. It was a dull autumnal day, probably going to rain later. A middle-aged woman walked by with a small dog on a long lead. An elderly couple walked past in the opposite direction, in animated discussion. A couple of cars drove by, but it was clear this estate was off the beaten track, not on any major route, not even a convenient 'rat-run'.

Around half past three, two teenage girls walked up the path of number twenty-three. The older one got something from her bag, presumably a key, and they let themselves into the house. On my phone, I checked the photo of the Greenes' address-book page. Christine's two daughters were Karen and Kate. I had two of Stephen's granddaughters in my sights.

It was only then that it occurred to me that we might be related. Some sort of half-sisters would we be called? Although that didn't seem right, seeing as there was an extra generation involved. I dismissed the thought. After all, it was only a possibility.

My plans hadn't gone beyond finding them. I wanted to talk to them, but I needed to ask about their grandfather, and it wasn't clear to me how I could make that sound like an innocent enquiry. So I drove home, needing to devise a strategy.

By the time I drove to the area the second time, a few days later, I had a strategy. Sort of. It wasn't a great plan, but it was the best I could come up with. I arrived later in the evening, hoping the mother, Christine, would be home. It was the girls I wanted to talk to, those girls whose photos for some reason were excluded from their grandparents' mantelpiece, but doing so in the presence of their mother felt safer, less likely to raise suspicions. The entry in the Greenes' address book listed Christine and Edward Banks, but the Edward Banks had been scribbled out and replaced by the surname 'Greene'. I parked on an adjoining road, locked the car and walked round the corner. If they thought I was some dubious character, I didn't want to risk them making a note of my registration number.

This time I'd come prepared. I was wearing a white shirt, black tailored jacket and black pencil skirt. A neat black briefcase and the fake glasses completed the image I was aiming for. I strode to the door of number twenty-three and rang the bell. Christine answered.

'Good evening. I wonder if I could have a word.'

'You are?'

'Sorry, Ms Greene.' I extracted a card from my inside pocket and held it up for a moment. It was a photo ID for my local gym, but I didn't give her long enough to scrutinise it properly. 'Catherine Morland. Social Services. But it's nothing to worry about. Just routine.'

'You'd better come in.'

Once inside the hallway, Christine turned to me. 'What's this all about?

'It's really your daughters I need to speak to.'

'Hope they're not in any trouble. They're good girls.'

'Oh no. Nothing like that. As I said, just routine.'

Christine called to her children and we all went through to a small front room. The girls sat together on the sofa, I was offered the easy chair and Christine sat on a dining chair near the table.

I opened the case on my knee and took out a notebook. 'Before I start, let me make it clear that this is all confidential. At this stage. It's a sensitive issue. Both legally and personally. So I must ask that you don't talk to anyone about this visit.'

The three of them nodded.

'It concerns a matter at school, Harrington Academy.' I looked at my notes. 'You, Karen, are in year eleven I believe, and Kate, you're in year nine?' There was more nodding. 'The issue concerns a teacher who we believe...' I paused. Adjusted my glasses. 'There have been reports, unsubstantiated at this stage.' Another pause. 'He has allegedly been behaving inappropriately.'

It was a guess, but it hit the mark.

The two girls looked at each other, nodded and spoke almost simultaneously: 'Mr Phillips.'

I raised my hand. 'Please. No names. In the fullness of time, there will be a process, evidence will be gathered, analysed and so forth. The police will be handling all that. But for now, we must avoid doing anything that might prejudice future prosecution. Should it come to that. Hence the need for confidentiality. My concern, our concern, at this stage, is solely the well-being of the students.'

'Why have you come to us?' Christine looked at her daughters. 'Has that Phillips guy done anything, said anything, to either of you? Touched you?'

'Please, Ms Greene. By all means discuss this as a family once I've gone, but I do not want to know any details. Not at this stage, as I explained.' I held up a hand again. 'But be assured, you haven't been in any sense singled out, or specifically identified. We will be visiting all the children who might – and I stress *might* – have been affected.'

'So how can we help? If you don't want us to talk about ... you know what.'

'The important thing is to re-assure the girls – all the girls. And that's why I'm here. Sometimes girls don't want to talk about such things, and that's perfectly fine. But if they do want to talk, we need to be sure there is a strong network around them, listening to them, supporting them, keeping them safe. So girls, you can talk to me at any time, in private. I'll leave my card with your mother. Obviously, you have your mother. I believe Mrs Greene that there is no Mr Greene.'

'Correct, but ...'

I interrupted. 'And you are not always here when the girls get back from school, you work I believe?'

'Yes, but ...'

'So is there anyone else they can turn to? Should an emergency situation arise? Of course we hope that won't happen, but we need to be ready. Worst case scenario.'

'There's Eddie's sister, Auntie Rachel who lives in Princess Drive, just round the corner.' The girls turned to each other and pulled faces before giggling.

I made a show of flipping through pages of my notebook. 'There are grandparents I believe. Living in Hounslow? Quite a distance, but on the phone?'

Suddenly it felt like a blast of arctic air had blown through the room, showering icicles on the woman and her daughters. The girls were wide-eyed in shock as they turned to their mother. The mother stood up and then sat down again. She turned away, patted her hair. The pause stretched into awkwardness, and then a small thaw brought the atmosphere back to near normality.

'Yes,' said Christine, speaking carefully. 'My mother. My father. But the girls will not be going anywhere near that man. There is no need. We have all the family we need without them. Those two are not part of this family.'

## -46-

Once I got back to the car, I sat behind the wheel, closed my eyes and breathed deeply. I'd got away with it. Mind you, once they thought back over my visit, they'd soon realise how none of it made any sense. They'd realise I'd 'forgotten' to leave my card behind. And once the girls talked to their school-friends, they'd know my tale of visiting everyone was untrue. Probably not the best scheme I'd ever devised, but I'd got out with no damage done and gained some information about Stephen Greene. Now all I needed to do was interpret that information. *What did it mean*?

The rift ran deep. That much was clear. There was no way the daughter and *her* daughters would be seeing their father/ grandfather any time soon. I wished I could have probed further, asked what it was all about, but that would have stretched the pretence too far. It was the girls I was supposed to be caring about, not their grandfather.

After their reaction to my mention of the Hounslow connection, I'd brought the meeting to a close as quickly as I could. I'd re-assured them that the girls' safety was our (i.e. Social Services) priority; I'd reminded them to keep the meeting confidential, although I knew that was unlikely to happen; I repeated that legal proceedings would follow in due course.

I knew they'd be suspicious, but if they reported me there was no risk that anyone in authority would pursue it. I was well-disguised, my car was unobserved, my motives unclear. If I represented a scam, what I hoped to gain from it would be seen as an un-resolvable mystery.

But it wasn't my greatest day, I knew that. A convoluted escapade with very limited reward. What exactly *had* I learned about Stephen Greene? He had offended them in some way, some big way, either the girls or their mother, or all three. So much so that he was deleted (I was guessing) from any future family gathering, deleted from Christmas card list. Cancelled, to use the modern vernacular.

I had an explanation, but it was speculative. When the mother was making it clear that the Hounslow grandparents were excluded from any safety net, the older girl, Karen, whispered something to her sister. I only half caught it, and couldn't be sure I'd heard it right. But it might have been, 'Out of the frying pan...'

If I'd heard correctly, it gave me a possible explanation. The trouble was, it didn't fit with the mild-mannered intellectual which was how I regarded Stephen Greene, the bland, train-loving nonentity. But then again, what do paedophiles look like when they're not fiddling with kiddies?

I thought about the shed and the trains, with its comfortable corner. There was a picture forming in my mind, but it had nothing to do with 1966.

Until the trips to Upminster, my enthusiasm for my mission had been beginning to wane. Stephen Greene had come across as so ordinary, so nice, in the most neutral sense of that adjective. Whatever he'd done forty or fifty years ago was strangely irrelevant. I even thought, perhaps I was being vindictive in a petty-minded way, to be pursuing some sort of vengeance all these years later. If he had committed a crime, he knew it and had lived with the guilt throughout his life. Was that not punishment enough?

But now.

Two granddaughters who didn't want to see him again.

Whose mother didn't want them seeing him again.

'Out of the frying pan...' (perhaps).

A bottle of brandy underneath the coffee table in the corner of the shed, with two glasses.

'The boys usually get excited.'

Now, my mission was back on track. I needed to get to the truth about Stephen Greene, for Diane's sake, but also (I feared) for the sake of other victims, victims who were still alive, still young.

# -47-

This time, I was there first. It was early evening again, so *The Crown* was near enough deserted and the corner table was once again vacant. By the time he arrived, I'd bought drinks for both of us.

'Thank you for coming, Dr Greene,' I said, standing up and indicating the chair with the pint of beer in front of it. 'This probably seems a little strange.' We both sat down. I took a sip from my glass. Stephen left his alone.

'What is this all about Ms Elliot? What do you want from me?'

'Well, as I said in my text, I've given up on the maths. To be honest I have no interest in the subject, never had. I hoped it would help me get to know you, which is why I pretended to want to learn it.'

Stephen's face showed bewilderment. 'That's what I don't get. Why would you be interested in me?'

'Let me explain. I'm a student. Studying for a PhD.' I mentioned a random London College. 'No, not maths, surprise, surprise! My subject is social history and the broad area of my research is the 1960s. A fascinating period in so many ways, as I'm sure you'll agree.'

Stephen gave a sort of shrug. Now he drank some of his beer.

'There have been tons of studies, lots of literature I've had to wade through. Most of it is concerned with the large-scale, global events, trends and fashions, society's reaction to the evolutions, the revolutions, the trends that marked that decade. But my particular focus is on the personal. Personal relationships and attitudes, personal reactions, those are my themes. Fortunately there are still people around who remember that time, who lived through those years. It's important to capture any memories and record them. Before it's too late.'

'Before we die off, you mean.'

'Well yes. Not to put too fine a point on it. Time marches on.'

'But there are plenty of us who've survived, it's not that long ago. Doesn't explain why you've come to me in particular. I'm nothing special.'

'We picked your old school at random, one of the many which fitted our criteria. It had some useful attributes: the right size, location, other things.' I gestured vaguely. 'I won't bore you with the technicalities, there are complicated processes we use to profile sources. Then it was a case of narrowing down to individuals. Some of the old boys - Old Rubicunds they're called, aren't they? – were easier to track down than others. Some of them were dead, as you can imagine. Despite what you say, we're talking a passage of forty years or more. Others have emigrated or fallen off the radar for other reasons, so we couldn't trace them. In the end the short list ends up ... well, short.

'A couple of weeks ago I had a long and particularly useful conversation with one on the list. He was from your year, Richard Wright? Comparing your memories with his would be a useful triangulation exercise. Do you remember him?'

'Old Dickie. Goodness. I thought he was dead.'

'No. Alive and kicking. Living in Norfolk.'

'Might as well be dead! Sorry. Joke. Poor taste.'

'No, you're right. Going to that county's a bit like travelling back into the last century. Old-fashioned and stuck in its ways. Suits your friend Richard down to the ground.'

Stephen stared into his beer. 'Old Dickie, eh? Haven't spoken to him for years. Funny how you lose touch.' He turned his glass round, watched the liquid move. 'You think you'll always be friends. Then suddenly you find you haven't spoken for years. You're not friends any more. You're not anything.'

'He mentioned your name. Among others. Back then, at school, you were close?' I got out an A5 notepad from my bag. 'Do you mind if I take notes?'

'Look. Miss Elliot...'

'I've said before. It's Anne. Now I'm no longer your student, surely ...'

'Miss Elliot.' He removed his glasses and polished them, deciding what to say. 'I'm finding this very strange. You first approached me, out of the blue, seeking tuition in mathematics. I was reluctant, for reasons I explained at the time, but you were persistent. I admired your keenness. Now it turns out that's not what you wanted at all. Why didn't you say straight out that you wanted me to help with your research?'

'Sorry Stephen. Of course, you're right. That's what I should have done. I shouldn't have deceived you. The truth is, there's this Matthew Christiansen in UCLA did some powerful work a few years ago that showed how a social science researcher gets more consistent, more honest, more useful answers from the subject – sorry, that's you, jargon I'm afraid. Anyway, he proved that if the subject doesn't know the purpose behind the questioning, there's a more relaxed atmosphere, better rapport between researcher and subject, and ultimately more accurate data emerges.'

Stephen put his glasses back on and shook his head.

'So what I hoped was that I could work my questions into our lessons, and so avoid it appearing like a formal question-and-answer session. But that didn't work out. The truth is Stephen, you're too professional. No, it's true. I paid you for maths classes and that's what you gave me. You allowed no space for informality and so there was no way for me to wheedle information out of you. So I've had to ditch that approach and come clean. Do you want another drink?'

# -48-

This was going well. I'd taken a chance on Richard and Stephen no longer being in contact, and that Stephen wouldn't have heard that Richard had died. That worked. I was also proud of referencing the fictitious American, Matthew Christiansen. And emphasising that my failure was due to his professionalism was another masterstroke. After a bit of a wobble, I felt I was getting away with it.

Stephen continued to resist, but as the second drink went down, he softened a little. It was finally flattery that did the trick – isn't it always? I implied that his profile was a perfect match for my needs, and that I wouldn't be able to complete my dissertation without his help. How could he refuse? He didn't.

I asked a range of questions that I thought a social historian would ask. His views on the key events of the day, like Macmillan, Kennedy, the Vietnam war, Wilson's 'pound in your pocket' speech (I'd done some research). I asked about TW3. By that time I'd found out it was a TV satire programme which divided opinion at the time.

I gradually brought the questions round to more personal issues, his friends, his relationships with his parents and siblings, teachers. His answers were uniformly bland. If I'd been a genuine researcher, I could imagine becoming increasingly frustrated. Was he telling the truth? Possibly, but more likely his memory was poor and he was feeding me the answers he thought I was expecting. Matthew Christiansen may have had a point!

I mentally took a deep breath. Crunch time was approaching.

'That chap I spoke to in Norfolk, your classmate Richard Wright. Would you say he was a close friend?'

'Oh no. Not close. Dickie and Deffo were the high-flyers in our class, as thick as thieves. The rest of us sort of orbited around them. Tried to get some reflected glory, picking up crumbs from their table.'

There were some mixed metaphors there, but I got the gist. 'When I spoke to him, one of the things he told me about was a party. Seemed like quite an occasion. It was in 1966. To celebrate the football.'

'I'm not a football fan. Never was, and these days... Well, don't get me started on their antics. Rugby is more my game.'

'But 1966. The World Cup?'

He picked up his glass and stared into the beer. I thought perhaps he hadn't heard me. 'People talk about 1966, especially those who weren't there. Weren't even born.' He flicked a hand, gesturing to me.

'Guilty as charged, your honour.'

'Probably not you personally, but other people, especially those into their football, talk about 1966 as though it were a golden age. It passed me by, and I wasn't the only one. It wasn't so big in those days, you see, football itself, and even the World Cup only merited the odd half-page in the papers. I didn't watch the final. I heard that we won, but so what? England beat West Germany at football. Big deal.'

'But do you remember the party? Richard said it was to celebrate England's victory. Did you go?'

'Did he say I was there? I wasn't much of a party-goer in those days, but we did used to get together sometimes as a group, at weekends or during the holidays. Gatherings more than parties.'

'He definitely said you were there.'

'In which case, I probably was. A long time ago, memory not what it was. It does ring a vague bell. Was it the one at Andy's place?'

'Yes.' Diane's diary had mentioned a boy she designated 'A'; could have been Andy.

'Andy's someone else you should talk to. I could send you his email address. We're still in touch. From time to time.'

'Thank you. That would be useful. But I'm more interested in the girls at this party. Do you remember a girl named Diane?'

It was as though I'd punched him in the mouth. Or stood on a chair and taken my clothes off. Or told him he had five minutes to live. This was a name that shook him to his roots. He tried to hide it, took off his glasses and polished them. Put them back on and raised his beer to his lips, taking a long gulp. The wide, blinking eyes gave him away.

Once he'd composed himself, he replied. 'Yes,' he said, simply. 'I remember Di.'

I waited. I was sure he wanted to tell me more. I could almost see the memories crowding in behind his eyes. All I had to do was wait. I was right.

'I feel very foolish,' he said, eventually, putting his glass down, leaning back, hands behind his head. 'An old man. Knocked off kilter like that. It was all so long ago. But Di.' He let out a long breath, puffed his cheeks. 'She was the love of my life, you see. I guess I never properly got over her.'

'They say you never forget your first love.'

'True. So true. She was. Oh, anything I say now will seem false, mere fantasy. She was perfect. Through my eyes. At that age. Perfect, absolutely perfect. Such startling blue eyes. Long blonde hair.'

'You met her at the party?'

It took him a while to reply. He was still in a dreamy world set in the distant past. 'If it's the party I'm thinking of, then no. That wasn't the first time. I'd met her before.'

## -49-

'We gathered at Andy's. There was plenty of beer. Cigarettes passed around, music on the record player. But what I mainly remember is me and Di. I'd admired her from afar since junior school, too scared to do anything about it. But that night, with a few pints of beer inside me, I finally found the courage to ask her to dance. I expected a brush-off. She was usually quite rude to me. But no, she smiled, such a smile she had, and said she would. We danced. We danced a lot. Fast numbers and slow ones. Then we stopped and she sat on my lap. We kissed. It was late when we went down onto the beach, under the pier. I laid down my coat, so she wouldn't be lying directly on the stones. The best night of my life.'

'So she was your girlfriend?'

The glasses received another polish. 'For those few hours, yes she was. I don't know how it happened, why it happened. Before that night, she wouldn't even look at me. I wasn't much of a catch, you see. I was shy, spotty, wore glasses.' He pushed his glasses up his nose with his middle finger. 'I'd always fancied her like crazy. She was stunning. Beautiful skin, and those beautiful eyes. She always wore short skirts, very short skirts. Then that night something sparked between us and for a while I really thought it was going to work out.'

I sipped my drink and waited. I expected him to tell me more, but he seemed lost in his own world. He drained his glass.

'And afterwards?'

'She was the same as before. Ignoring me, or making nasty comments about me. As though that night had never happened. It broke my heart.'

I waited again. Stephen picked up a beer mat and tapped it against his empty glass. He looked as though he was about to burst into tears.

'Sorry, Ms Elliot. None of that's very helpful. The nostalgic ramblings of an old man.'

'Not at all, Stephen. Everything's grist to the mill. Emotions and their consequences. Relationships. All useful. Contextualisation we call it. So, do you remember Richard and Grahame? At the party. What were they doing? Did they pick up girls?'

Stephen looked blank.

'Dickie. And Deffo, was it?'

'Oh, of course. Those two. They'd have been at the heart of it, I'm sure of that. Just their sort of thing. A happening, that's what we used to call it, an event like that.'

'Did they come with you to the beach?'

'Oh no. Of course not. That was just me and Di, private. We were alone in the moonlight. I put my coat down for her. Over the stones.'

# -50-

Once home, I got changed and went for a run, even though it was already dark and cold and my preference is to run in the early morning. Sometimes you just need to run. It's a good opportunity for thinking and I had a lot of thinking to do.

An hour later, showered and wrapped in a loose towelling robe, I fried a pork steak, adding a creamy mushroom sauce and mixed vegetables. Sauté potatoes. A glass of chardonnay.

And did some more thinking.

I had finally managed to get Stephen Greene talking about the past, about 1966, the party, Diane. But what he'd said had been nothing like what I'd been expecting, I'd anticipated some sort of admission of guilt. Perhaps some attempt at explanation, he'd been drunk and got carried away, he'd been egged on by the others, something like that. But no, I'd got nothing of that sort at all.

It was taking a while to assimilate. Yes, I'd had the conversation I wanted, but it had resolved nothing. His version of the events of that night didn't match with the version I'd pieced together from Diane's diary entry and old Mum's explanatory letter.

And the way he'd spoken … Not like the Stephen Greene I was used to, so confident, authoritative, in control. As he told me what had happened, he'd entered some sort of dream-like state. Eyes gazing into the distance, not at me. Fractured narration, barely coherent.

I regretted again not getting more from Richard Greene. He'd told me about the football, the drinking, the dancing to the Rolling Stones, but not the detail I needed. What had Richard remembered about Diane? What had he remembered about Stephen? What was his memory of what happened on Brighton beach that night? I had no way of finding out now.

The most logical conclusion I could come to was that Stephen Greene had reconstructed a rose-tinted version of the events of that night. What he thought was true was in fact a false memory. Given his nature, especially back then, by his own admission shy, self-conscious, naïve, if what happened was anything like I'd imagined, it would have caused deep shock, lasting trauma. That night was probably his first sexual encounter and if it involved gang rape, that would have had a profound effect on him. Therefore he had invented, in his head, a scenario in which

Diane, his 'Di', was a willing participant, where the occasion matched his dreams, his imagination: he and Diane as lovers. Everything else, the involvement of the other two, the coercion that slipped, then sank, into brutality, none of that had any part to play in his idealisation of that night. So he'd rejected it and then forgotten it.

Was that possible? Did my cod-psychology carry any credibility? I had no idea.

On the other hand, perhaps what Stephen had told me was what really happened and there had been no rape at all. How could I tell? Was Diane, my grandmother, to be relied upon when she named those three men in her diary, when she told her daughter that she'd been raped three times? Was my mother to be trusted? Was her recounting of the conversation with *her* mother accurate? Maybe she didn't want Diane to come out of the story as a loose woman, as an instrument of her own 'downfall'. Better that she was a victim.

There were too many potentially unreliable narrators contributing to this story.

I finished the wine.

I found some sorbet in the freezer. Put the percolator on for some coffee.

Then there was the other thing, the other thing I had yet to unravel. Nothing to do with Diane, nothing to do with 1966. Everything to do with boys and girls in the twenty-first century. Two granddaughters. Maybe others. Young boys interested in trains. The more I thought about it, the more I began to realise that these young victims, possible victims I ought to say, were more important. More important than who was telling the truth about events over forty years ago. More important than whether or not Stephen raped my grandmother. What mattered was what he was up to now, in this century, in the present, and possibly in the future. Did that man carry a greater guilt, a more recent guilt, an ongoing guilt?

I needed to find out.

# -51-

'Good of you to meet me again, Dr Greene.'

'Pleased to be of help.'

Same pub, same hour of the day, same table. Same drinks. A couple of weeks later. I'd had lots of thinking time but had come to no conclusions. I was hoping, as last time, that the beer would loosen Stephen's tongue and he'd reveal more answers. I needed more answers.

As I was waiting for him, I'd mused over the change in our relationship. When we'd first met, in this pub, at this table, I was submissive and compliant, seeking his approval, so that he would accept me as a pupil. He was dominant, in his understated way, masterful. Then, the last time we'd met, I'd turned that around: it had been me in charge. I was pretty proud of myself. My negotiating skills had persuaded him to open up, to talk about Diane and the party. What would it be like this time? I'd still be calling the shots, but the agenda was rather different. To find out what I needed, I'd have to get him under pressure. That was the only way he'd give himself away, say more than he intended. I recalled the episodes when Vera outwitted confident and devious criminals. Could I emulate her? I was confident I could.

'Bet you're pleased to get out of the rain,' I said. 'It's a monsoon out there.' I resisted calling him 'Pet'.

Stephen shook out his umbrella and propped it in the corner.

We exchanged a few more words about the weather, the chances of the rain turning to snow. I kept the small-talk going, mentioning the gruffness of the landlord, the run-down nature of this part of town. I risked a political reference, knowing that the education minister had recently announced some sort of exams initiative. As I expected, Stephen was quick to pick up on that. He had a strong opinion: the minister was not his favourite person. Teachers always hate education ministers. I got him to talk about his work, his school. He told me he was Head of the Mathematics Department. When I suggested that might be quite a burden, he confessed it was, but then, as he was about to go into more detail, he stopped himself.

'This is all very interesting Miss Elliot, but I'm sure you didn't ask me here to merely chew the fat.' I'd already bought a second round of drinks.

'No indeed. But background information is important. Virtually none of it will be used directly, but context is essential. Like any writer, I need to know my characters. That's you again: character, subject.' He smiled. 'I should have said before, anything you tell me will not be attributed to you personally in my thesis. Inclusion in the acknowledgements will be the only mention of you by name. Not even that if you'd prefer not.'

'I assumed that would be the case.'

'I think you said before, Stephen, that you used to be an academic? Before you turned to teaching?'

'Yes, correct. I read for a PHD. Cambridge. Had research papers published.'

'Pure Mathematics?'

'Algebraic Number Theory. Don't ask me to explain. It's boring.'

'I'm sure that's not the case.'

'Oh, all a long time ago. Not boring at the time.' He stared into his glass. 'But now? Very esoteric. Fairies dancing on a pin. You know.'

'But you understand the academic world, and that's why I'm so pleased you're willing to help me like this.'

'Yes. I do appreciate the demands of high-level research. I know what it takes. Not that I ever needed to grill any 'subjects' or 'characters' as you call us. Research in pure mathematics is a rather more antisocial activity. Insular. But yes. I'm pleased to be able to help.'

'What I want to do is get a bit more detail about your attitudes to the changes of the 1960s. There was so much change. Abortion. The age of consent. Homosexuality. How did you feel about all that?'

Stephen picked up a beer mat. Flicked it against his glass. Shrugged. 'It's hard to say.'

'How do you mean?'

He replied carefully, as was his usual manner. 'You see, Miss Elliot. When you're living through it. It's just life. You don't think of it as anything special. Those were my teenage years, they were the only teenage years I had. I knew nothing else. And that's how it was for all of us.'

'It didn't feel special?'

'Well, yes. We knew times were a-changing. Bob Dylan told us that. The past – you know, the war, national service, rationing and the rest of it. That was the province of the old people. That's what they talked about, but for us it was irrelevant history, dead and buried. For us, the present and the future was all there was, all that mattered.'

'That's what made the 1960s so special.'

'I don't understand.'

'Well, it's a common enough feeling among the young these days, the certainty that they are the future. The punks, Generation X, the millennials. They've all had revolution in their blood. And now, to the young of today, which I count myself as part of, can't remember what they're calling us. Whatever. But the thinking's become routine, to feel like we're the ones waving the banner, leading the march. But your generation, the youth of the 1960s, you were the trail-blazers, the first ones to feel that.'

'I suppose you're right.'

We sipped our drinks and I made a show of referring to my notebook.

'To come back to my question. The sexual revolution, so-called. Were you in favour?'

'Of course. It made sense. What was wrong with sex before marriage? Why shouldn't homosexuality be decriminalised? Why shouldn't girls take the contraceptive pill? The counter argument was virtually non-existent. Those who opposed changes only did so because it *was* change, because it upset the status quo. But most of us thought change was good. Let's start afresh. Greater freedom, less rules. Do your own thing. As they say these days, what was not to like?'

Into his third beer, Stephen was beginning to speak more freely, to open up about his opinions on these topics. Sex, drugs and rock-and-roll. He may not have been an active participant but he had enjoyed being on the periphery, observing. I pretended to be making copious notes. Eventually, I moved on to the crucial question.

# -52-

'Here's an interesting question, Stephen. When I was reading about those years, I came across an intriguing aspect that hasn't been much discussed. There was one change that was expected in some quarters but never actually occurred. It was as though the society of that era drew back from the brink, saw it as one step too far. In contrast, that is, to the ever-increasing permissiveness you've talked about.'

'I'm intrigued.'

I made sure I was checking his face for any reaction as I gave him my revelation: 'I'm talking about paedophilia.'

He took off his glasses and polished them on a tissue from his pocket. It was his favourite stalling technique, giving him time to think.

I continued, still watching him. 'These days, of course, paedophilia is regarded as the worst of crimes, despicable, unforgivable. Pick your most extreme word of damnation and it applies. But back then, there were serious people, serious people campaigning for it to be legalised.'

'Were there?' He spoke slowly, carefully, 'I don't remember that.'

'PIE. It was a newspaper. The letters stood for "Paedophile Information Exchange". It was openly available, not under the counter, nothing secretive about it. Even discussed on TV.' My research had told me this didn't actually happen until the late 1970s, but I had no compunction about stretching the truth in order to help the point hit home.

'No, that all passed me by.'

'Their argument was that pre-pubescent children could derive pleasure from sexual activity, so it was legitimate for them to be introduced to this pleasure. Why not? Pleasure is good. Where's the harm? It sounds a quite revolting, horrific idea. But that's to modern ears. Back then, with barriers coming down, progressiveness and permissiveness as the catch phrases, like you said, greater freedom, less rules, there was a lot of momentum behind it, so yes, legalisation of paedophilia was actively discussed and considered.'

'No.'

Stephen had been growing increasingly edgy, I was touching a nerve. He stood up.

'You're making it up.'

'I'm not. Anyway, why would I?'

'I don't know. To shock me, perhaps. Playing some sort of game.'

'How did you feel about paedophilia in those days?'

He shook his head. 'I think I've told you all I can.'

'Did you think it should be legalised? That the age of consent should just be abolished?

He didn't answer.

'Did you subscribe to that magazine? PIE?'

He took off his glasses and rubbed his eyes. Raked his hand through his thinning hair. He was on the point of leaving. I needed to be quick.

'What is your opinion of paedophilia now, Dr Greene?'

'The same as everyone. It's horrible, terrible, repulsive.'

'How do you feel about your granddaughters, Dr Greene? Karen and Kate. Lovely girls, aren't they?'

He raised his eyebrows, blinked rapidly. 'What have they got to do with anything?' He was breathing heavily, frowning, shaking his head.

'And the boys from school? How do you feel about them? When you invite them to come and play with your trains?'

That's when Dr Stephen Greene left the pub. He bumped into his chair as he went, nearly knocking it over. He forgot his umbrella.

## -53-

He'd admitted nothing. But that didn't mean he hadn't given me information. His reaction told me all I needed to know. The concept of paedophilia was unsettling for him. He wouldn't be the only one, but I knew it wasn't simply normal abhorrence he was displaying. There was something more complex going on in his head. It convinced me that my speculation about him was correct. But what could I do with that information?

For a few days, I settled back into my normal routine. I needed some normality to counter the images that came dancing into my brain whenever I relaxed too much. Images that were probably worse because I had no specific knowledge, nothing but my own imagination and Stephen's reaction to build from.

Not having any more maths homework was a relief but that left space to fill. I re-read some Jane Austen novels. *Northanger Abbey* is probably my favourite, even though the critics regard it as rather light. I like the way the reading habits of the characters inform their behaviour.

I had a CD of Rolling Stones hits, and played it good and loud. It's easy to forget how brilliant their early work was, every track energetic and memorable, the whole an anthem to youth and a vibrant future. Yes, music of the 60s.

I stretched my morning run, a little more each day, until I was close to ten miles. I thought about entering a half-marathon. That would be a good challenge.

I treated myself to a meal at a classy restaurant, but glancing at the menu, I ignored their fancy dishes and plumped for a simple steak and fries: it tastes so different when delivered by a proper chef, one who knows what they're doing, one who knows what 'rare' actually means.

All this time I was trying to decide exactly what I should do about Dr Stephen Greene, while not letting my mind imagine too wildly. The police came back into the frame. My investigations a-la-Vera were hopelessly amateur. The police, with their depth of experience and resources, would get to the bottom of what Stephen Greene was up to.

But would they? Would they even listen to me? My evidence was mostly about how he reacted to my mention of the word paedophilia. But 'the look in his eye,' the sweat on his brow, the frequent cleaning of his glasses: they didn't stack up into much by way of evidence. The police could question Stephen's granddaughters, more directly and more pointedly than I was able. But would the girls talk to the police? It's one thing being committed to a family rift, quite another to reveal the reason for that rift to figures in authority, to hand your grandfather over to them. Would the police question the boys at Stephen's school, even without any formal complaint?

Perhaps I should try to get more evidence. I felt that's what I needed, but after the last time I couldn't imagine Stephen agreeing to meet me again. I'd sucked that source well and truly dry. Perhaps I could seek out some of the boys at the school who had an interest in trains. How could I do that without raising suspicions regarding my own motives? Perhaps I should simply try and spy on the man, undergo real surveillance.

Then I got the email.

## -54-

This journey on the underground feels different. Partly that's to do with the different time of day, I've never travelled out to Hounslow mid-evening. But the other difference is my frame of mind. Previously, I've always had a plan, known what I was expecting to find and what I was going to do about it, even when my objective was merely to attend a maths lesson and try to be friendly. Now I have no plan. Now I know nothing. I am in the dark in more ways than one. I don't like this lack of control.

The back streets of Hounslow are quiet, there is no traffic, no kids playing, no dog-walkers. Of course, not really 'quiet', Hounslow's never quiet for long. The aircraft still pass overhead with metronomic regularity, but you get used to it. Through my visits during the past few months I've made progress. The locals genuinely don't notice. Newcomers get a sore neck. I'm somewhere in between: I react to the sound but try not to look.

So yes, there are aircraft passing overhead, but otherwise the night is quiet. I arrive at Stephen's home. The house is in darkness as his email had said it would be: his wife's away. Following his instructions I walk down the passageway by the side of the house. It's very dark here, but when I reach the end, the light from the shed's window illuminates the back garden.

Ever since I opened his email, I've been wondering what he was going to say. Obviously, it would be related to our last meeting, when I harassed him relentlessly and he walked out on me. I recall the look in his eyes. He knew what I was getting at, even though he didn't know how much I knew. So what happens now? Is he going to confess? Is he going to warn me off? Or maybe he'll try to explain, explain how I've got it all wrong and nothing is as it seems. That he's perfectly innocent. *Hmm*.

Until now, although unhappy at not being in control, I've nevertheless been full of anticipation, eager to find out how this was going to play out. Now, as I stand in the emptiness of Stephen's garden, the dark house behind me, the shed with its ominous potential standing before me, the light from the window highlighting stray bare shrubs, I begin to feel nervous. I've brought my bag. It's not empty. I feel its re-assuring heft. But that's not really the problem. I'm not nervous about my own safety, I don't believe I'm in physical danger. After all, it's only meek and mild Stephen Greene I'll be meeting. He's never struck me as an intimidating figure. Of course, he might have recruited a team of local heavies to give me a good hiding. Perhaps, but no, it doesn't seem likely. My fear is simply fear of the unknown. Fear that I might not have the ability to cope, not be able to produce whatever reaction, retaliation, is called for. I don't like being taken by surprise. I like to be prepared.

There's one thing for sure. Standing here and thinking is going to resolve nothing. And I haven't come this far to turn and walk away.

I approach the shed. The door is shut. I hesitate. Should I knock? Stephen said I should come to the shed. Did that mean walk right in?

I knock. Stupid! I've done one of those girlie taps which are hopeless, because when you get no response, you don't know if the person has heard you or not, so don't know whether to knock again.

I knock again. A proper rat-a-tat. Not ignorable.

There is no answer.

I push at the door and it swings open.

## -55-

The scene looks familiar: an elevated network of train-tracks laid out across the length and breadth of the shed. But it's not right, and it gradually dawns on me what's not right about it. It's broken, all broken. There are jagged ends of tracks sticking up at strange angles, engines and carriages lying on their sides, off the rails; others broken into pieces. There's debris covering the floor, I'm standing on broken figures, parts of coaches and other unidentifiable fragments. The whole thing's a mess.

The control panel is split into several pieces. I picture Stephen standing there, like he was last time, excited, eyes shining brightly. He's not there now. He's no longer in charge of this broken system.

My eye drifts to the sitting-room corner. That looks intact, much as I remember it. I take two steps, two crunching steps, and see the envelope on the table, beside the empty tumbler and a mobile phone. Then I see the other thing, casting a shadow, in the other corner.

I see first a pair of grey socks on shoeless feet. Suspended in mid-air. I look up and see the figure of Stephen Greene, hanging from a rafter, a striped tie around his neck. His face is directed away from me and I'm pleased for that. The body slowly rotates. I look away.

Two more crunchy steps and I pick up the envelope. It has my name on it: Frankie Jackson. Not Anne Elliot. I rip it open. It appears to be a list, typed in black ink. 'I'M SORRY' it reads at the top, capital letters. Then 'Sorry Karen'. Then 'Sorry Kate'. And the list continues: 'Sorry Wayne. Sorry Charlie. Sorry Ed...' Line after line. I turn the page over and find another column of 'sorry's. On the bottom of the second page there's another capitalised line: 'I'M SORRY' before one more line: 'SORRY, SORRY, SORRY.'

## -56-

I took another trip to the tattooist. He's called Kyle, or at least, that's the name over the door. I asked him to insert a figure '2' next to the '1' inside Diane's curly D, but to be sure to leave space for one more figure.

I felt light, as though I was about to lift off the ground, to levitate. I hadn't realised the heaviness of the burden I'd been carrying, the burden that was Stephen Greene, his crimes of the past, his crimes of the present, the mysteries surrounding him and his family. My brain had been thick with thoughts of him, still was, would take weeks or months to declutter, to shrug off the complex ramifications. But that process had begun.

I knew what I needed and that was some semblance of normal life. I ran and ran again, I ate well and drank well. I took long leisurely baths. I watched mindless television late into the night, then slept well, woke early and went running again. I threw myself into housework, finding corners that hadn't been relieved of dust for months, while my ears were bombarded with *Black Sabbath, Metallica, Tool.* I helped Jake in the garden, despite his vigorous attempts to dissuade me, his chastisements when my weeding was insufficiently discriminating. It was an important time of the year, he told me, preparing for next season. I tried to make my endeavours appropriately serious.

I decided it was time I read some of those Dickens novels that I'd never got around to: *Barnaby Rudge, Martin Chuzzlewit, Dombey and Son.*

Yet still my mind wouldn't allow itself to be wholly distracted. It still found time to think about Stephen Greene. I'd phoned the police from the shed, using Stephen's phone, but hadn't given my name. I'd left the list of 'sorry's, but taken the envelope with my name on it. I was guessing the police wouldn't bother to check the shed for fingerprints or DNA, it being a clear suicide, no need to waste precious police resources.

I hadn't killed him, but then again, I suppose in a way I had. My rant in the pub had clearly hit home. I never threatened to go to the police, but he may have assumed I would, not knowing whether I had concrete evidence to back up my suspicions. He'd chosen an end he felt preferable to the hell that prison can reputedly be for men of his persuasion. I'm sure it was cowardice that was the driver rather than genuine remorse, despite the note.

I wondered how much his wife, Caroline, knew. She surely knew what had happened with the two granddaughters, whatever that was, because the reaction of their mother suggested a major bust-up, involving all parties. But was she aware what happened in the shed with the boys from school? Of course, I didn't know precisely what had gone on, but the suicide and the apologies were strongly suggestive. Whatever happened went beyond innocent play. Whatever had happened, shouldn't have happened, that much was clear.

Then there was my core mission, my revenge for Diane. Had Stephen raped Diane in 1966 as her diary implied and my mum's letter made explicit? Or had that night seen a romantic consensual coupling, as Stephen reported. I hadn't been there and had no access to any reliable witness. So I didn't know. His more recent behaviour pointed to a complex sexual problem, in which he needed children to satisfy his desires. For that to have stemmed from an early traumatic sexual event, such as a gang rape, was conceivable. More cod-psychology? According to old Mum's letter, Stephen had been the last of the boys to rape Diane and only did so responding to pressure from the other two. She had given more details. According to her, they had held her down. Stephen had folded his coat and placed it under her head. He had laid on top of her and tried to fake an orgasm. The other two had seen through his pretence and under their belligerent urgings he had gone through with the rape.

I had no doubt that was the true version. That is what happened. And for that, despite the mitigation, Stephen Greene deserved to die. If he had also committed the recent crimes I suspected him of, his death was even more justified. I was proud of myself.

## -57-

The news that Joe, my former father, was dead, had hit the street. I tried to look surprised, even though this was another death I wasn't mourning. Mo broke the news to me and accompanied it with a long tale about the problems the authorities had encountered over the funeral. According to Mo, they couldn't find a next-of-kin, or indeed any family at all, so there was no-one to organise (or pay for) a funeral. I wasn't concerned: they could chuck him onto the Council tip for all I cared.

Even though Joe was dead, I still got nervous when the doorbell rang. There was no reason to because the ringing rarely signalled any interesting visitor, certainly not anything to worry about. It was usually a delivery, and if not that, it would be someone trying to sell me something I didn't want: dish-cloths or a brand of religion or a political view. I had no compunction in telling whoever it was to go away, choosing whichever phrase best matched my degree of irritation at the time.

The doorbell rang and I went to open it, with these thoughts in my head, safe in the knowledge that it wouldn't be Joe, but nervous anyway: after Joe I couldn't stop being nervous.

It was Caroline, Mrs Greene, Stephen's wife. Stephen's widow.

'Hello.' She seemed less sure of herself than when I last spoke to her. Her face was pale, her hair was hanging limp on her shoulders, her voice was timid. Her clothes had a lived-in look. She was no longer smart.

'Hey,' I said, hesitating. Well, she was the last person I expected to meet again. 'Do you want to come in?'

I played the part of a welcoming hostess, despite being rocked by the unexpected appearance of this woman. What was she doing here? I offered tea, digging out a proper tea service that hadn't left the cupboard since the Jacksons had died, and provided a plate of biscuits on a matching plate. I apologised for the lack of cake.

I wrestled internally over what was the right way to start the conversation. Eventually, I put on a sombre face and a sombre voice and tried: 'I was so sorry about ...', but Caroline quickly interrupted me, waving a hand with some vigour.

'Yes, yes. Forget all that. Take it as read.'

I raised my cup to my lips.

'The funeral's over, such as it was. Time to move on.'

'Did your daughters come?' I thought she'd at least want to talk about the funeral.

'Oh no. Small affair. A couple of teachers from school. Alistair from next door and his frumpy wife. That was it.' Another wave of the hand.

I held out the plate of biscuits and she took one. I waited. Why was she here?

'You're probably wondering why I've turned up like this, out of the blue. I got your address from Stephen's phone. I'm trying to remember to call him that, Stephen. Like I said, it's time to move on. Still, I felt …' She chewed on a finger nail and didn't finish the sentence. 'I need to draw a line under … under all this…' She lifted her hand into the air again but left another sentence unfinished. 'It seems to me that you're a part of it, that's the truth. So I need to clear the air with you. Explain a few things. Get some answers.' She drank from her cup and replaced it on the saucer. She seemed to draw herself up, took a deep breath. I felt we were coming to the reason for her visit. 'Let me speak frankly. Who exactly are you and why did you come into our lives?'

I made a show of chewing the biscuit in my mouth, clearing my mouth of crumbs, swallowing. Thinking time. I hadn't expected her to be so blunt. 'No big deal. I'm sure your husband explained. I'm a Social History student, studying for a PhD, and as part of my research …'

'Bullshit. Imperial College has never heard of you. They have no record of any Frankie Jackson. Nor indeed of Anne Elliot.'

'These admin departments.' I shook my head. 'They don't know their... bottoms from their ...'

Caroline interrupted me. 'They're not to blame, it's you, it's always been you and your make-believe. I mean, "Anne Elliot," come on! You must think we were born yesterday.'

I held my hands up. 'Sorry. Yes. Silly idea.'

'And what about all the other lies you told us?'

I didn't answer.

'Stephen was always suspicious of you. He said your maths ability was ridiculously weak for someone with aspirations to A-level. There was something about you didn't ring true with me either, and it wasn't just your name. But we indulged you. He was for telling you to get on your bike, but I was curious, especially after the second invention, the one about doing research. I'm still curious.'

I gave a weak smile and a small shrug. Not much I could say.

'Tell me, Miss Frankie Jackson, assuming *that* is your real name, are you some sort of private investigator? You seem too young, but you never know these days. I don't think you're police, they're not so conniving. So who's your employer? Who's paying you to look into our affairs? Someone foreign, I'm betting.'

I hesitated. I couldn't see any way to get onto the front foot. And I don't like not being on the front foot. I waffled. Suggested she'd been very clever to have sussed me out. I asked how she knew my real name and she said they'd checked my driving licence, which I kept in my bag. So my trips to the loo had been opportunities for them as well as for me.

When she accused me of dodging her questions, I said I was subject to a confidentiality clause, I couldn't reveal who I was working for. I tried to make it sound plausible. I re-assured her that any investigation I might have been involved with was now at an end. Stephen was dead. That brought everything to a conclusion.

I thought I was in for further bombardment, but then the fight seemed to drain out of her. She didn't press home her advantage, merely sank back into her chair and clasped her hands together. It was as though she'd made the gesture, but when it came to it, she couldn't be bothered. Or maybe she was playing a different game.

'Not that it matters, not anymore. It's not important. Whatever your reasons for doing so, you dug away and eventually found what you were looking for. I guess.' She looked at me, questioning.

'More tea? I always find a cup doesn't hold enough. That's why I normally prefer a mug.'

The break for more tea seemed to get Caroline back on track. When she spoke again it was with a more conciliatory tone. 'I may have given you the wrong impression. I'm not here to start a fight. Honestly. I did want to understand you, but more important than that, I wanted to thank you.'

I hadn't been expecting that.

'Thank you for texting me. Before you phoned the police. How did you know my number?'

'Stephen's phone.'

'Of course. I was able to get to him before the emergency team arrived. I took the note. Burned it. I couldn't see how giving it to the police would help anyone. It hasn't stopped the rumours going around, no surprise there. But largely his reputation is intact. Apart from those who know differently and I don't think there's any among them eager to spill the beans. Something of a conspiracy of silence. Unless you're intending to spread malicious rumours?'

'Oh no. Definitely not.' I suspected that, like Stephen, she had an inflated picture of what I knew. In fact, I knew very little, although I suspected a lot.

Caroline looked out through the conservatory to the back garden, lost in thought. I can't say I was entirely content. Why should Stephen Greene's reputation remain intact? Why should he be remembered with fondness? Then again, it wasn't something I wanted to concern myself about. His death was the important thing.

'Can I say, Caroline? You seem to be taking it very well, the death of your husband.'

'Am I? Yes, I suppose I am. Like I said, it's time to move on, I'm not one for dwelling on the past.' She seemed to be considering whether to tell me more.

I gave her a prompt: 'You were married for a long time. Did you love him deeply?'

She smiled. My words didn't fit with her feelings. 'We weren't very close, if you must know. Companionship was probably the best way to describe the relationship we shared through the later years. We had been close, we'd been friends, dear friends. But in recent years, we travelled our own paths. I had a few women I met with for coffee, the lace-making and one or two other hobbies. He had his job, his trains and his … predilection.'

'You knew about that?'

'Oh yes.' There was another pause.

'Friendship, close friendship at the start. Never lovers, not in the normal sense.' She saw the look on my face. My too-much-information face. It didn't put her off: 'You might as well know everything.'

# -58-

'He always had problems, in the bedroom department. He needed unusual stimulation and even then ... I won't bother you with all the details.'

'But you had children. Two children.'

'They're not his. He thought they were. We'd laid together, to use that rather quaint expression, and he thought he'd done enough. He hadn't. I had a lover and it was him who impregnated me. Twice. Stephen never knew. Or if he knew he never said.'

'I don't know what to say. Did your lover want you to leave Stephen?'

'No. Not at all, it was never mentioned. He knew I wanted children and I told him Stephen couldn't do the business, so he stepped in. So gallant. Then, after I got pregnant the second time, he disappeared.'

'Never wanted to know about his children? Never took any interest in them?' Despite my personal aversion to children, I thought it was a given that those who had progeny were generally interested in how they turned out.

'No. I kept in contact for a while, at a distance, through mutual friends. I believe he got married. Don't think they ever had children. He must be old now.'

'It all sounds rather peculiar.'

'Didn't seem so at the time. He was a friend of Robbo's ... Stephen's ... an old friend. They were at school together.'

Fascinating though Caroline's life-story was turning out to be, I'd felt it drifting further and further away from anything I was personally interested in. I was surprised Stephen wasn't the father of the children, but it didn't matter now. Other people's lives ... so what? But then, when she mentioned Stephen's school. everything changed. This put a totally different complexion on her outpourings. Caroline's lover was Stephen's schoolfriend. Was he therefore another attendee at that party in 1966? Was he a participant in the activities that took place that night? Or was he a witness? Could this mystery man provide the detailed information I sought?

I had no more interest in Caroline, now her husband was dead, but I was very interested in her lover. Then my brain clicked one notch further. Perhaps I was being too hasty in disregarding Caroline herself. She was connected now to two former schoolfriends who were both 'of interest' to me. Could Caroline herself have been one of the girls at the party? I tried to remember Diane's diary. She'd mentioned other girls, usually by initial. Had there been a 'C'? I felt sure there had been.

As my brain tried to unravel these complexities, Caroline had been continuing her confessions, describing the double life of her early years, married to Stephen but having regular sex with another man, his friend.

'Do the girls know Stephen is not their father?'

'No. Although I'm thinking now, maybe I'll tell them. It might help patch things up if they realise that they owe nothing to Stephen, not even their existence.'

'Do you still see the father?' I was pretty sure she'd said she didn't, but now I was more interested in him I wanted to be sure.

There was the briefest of hesitations that I didn't understand because her response was definite. 'Oh no. That all ended donkeys years ago. Once I was pregnant with Kate, Grahame disappeared. I heard he got married. Moved to Sussex. Back to his old hunting ground.' She did that looking-out-of-the-window thing again. Chewed on a finger nail. I couldn't figure her out. She gave the appearance of opening up, telling me her secrets even though I hadn't expressed any desire to know them. Opening up, yes. But telling the whole truth? I wasn't sure.

Two things she'd mentioned lodged in my mind. Sussex. And the name Grahame.

'This has all been very boring for you. Sorry to unburden myself on you like this. I didn't mean to. All I really wanted to do was first of all to thank you, which I've done, and then to find out what you were intending to do.'

'How do you mean?'

'Are you going to tell the police? Or blow the whistle in some other way, some social media trolling? So everyone knows about Robbo, about Stephen.'

'No. Never occurred to me. Nothing to do with me what he got up to.'

'So. Let me ask you again. Why did you come after us? After him?'

I nearly told her the truth, about my grandmother, the party and all that, and about my mission, my plans for revenge. Perhaps she would be able to help. But I didn't. I didn't because of the name she'd given her lover, Grahame. If that was Grahame DeFreitas, he was the third man I was after. No way would she help me seek him out if he was the father of her children.

# -59-

I didn't tell her the whole truth, but I opted for a partial version. 'I can't tell you, I'm afraid. Let me just say it was a personal matter.'

This was an opportunity, perhaps my last opportunity, to extract more information from Caroline. I dared not waste it.

'To put my mind at rest, perhaps you could tell me. I'm intrigued as to how you came to meet Stephen, your Robbo. You don't seem particularly well suited.'

Fortunately, Caroline was still in an effusive mood, keen to keep talking, to tell me her version of history. Whether or not it was genuine I could mull over later.

'Oddly, it was through Grahame. We were all young, very young. Grahame wasn't my boyfriend but he was sniffing around, like boys do, and I didn't mind. We flirted in that naïve way teenagers have, knowing and unknowing at the same time. The boys had organised a party to celebrate the football. You know, the World Cup? 1966 I think it was. Grahame invited me.'

I tried not to react. She remembered the party! I needed her now to tell me all she remembered. But if I pushed too hard, she might get suspicious again. I kept my breathing even and gave her encouragement through my facial expression.

'At the party, everything went great. Grahame and me danced and after a few drinks, ended up kissing and cuddling. I thought this might signal the start of a proper boyfriend/girlfriend relationship. But I'd had rather more to drink than I was used to, well, we all had, and there were a couple of hours when I remember nothing. I presume I fell asleep. When I woke up, everything had changed. Grahame was nowhere to be seen and Robbo was sitting in a corner, head in his hands, sobbing his heart out. I sort of knew him, our friendship groups overlapped to some extent. He was a bit weird, a bit of a geek, a boy whose favourite subject is maths. You can imagine! So most people made fun of him, but I felt sorry for him. Especially seeing him there, so upset, all alone. I comforted him, tried to get him to tell me what the problem was.'

I nodded. Raised my eyebrows.

'Anyway, long story short, we started going out, and Grahame dropped off my radar. Robbo and I stayed in touch when he went off to university, met up in the vacations. I expected him to meet some nerdy academic and forget me, but he didn't. He came home seven years later with his PhD but no desire to continue with a university career. He wanted to teach. He became a maths teacher. I became his wife.'

'So how did Grahame come back into the picture?'

'He'd stayed friends with Robbo and there were times when the old group got back together. That gave Grahame and me opportunities to get close. He was still keen on me and, like I said, me and Robbo weren't exactly in happy-ever-after territory, so I was happy to reciprocate. There were opportunities and we took full advantage of them. All boring stuff now, ancient history. Like I said, I've not seen Grahame since I was pregnant with Kate. After that Robbo and I concentrated on bringing up the girls. They were our focus. Once they left home, that's when our real problems began.'

Caroline had said far more than she needed to, and I was grateful, although I didn't really understand why she'd told me. Was it just to get things off her chest? I got the impression she didn't have many friends; at least, not the type she could share with. I was a stranger, non-judgemental. I certainly didn't pass judgement. Or was there another agenda at play, here? Something of which I was totally unaware.

'Can I ask you, Caroline? Probably seems like a strange question. But what was Grahame's surname.'

'DeFreitas. Deffo the lads used to call him, back in the day. Why do you want to know?'

'Oh, no real reason. I thought I might know him. Different Grahame.'

Not sure if I'd got away with that, but it didn't matter: Caroline had confirmed his name.

We'd finished our second cups of tea, and cleared another plate of biscuits. The visit had completed its natural course.

'So what are you going to do now?' she asked

'What do you mean?'

'I can see.' She gestured to my bare walls. 'You're not intending to make much of Christmas.'

'Oh no. I can't be bothered with all that. I'll be on my own, no little ones to wrap presents for and feed sweets to until they're sick.'

'Christmas doesn't have to be like that. But then. New year, new plans? Does your 'employer' want you to investigate any other old Rubicunds?'

I made an instant judgment that she'd dropped that word in to test my reaction. I ignored it. 'Wait and see. That's about as far as my plans for next year go. Let's see what tomorrow brings. What about you?'

'A holiday, I think. Somewhere near the coast. I've always liked the seaside.'

# -60-

She left soon after that. It was an altogether strange visit. As I realised later, there was more to it than I was aware of at the time.

But for now, I had another version of the party-story. Or was it simply a continuation? Why had Stephen been so upset? Because he'd been forced to rape a girl? Or because he'd made love with the girl of his dreams and then she'd rejected him? Or for some other reason? Caroline hadn't given me any more detail. I didn't feel able to push her further, I'd already overreached the role of an uninterested third party.

I wondered again what would have happened if I'd come clean, told her my story in return for hers. I nearly had done, but on reflection thought I was wise not to. I was sure she'd have made things difficult for me. She was loyal to Stephen, and probably (and this was worse) loyal to Grahame too, even though she claimed not to have seen him for years. Whether that was true or not was irrelevant:

he was the father of her two daughters, and that would count for a lot.

I was suspicious of everything, of everyone. Who had told me the truth? Had anyone told me the truth? Caroline's tale in particular seemed quite bizarre, but I couldn't think of any reason why she would make it up. I've always thought that in Ann Cleaves's 'Vera' stories, families that appear to be 'normal' often turn out to be hugely complicated, involving intricate relationships, and it's from there the acrimony arises, leading to murder, or at least suspicions of murder. Families aren't like that in real life: that's what I've always thought. But now I was re-evaluating Cleaves's work: the secrets and lies in the Greene family were every bit as improbable as any fiction.

It was soon after Caroline's visit that I met Scott. Or James as he called himself at the beginning. That changed everything. A few weeks later I was awarding him a nine. I never award tens, but he certainly earned the nine and had the potential to achieve a nine-and-a-half.

By then, we were into a new year and I'd had enough time to indulge myself in my favourite activities and to feel more in control of my life. Caroline's visit had knocked me off balance with her startling revelations. But with time to consider, I fell back on the core narrative, the one I felt was most likely. Richard, Stephen and Grahame had all raped Diane on the beach, at the party in 1966. Richard and Stephen had now paid for their crimes, I had the tattooed figures '1' and '2' as mementoes. My next target would be Grahame DeFreitas. According to Caroline, he was living in Sussex, on the coast. I needed to find him and confront him and make him also pay for his crime. Simple.

Simple was also the word for my Christmas and New Year celebrations, or rather non-celebrations. To be honest, I hate the whole shebang, and can never wait for it all to be over and for life to return to normal. I have no memories of warm and loving Christmases past. Also my view must be coloured by my lack of family, and especially my lack of children and lack of affinity towards other people's children. I'm often told that Christmas is a time for children. To me it seems more a time for the sellers of things of little importance or use to beef up the hype and try and sell us even more of those wretched things, whether we want them or not.

So I allowed myself to indulge in a little more alcohol than usual, but other than that attempted to continue with my usual lifestyle: running as usual, listening to loud music as usual, watching old movies as usual.

New year would bring a return to normality. Except that it didn't, because of James.

## -61-

'Do you think people-watcher watching is a thing?'

I was sitting at the corner of the bar in the *King's Head*, the same seat I'd occupied when I picked up Danny the previous summer. I hadn't seen Danny for a long while. I hoped he'd used his windfall to move out of his mum's house, taken the opportunity to leave the area and begun to build an independent life. He'd stopped texting me, which was a good sign.

I'd gone to the pub for a drink and a change of scenery, nothing more. Jeans and a jumper and no make-up, hair roughly combed. I wasn't trying to pick up anything. Customers were thin on the ground. I was guessing the regular drinkers were still nursing hangovers from New Year's Eve celebrations.

The voice came over my left shoulder and I turned that way. He was old. Well, not old like Richard or Stephen, but well beyond the normal range that would attract my interest – later thirties, early forties?

He explained: 'Only, you've been checking out the drinkers.' He gestured. 'The nervous young couple in the corner on what looks like a first date; the spat about the spilt beer at the far end of the bar that looked like it was going to flare up; the middle-aged couple sitting in silence. So, you're a people-watcher. And I've been watching you.'

If it was a chat-up line, it had originality going for it, but not much else. It didn't deserve a response. I reached for my drink and took a healthy gulp.

The man continued to talk. He didn't seem to be addressing me directly, yet the soft pitch of his voice wouldn't be audible to anyone else in the room. He wasn't bothered that I wasn't paying much attention. At least, he didn't *seem* to be bothered that I wasn't *appearing* to pay much attention. He talked about a film that had been released recently, and had caused a bit of a stir. I hadn't seen it, but his observations sounded knowledgeable, as though he were not simply a punter, more likely a critic. He talked about a couple of TV programmes in similar style. Then he moved on to football, a brief mention of a recent London derby, then his thoughts on last year's failure of the England team. *Big yawn*. He touched on politics, but kept his comments theoretical, couched in general terms and avoiding the prejudiced clichés that those on the extremes so readily fall back on. He spoke about a hilarious YouTube video that I hadn't seen.

The whole episode, lasting well over half an hour, was weird. I didn't respond to anything he said: he gave me no opportunity to do so. He never asked any questions or invited me to express an opinion. He finished his drink and placed the empty glass on the bar next to mine. Then he left, calling over his shoulder: 'Nice talking to you, Frankie.'

Once he'd gone, I wondered if I'd dreamt it all. I was used to men coming on to me and knew how to deal with them, how to encourage or not depending on my opinion and my mood at the time. But this wasn't like that. He'd remained distant, not engaging with me at all, not trying to get me to engage with him. If that was his way of impressing me, then I suppose it had worked, because at least it was memorable. But I wasn't clear what he'd been trying to achieve, and whether or not, in his terms, he'd been successful.

The most concerning aspect was that he knew my name. This had not been a random bar-room encounter. He'd come looking for me and he'd found me. Now he'd found me, what would he do next?

I didn't have long to wait. I returned to the bar two nights later. Twice a week at the same pub was unusual for me. Was I hoping the mystery talker would return? Maybe, although my main focus was trying to clear my mind of all the Stephen and Caroline Greene baggage, so that I could move on to phase three of my mission, the search for

DeFreitas. I took my well-worn copy of *Wuthering Heights* to the pub as a change from Austen, and found a corner table away from the bar. The room was quiet, even quieter than before. The same as on my previous visit, I'd made no effort with my appearance; I was still not looking to impress anybody. On the other hand, I had chosen one of my fancier bra-and-pants combos. *Well, you never know.*

He was a large man, not particularly tall, but with broad shoulders and an undeniable presence. Smart grey jacket over an open-neck patterned shirt. When he came through the door, he made straight for my table and sat down opposite. It was as though he knew I'd be there. 'May I join you?' Seeing him straight on for the first time, I registered a squarish face, high forehead, thick hair in need of a cut. Not unattractive. His eyes seemed unusually large and I couldn't figure out why. Was it the broad forehead, the sparse eyebrows? Or merely that he had big eyes (all the better to see you with)?

'Well.' I indicated the open book in my hand. 'I had been hoping for some peace and quiet.'

'I can do quiet,' he said, putting his finger to his lips. He went to the bar and returned with a glass of what looked like whisky. He sat down and said nothing.

I read, occasionally drinking from my glass. He also drank and looked round the bar. True to his word, he said nothing. After a while he went to the bar for another drink, and returned to sit in silence once again.

It felt like some sort of game, 'Grandma's Footsteps' is it called? Who would be the first to move, to look, who would be the first to look away? Despite my eyes being locked onto the page, my reading wasn't progressing. I was familiar with the story, but the words were not making it through to my brain. It was me who blinked first.

I closed the book and placed it on the table. 'Okay. I give in. Who are you and what do you want?'

'*Wuthering Heights* is one of my favourite books. Such complex layering, there's always more to find every time you read it. Nellie Dean is a particularly interesting character. She always seems to be in the right place at the right time, to overhear a crucial conversation so she can relay that information to Lockwood.'

'I didn't ask for a critical appraisal.'

He ignored me and went on to give his verdict on other characters, and then moved on to tell the tale of the Brontës, how they first published under male pseudonyms, using the surname Bell, and the widespread opinion of many readers that the three of them were in fact one and the same. I knew most of this. He then told me something I didn't know: apparently Emily had written another novel, but when she died, her older sister, Charlotte, had destroyed the manuscript. I knew that when it first came out *Wuthering Heights* had been attacked by critics for being depraved, and apparently her second novel was even more likely to attract such criticism; Charlotte wanted to avoid more scandal.

'Fascinating,' I said. 'You're a keen reader, then?'

'Oh yes.' I'd already guessed that it wouldn't take much provocation for him to wax lyrical on any topic. I was right. He listed the classical authors that he claimed to enjoy and then swiftly moved on to more modern novelists. To my surprise, he mentioned Margaret Atwood, Jeanette Winterson and Sarah Waters, three of my favourite authors. It was unusual for a man to take such an interest in female writers. A calculated lure, I assumed, temptingly dangled.

As on the earlier evening, he left without seeking my opinion on any topic.

He was an interesting man, well-read, well-informed. Of course, he may have googled *Wuthering Heights* on his phone when he went to the bar, but somehow, I thought not. Before he left, he scribbled a name and number on a beer mat. He didn't ask for mine. 'James' was his name. The number was a mobile.

# -62-

I tried various spellings, and had to rule out a few false leads, but in the end, as far as I could tell, the Grahame DeFreitas I was after had no social media presence, nothing on Facebook, Instagram, Snapchat. Googling the name threw up a web-page that was nothing more than a rather minimal CV. After a BSc at Manchester, he went to the States for his post-graduate studies, attending Stanford University. He was involved in the early days of computer technology, and was a participant in the growth of Silicon Valley, as it spawned numerous rapidly expanding companies. By the time he returned to the UK he had enough experience to set-up his own IT company, a company that was soon worth multi-millions of pounds. He married and had one child, a son. He was a rich man when he retired. However, his health had since deteriorated rapidly and he now lived (according to the web-site) in sheltered accommodation in Sussex.

The bad health dimension made me stop and think. Does there come a point when confronting an ailing pensioner with misdemeanours from their past becomes inappropriate, no more than cruel and pointless vindictiveness? Perhaps, in general terms, that was a valid argument. But not in this case. Grahame DeFreitas was a rapist, and as I'd told myself before, being a rapist is not something you grow out of. If he was ill, that meant I was more likely to be able to catch him; it certainly did not exempt him from my revenge.

I sent a single character text to James: "?" That way, he now had my contact number and could do what he chose with that information. I was curious about the man. Despite my experience with Joe, another man who had entered my life uninvited, I had no feelings of fear towards James. I couldn't be sure why, but despite his actions having all the hallmarks of a stalker, he simply didn't strike me as a dangerous man, and I had confidence in my judgment. But then again, nor was I particularly eager to get involved with him, sexually, romantically, or indeed in any other way. He wasn't repulsive, but neither was he the stuff of dreams.

I put James to one side and thought about DeFreitas. I contemplated heading off to Sussex in order to track him down. It wouldn't be as easy as with Richard, nor Stephen. I had no leverage to work at, no leads to follow. 'Sheltered accommodation' was (I was guessing) prolific in the area. I needed more, before chasing round the south coast like a headless chicken on some random quest.

It occurred to me that the electoral register could be a potential starting point. I needed to guess a town, so I plumped for Brighton. An old man returning to the town where he grew up? Seemed likely. Or, if I felt more dramatic, a criminal returning to the scene of his crime.

James texted me. I wasn't surprised when he didn't explain anything, didn't answer any of the questions implicit in my "?". He invited me on a trip to the British Museum. Once again, I had to give him credit for originality – not a drink at a bar, not a meal at a fancy restaurant. If his intentions were in any way romantic, this was not the obvious venue for a first date.

I declined his kind offer.

The electoral register provided only minimal return. It confirmed that there was a Grahame DeFreitas, of about the right age, living in Brighton, but as far as I could gather, getting any more information – such as address or phone number – would involve a lengthy process and was likely to be unproductive. Not sure if 'ex-directory' is a term that's used anymore, but whatever it's called, that's what he was.

James was not easily put off. Again, I was not surprised. He suggested the Science Museum, the V & A, a couple of other tourist hot-spots, none of which appealed to me. Then he wrote that he lived near Greenwich, and why didn't I take the DLR out there on Sunday and 'we'll see what happens.' I gave in. Like I said, I was curious about the man and not fearful. If events turned in a direction I didn't want, I knew how to repel a pest. My trusted bag contained the wherewithal to respond appropriately in the event that any emergency should arise.

## -63-

It was cold but sunny on that February Sunday and I enjoyed myself. I wasn't expecting to, but I did, and James gave the impression that he also enjoyed the day. We went around the Cutty Sark and the Maritime Museum; we walked up the hill to the Observatory. We read the information plaques together and (inevitably) he added his own contributions. Did that man know something about everything? We took photos of each other with one foot in the east and one foot in the west. We wandered around the market, finding plenty to laugh about. We ate lunch and dinner at establishments James recommended: the food was fine.

And that's how it started. That night he scored his nine and, to my surprise, that didn't signal the end. I'm well aware that giving a man what he's after can well lead to the end of a liaison, but as it was what I wanted as well, I was prepared to accept that. In fact it was only the start, nowhere near the end. He wanted to spend more time with me (he said) and I wanted to spend more time with him. So it became a relationship, a romance, an affair. Couldn't decide quite what to call it, couldn't at the time and still can't now.

I didn't know much about him, and he knew even less about me. I believe normal people in such a developing situation ask personal questions of each other and get increasingly intimate replies, and that's how they get to know each other: we did not. I wondered if he might be married, but soon decided it didn't matter. It was none of my concern. It was *his* concern, and if he was married it was his wife's concern. But it had nothing to do with me. The flat he took me to was undeniably a bachelor pad, of the minimalist kind. Not that that proved anything: he gave the impression of having sufficient wealth to own several residences.

I had nothing to compare our friendship with, apart from what I'd read in novels, and our relationship didn't follow the trajectory of any liaison I'd read about. We were in some ways together, in some ways not. We enjoyed each other's company, but we also enjoyed being apart. Infatuated we were not.

It lasted through to May, three months, give or take. *Happy days*! It threatened to be a distraction from the main purpose of my life. At least, some of the time; and, I was surprised to find, I didn't mind that it was so.

# -64-

James was unpredictable, liable to do things and say things that I wasn't expecting. At first, I wasn't happy with that, it unsettled me. I always like to know where I am in all matters, financial, emotional, physical, mental, but especially in my interaction with people. I need to be in control, taking the lead, making the important decisions, running the show. But with James that wasn't possible. As soon as I thought I'd got him pigeon-holed, cornered, safely harnessed, he'd leap away, fly up, head off in a different direction.

He never allowed our relationship, our affair if you like, our liaison, he never allowed it to slip into any sort of pattern. If, for example, we met up in some pub on a Monday, it didn't matter how that went, whether we had a good time or not, the next week would be different: we wouldn't meet until Wednesday (say), and that would be for a walk through the woods, or a trip to a shopping centre, or a random bus ride, just to see where we ended up. Wrong-footed. That seemed to be the state he wanted me to be in and I didn't like it.

Then, in time, I became used to it and eventually even to like it. In the end it was the unpredictability that became the predictable aspect of his character, and I learned to endure the ride, and, eventually, grew to enjoy it.

I don't mean to imply that he was domineering, that he played the role of some masterful, macho male, ruling the roost. If he'd been that, I'd have headed for the hills super-fast. Yes, he sometimes chose what we'd do, but just as often it was me who did the choosing. Here's an example. One time I remember he'd got us tickets for some film, a new release and the tickets were like gold-dust. As we were about to enter the cinema, some swish place in the West End, I told him I didn't fancy sitting in the dark for three hours, that I felt like going dancing. We went to a club and danced. Normally, neither of us was much into dancing. So it was no surprise that my enthusiasm waned after a couple of dances, and an hour or so later we left the club. But there were no recriminations. No shouting, no anger, no sulking. I'd spoiled his plans but he didn't seem to mind. We went back to mine and straight to bed.

I know the way intense emotion can come to dominate a life. A romantic relationship can become the most important thing, and then grows further into being the *only* thing. That was not how it was with James and me, and I was pleased that was the case. When I wasn't with him, I made sure I continued with my own life. I had my music, my running, my classic movies; my eating, my drinking, my reading. Then he'd text me, or I'd text him, and we'd do something together. Maybe it would be a date. Maybe it would be simply two friends spending time in each other's company. Maybe we'd have sex.

That's another aspect which was hardly normal, like everything else about the affair. We enjoyed sex but it was unpredictable in both its frequency and intensity. I know how much of a driving force sex can be, especially (so it seems) for men. I had no reason to believe James was any different in that regard. His flair for sexual activity was admirable: that nine was testimony to that and it was no flash in the pan. But when we spent time together, on a date or a non-date, it would sometimes end with a doorstep kiss and a wave goodnight, and then on other occasions we'd spend the night together, a night full of heat and passion. Usually we agreed which it would be without needing a discussion: the mood would determine how the evening would end. On the few occasions we disagreed, there was still no problem. I could ask and he'd refuse, or vice versa, and that was fine. No anger, no sulking, no petty point-scoring.

Another ingredient that my reading implied was inevitable after a certain period of time, was the use of the

'L' word. But not only was that word never uttered by either of us, there wasn't even an occasion when it came close to being uttered. It did sometimes enter my thoughts when I wasn't with James, wondering where the relationship was headed, but it was only in trying to put a word to how I felt, or how I might feel in the future. There was no need to share these feeling with him. I was confident that his attitude to that word was the same as mine, although we never discussed it.

The other thing I thought about, when lying in the bath, or out on an extended pace run, was the idea of the relationship lasting. Lasting into the long term. Not becoming permanent, that was ridiculous, and I certainly couldn't imagine that. But continuing into next month, even next year? Yes, I could imagine that and would welcome it: having James as part of my life was preferable to the alternative.

That 'part' was a crucial word, an important qualification. It would be accurate to describe us as a couple, an item. But we never merged into one person as some couples do, never permanently close, there was no being 'joined at the hip.' When we were apart there was no frantic texting or messaging, no reaching out, trying to grab the attention of the other, no twee emojis. We had each other's number on speed-dial, but rarely called except to arrange the next meeting. That might be the next day, the next week, or sometimes even longer. And neither of us made demands on the other. We respected each other's privacy, agreed, without actually saying the words, that we were each entitled to our own space. If I could sum up our pairing, I would use the word 'natural', there was nothing false about it, no contrivance. Also, the word 'grown-up' would seem to fit. Adult, mature, not juvenile. That was why it was sustainable. I could never be part of a clinging, angst-driven, selfish relationship.

Perhaps we were right to steer clear of the 'L' word.

## -65-

So far, so perfect. Except, of course, it didn't last.

At heart I always knew that it wouldn't. I thought a lot about the positives, but the negatives returned from time to time. That weird beginning, where he'd joined me in the pub, already knowing my name. Then there was *his* name. James was okay, but James Benwick? Really? The inference was that he knew far more about me than he should have. No, the warning signs flashed bright and loud. But most of the time I ignored them.

Meanwhile, when not with James, I kept returning to my mission: finding DeFreitas. Or a better description might be planning for how I might go about finding him. I was determined that James would not divert me from that project, or at least if he did, it would be no more than a temporary diversion.

I could easily travel down to Brighton, but the Parkrun trick would not work. If DeFreitas was as ill as it sounded, his days of 5k runs were long behind him, if indeed they'd ever been in front of him. I needed to get a list of places that provided sheltered accommodation, whatever that was. Then would I phone all of them? Might be a long process, and anyway, would they tell me if he was a resident? Probably not, everyone's so scared of data protection and identity theft these days.

If I did find him, how would I talk to him? I wasn't keen on using the 'social historian' line again, it hadn't proved a great success with Stephen. According to Caroline, the pair of them had seen through me very quickly and only played along to find out what I was after.

No, my plans for finding DeFreitas were not going great. It was frustrating. Fortunately, my dark thoughts kept getting brightened by a fresh encounter with James. That helped, while it lasted.

The relationship with James ended strangely. It did not end with a flaming row: that would have been entirely inappropriate because we never had any significant disagreement, indeed it was rare for either of us to use a raised voice. Nor did it quietly fade away, another ending which was unlikely. It ended by lurching in an unexpected direction, into unsustainable territory. Our coupling broke.

We were having dinner at my place. I'd cooked a few times for us, as had James. We both enjoyed eating and didn't mind cooking. I don't remember what we ate. I do remember the wine, a particularly fine Chianti.

We'd finished the meal, but were still sitting at the table, opposite each other, nursing a final glass of wine. 'So, Frankie,' he said, wiping his mouth with his serviette. That was the first flag of warning: he rarely used my name. 'Tell me. What is it you actually do?'

I assumed we were in bantering territory, as we were most of the time, our conversations being generally light and jokey. 'Oh, this and that. You know. I eat and I drink.' I raised my nearly empty glass. 'I read and I run.'

'Yes, yes,' he said, looking more solemn than I was expecting. 'I know all that, but what is the *purpose* of your life? What's your life for?'

I was still trying to keep the mood light. 'Nothing important,' I said. 'I will try and achieve world peace next year. If that doesn't work out, I'll take up breeding pigmy kangaroos in Ouagadougou.'

He didn't smile. He didn't respond at all. I realised I'd been hearing the wrong music, singing the wrong song.

'Okay,' I said. 'Right.' I thought hard. 'Well, if you really want to play the deep and meaningful stuff ... then I suggest you go first. So, James. What do *you* do? All I know is that you wrote computer programs and you were so good at it you got promoted, helped by a father who pulled a few strings. You then had a job where you supervised other people writing computer programs. And you were so good at *that,* they gave you a stack more money, and now, at the tender age of forty-two, you're semi-retired, living a life of leisure on half your previous salary, which is still plenty. So what do you do? With the non-earning half of your days?'

'I have a project. A mission.'

Him using precisely the term I used for my own project, my mission, disconcerted me a little. Disconcerted me a lot, to be honest.

'You know my father?' I nodded. I didn't know him personally, but James had told me he had played a large part in James's career development, and that he'd fallen into bad health in recent years. I couldn't remember whether he had dementia or one of those other old people diseases, of which there seem so many.

'He's dying. We don't know how long, but unlikely to make it through to the end of the year. He has set me a task.'

I waited. I assumed he'd tell me more. Rather than doing that, he asked me a question. It was not a question I was expecting.

His big eyes seemed even bigger than usual as he stared at me, eyebrows raised. 'Do you know Diane?' It was not an off-hand question. This was serious stuff.

## -66-

It may not be a common name these days, but you still run into Dianes, especially among the older generation. There are plenty of people around who have that name, in addition to the one at the centre of my thoughts, the centre of my life. I stammered: 'Er, ... What does she look like? Does she have a surname? How old is she? Give me some help here.'

'Old. My dad's age. Late sixties, early seventies.'

'One of my neighbours is old. She's got grey hair. But I think her name is Phyllis or Fiona, something like that. Not Diane. I can't think of any Diane.'

'I don't believe you Frankie.'

I came to a decision. I needed to stop this right now, before it got hopelessly out of hand. 'This is so weird, James.' It was rare, too. for me to use his name: he was bound to have noticed. 'You're acting very strange. I don't know what this is all about.' I shook my head and scratched my hair. 'I suddenly feel very tired. I think I'll call it a night.'

He stood up, still staring at me, wide-eyed. It was unsettling. 'Fair enough,' he said. 'Let's leave it there. Meet me tomorrow. In the park. I've got a story to tell you.'

I was confused. Who was James? He wasn't the ebullient, easy-going, semi-idol I'd come to know, come to feel emotion towards. He wasn't the slightly odd-ball character with an oblique approach to romance that I'd bought into. He was not the heart-throb whose sexuality merited at least a nine. Or rather, he had been all those things, but only superficially so; there was more to him than that. But I had no idea who he actually was and what he was doing in my life.

Once he'd left, I tried to work him out. Our early meetings in the King's Head had not been accidental, that much I was sure about. I'd known it at the time – his calling me by my name had been a give-away – but I'd let that fact slip into the back of my mind. For some reason, he'd sought me out. He'd given me a false name, choosing a character from Jane Austen's *Persuasion*. I should have paid more attention to that. Then, for the last three months or so, he'd played me. Softening me up, maybe? Was that the plan? Leaving me weak, easy meat. Susceptible, vulnerable.

In that regard, it had not worked. However wrong-footed I might have been by the way the conversation went that evening, it was only temporary: it didn't take me long to get my balance back. And giving me twelve hours to get my head around the situation was a bonus. If he'd pressed home his advantage, he'd have surely made more progress, towards whatever it was he wanted to achieve. I had to admit, I had felt exposed when he dropped the 'Diane' bomb into the conversation.

I am a murderer. That fact will always be there, lurking beneath whatever else might constitute my life. I am confident that my murderous actions were justified. I am also confident that my part in Richard's death will not, in the normal course of events, be discovered. But that means I have a secret, a secret that has to be kept under lock and key, chained, buried. This affects how I interact with people, because the shadow of the secret always threatens to loom darkly over every word I speak. More so when I am involved in conversations that lap at the edges of that secret. I presume all murderers know this and learn to live with it. Maybe those who don't are the ones who give themselves away, the ones who get caught. I am not going to give myself away.

# -67-

The next day, walking in the park, I felt strong again, my secret safely tucked away under several layers of carefully-prepared misdirection. I felt ready for whatever was to come. I didn't know what that was, but I'd thought through a few scenarios. One factor I was sure of was that our two 'projects' to some extent overlapped: that was the key. The name Diane couldn't be a coincidence. DCI Vera Stanhope never believed in coincidences and I was happy to take my lead from her.

As I walked through the gate and began to walk up the hill, still wrapped in winter layers despite the warmth of the spring sunshine, I cleared my mind. I was going to have the choice of coming clean or constructing careful lies. I could go either way. I felt in control. I liked being in control.

James was sitting on the bench, where I'd met Danny, a lifetime ago, and given him his unearned cash. As I approached, James stood up and we embraced briefly, almost as strangers now, several layers of clothing between us, not as the lovers we had so recently been. We strolled together into the wooded area. I knew these paths well from my running, and I'd led James along them on more than one occasion, during the weeks of that winter and early spring. Walking with James, I'd become more observant, seen more of the verdant flora, directed to the highlights by his running commentary as he added his knowledgeable remarks to each sighting of flower or plant, each naming accompanied by extensive botanical detail.

That morning, he did not talk about the plants. There was plenty of new growth, spring blooms and fresh foliage, crying out to be named and explained, but James's thoughts were elsewhere. He wasn't as conscious as I was that as the natural world was coming alive again, our world, the world of James and me, was crumbling. Indeed, had already crumbled.

'Sorry for last night,' he said. 'I got a bit carried away. Too blunt. I didn't mean to scare you.'

'I wasn't scared.'

'Okay. Let me tell you the story. My dad's dying. I said as much last night. Knowing he doesn't have many months left, he asked me to track down an old friend of his. He'd wanted to get back in touch with her for years, apparently, but never got round to it. Her name was Diane. Or you may know her as Di.'

'I asked you last night and I'll ask you again. Who is this Diane?'

He turned to me but did not reply. We walked on for a few minutes of silence before he continued.

'He gave me names of some people who he thought might be able to help. To help find Di. These were all people he'd known back in the day, but had no contact with since, so he didn't feel he could suddenly get back in touch with them, out of the blue. The first name he gave me was Richard Wright.'

I didn't react. It was a shock, but I was expecting to be shocked. I sidestepped a large puddle in the middle of the path: there had been a heavy storm a few days previously.

'He lived in Norfolk. A small town on the east coast. Hunstanton. Do you know it?'

I nodded.

'I went there and tried to find him. I went in the first pub I came to and didn't even need to mention his name. He was already the main topic of conversation among the locals. He'd been killed. Murdered.'

'Gosh. Bet that was a shock.' This was stretching my acting skills. I didn't sound convincing, even to myself. Being prepared for anything is okay in principle, but when it came to it, this was hitting too close to home.

I tried to rescue the situation. 'So was that the end of your search? Or were there any friends or relatives you could talk to? That may also have known this Diane?'

'No. It seems he was something of a lone wolf. There was a wife, but nobody knew where she could be found. He was a member of various local groups, but actually no-one knew him, not really, he didn't have any close friends. No relatives.' He gave me another sideways look. 'So I moved on to the next name on my list. Two names, actually.'

I guessed what was coming.

'Caroline and Robbo Greene. Their address was in West London, Hounslow.'

'Did you have better luck with them?' I felt I had to join in the conversation, but every time I chipped in, James turned to me. My pretence of ignorance was a thin veneer and I was sure he was seeing right through it.

'Robbo had committed suicide.'

'You've not been having much luck, have you?' Perhaps adopting a light-hearted register would be more convincing. As soon as I said it, I thought: *Probably not.*

'I spoke to Caroline, Robbo's wife.'

'I bet she was pretty cut up. About the husband.'

'Yes. I suppose so. Anyway, she wasn't much help. Claimed to have never heard of anyone called Diane. Said Robbo had never mentioned anyone by that name.'

I felt bombarded with information. With data crying out to be analysed, from which to draw conclusions. To me,

Caroline had admitted being at that party, so surely she'd known Diane. To James, she had denied it. What was I to make of that? But there was no time right now to think things through.

'So where to next? Who was the next name on your father's list?'

'Not on the original list, but what Caroline told me enabled me to add another name. Frankie Jackson.' Of course. I should have guessed.

# -68-

'When Caroline realised I was seeking information connected with Stephen's past, she told me about a young half-caste woman who had often met with Stephen in the weeks leading up to his suicide. She said it was strange because this woman had first seemed interested in being taught maths, only she'd given them an obviously false name. Then she had come up with a pack of lies about being a post-graduate student at Imperial. When she said all that, I began to make a connection. The friends of Richard Greene had talked about seeing him with a young woman of Afro-Caribbean origin. Also with a strange name, although I couldn't remember what it was. So I pressed Caroline for more details. She gave me a name and an address.

'So tell me Frankie. Did you know Richard Wright? Did you know Stephen Greene?'

'There are plenty of us 'half-caste' women around, to use your rather non-pc term.'

'But most of them are not called Frankie. And most of them do not have your North London address. Nor your phone number. You're the only ... brown girl ... that fits all these criteria.'

We had emerged from the trees. The sun was warm. I took off my jacket and hooked it on my finger, hanging it over my shoulder. I stood still and after a couple more paces, so did James. He turned to face me.

I was trying to decide what to admit to. To be fair, he had me bang to rights. But no way was I about to confess everything to this James, for whom any feelings I might have had had disappeared literally overnight. I considered what portion of the truth, and what version of the rest, I could get away with. Whatever decision I came to, it was important that it gave me the initiative. I'm not the submissive type. I was not prepared to be entirely defensive, I needed to strike back. To that end, I had an assertion of my own to make, and that would give me some thinking time.

'So that's why you turned up at the *King's Head* and started talking to me. I think it's called stalking. That's why you wheedled your way into my life, telling me all sorts of lies. Why didn't you tell me all this right away? Why all the pretence?' I still hadn't decided what to tell him. This 'Why didn't you say?' line was a way of stalling as well as putting me ahead in the game, however temporarily.

'So you think I should walk up to a stranger in a pub – you – and accuse her of murder.'

'Murder? Whoa! Who said anything about murder? You just said you'd added me to your list, as someone who might be able to help in your search. You didn't say anything about murder. Do I look like a murderer? Come on!'

I walked on, stomping a little, kicking at a few loose stones. They splashed in a puddle. He followed, then came alongside. He was waiting for me to explain. I was still unsure what to tell him. If I confessed, I didn't think he'd go to the police, but I couldn't be sure. I felt I knew him well enough; he was, like me, no fan of authority. But could I be sure that the James I thought I'd come to know was the same as this new James, the one who was no longer my lover?

Anyway, how would confessing help me? The only reason to tell him anything was if he could help. I still had Grahame DeFreitas to find. James hadn't mentioned that name. Was it on his father's list? If so, perhaps we could join forces, find him together, despite the apparent differences in our motives.

'From the sound of it,' I said, 'I'm something of a distraction. Not someone on your father's list, so forget me. Move on to the next on the list, whoever that might be, start tracking him down.'

'A very pleasant distraction, if I may say so.'

'You may not. Let's be clear, here. Whatever we had going, up until last night, it has now gone. Finished, finito. You can't smooth talk your way out of this. You came on to me for one reason only. You used me. I don't like being used.'

'Is that a threat?'

'You mean, am I going to kill you? Like I killed Stephen and Richard? Oh yes, out here in the park, with no gun, no sword, no … blunt instrument. I'll throttle you with my bare hands, shall I? Break your neck with one swift blow from my lethal right hand.'

James stood at the top of the hill, looking down the path to the main road. 'I hadn't meant to deceive you.'

'Yeah, right.'

'I hoped, once we'd got to know each other. That maybe we'd be able to share information, like adults. Cooperate. Perhaps we still can.' He turned to me, looked me straight in the face with those big eyes. 'Think about it, Frankie. From the way my wanderings across the country have tracked yours, I'm guessing that you're also trying to find this Diane. If that's the case, we'd do better working together. Think about it. Let's meet again tomorrow.' He took two strides down the hill before turning back. 'And no, I don't think you killed those men. You're not a murderer. See you back here tomorrow.'

## -69-

Back home, I threw some random ingredients into a pan and made an easy meal. I opened a bottle of wine. I tried to understand. Were James and I competitors, rivals or potential collaborators? Were we on the same side or not? Was this episode with James an irritant, a period I had to see through and not allow myself to suffer too much damage, before moving on to my real objective? Or could James contribute to that objective?

Gradually, I managed to impose some structure on the confusion in my mind. James, for reasons I didn't know, but under instruction from his father, was searching for Diane. Presumably, this was Diane, my grandmother, long dead. His search had taken him through the same route as mine, to Richard Wright (deceased), to Stephen Greene (deceased), to Stephen's wife-then-widow, Caroline. It had led him to me and that was why he had befriended me (well, that's one word for it). He hoped, presumably, that I would reveal the whereabouts of Diane.

If I told him she was dead, would that be the end of his quest? He'd return to his father with the bad news and that would be the last I'd see of him? Maybe, but then again, maybe not. Depended really on why his father wanted him to find Diane.

He needed me, or thought he did. That was a good position to be in: I enjoyed it when people needed me, for whatever reason. He believed I was also looking for Diane, and so it would be sensible for us to pool our resources. He'd assume I knew more than he did. If, on the other hand, I convinced him that collaboration was not on the cards, would he simply bugger off? And if so, is that what I wanted?

I needed to focus completely on *my* mission, not James's fruitless one. I had one target left: I wanted to find Grahame DeFreitas. I wanted to know whether he remembered raping Diane on Brighton beach that night in August 1966. I needed to know whether he had any regrets, any remorse. Regardless of that, I needed to extract revenge on Diane's behalf. How did James's mission contribute to that? Well, I presumed the name Grahame DeFreitas was on his list, as one of the contacts that might lead him to Diane. He hadn't mentioned him, but that didn't necessarily mean anything. If he was on his list, he may have a lead that would help me. For that to work, I'd need to pretend I was also simply following a trail. If I told him my true motive, he might be less inclined to help.

I was going round in circles, no further forward. Was James a potential ally or a potential enemy? Or a potential irrelevance? I poured another glass of wine.

I came to a decision: I'd opt for a simple approach. I texted James. A simple question. Was Grahame DeFreitas someone he was looking for? Let James wonder why I wanted to know. I didn't have to explain. I could wait for his reply then decide what to do with that information.

The reply from James came almost immediately;

*No. Grahame DeFreitas is not on the list of people I have been instructed to talk to. A simple reason. By the way. James Benwick is not my real name. I'm sure you guessed that. My real name is Scott. Scott DeFreitas. Grahame DeFreitas is my father.*

## -70-

I'm not accustomed to sleepless nights, I've never suffered from insomnia, even when Mum and I slept on the pavement. But that night my brain refused to shut down, as the implications and ramifications of James's text chased each other through spirals of reasoning, some logical and some not so much. The one notion I couldn't let go of was that if Grahame DeFreitas was my grandfather, that made James a relative of mine. Half-uncle? Is that what it's called? Whatever it was called, it felt repugnant.

The next morning, I didn't go out to meet James: I sent him a text saying I was ill. I stayed home, and in the cold light of day tried to apply cold reasoning to the facts now in my possession. This new development threw all my previous reasoning out of the window.

On the face of it, this was an extremely fortuitous turn of events, to put it mildly. I had so far come up with no plan to find Grahame DeFreitas, and then, just like that, he'd landed squarely in my lap. I could find out from James (or Scott if that's what he wanted to be called) where his father lived and phase three of my mission could proceed.

I needed to go for a run. The sunny side of spring had temporarily departed and the temperature had dropped ten degrees or so. But it remained clear-skied, no rain, no snow. So, returning to winter gear, gloves and leggings and a long-sleeved top, I was ready to run. I took the path through the woods, thinking of the recent conversation with James. Scott. I still needed to assess him properly. He was clearly now going to be useful, but he remained a potential threat. Didn't he? If he knew what I'd done, I don't think any loyalty for me, or dislike of authority, would keep me safe. No, that was a mistake I must avoid: thinking of him having any loyalty at all, any feelings for me, forget it. Remember: he'd used me. He'd come on to me because I provided a potential route to Diane. That's all. I had to forget the other, forget the moments when emotion had reared its ugly head; any emotion had been solely on my side and I had to let those feelings go. Emotional involvement is always a weakness: I ought to have learned that by now.

Two days later, the doorbell rang. I knew it was James. Behind the locked and bolted doors I ought to have felt safe. But memories of Joe were never far from the surface of my mind, and a shiver ran down my back whenever the doorbell chimed. I hate being afraid of men, but what can you do about it? I whispered to James though the letter box in my best husky voice, telling him I felt rough, had a super-high temperature, and thought I had 'flu. I refused to let him in.

That gave me a few more days to sort out my thoughts and decide what I wanted to happen next. If I was going to use James – I should start thinking of him as Scott as presumably that was his real name – if I was going to use Scott, I had to give him some version of the truth, but there was no need to tell him everything. I certainly wasn't about to admit to murder.

A week later we met on the bench in the park, at my instigation. Spring had returned. It was a glorious day, warm and sunny. Felt like high summer, never mind early May. I was still dressed in jumper and jeans, scarf round my neck, playing the part of the recovering invalid. Scott asked after my health and I told him I felt much better, and then coughed to indicate that my recovery was not yet complete.

I had a question prepared. 'Tell me James. Sorry, Scott. Tell me why your father wants you to find this Diane woman.'

'I don't really know. She's an old friend. As far as I know he's not seen her for forty years, maybe more. Perhaps he still carries a torch for her, you know what first love can be like. But knowing him, it's more likely some grudge, something unfinished from the past. Before he goes, he wants it tidied up.'

I waited, hoping he'd say more.

'As you can imagine, it's a question I've asked myself a dozen times. Dad won't say: he just says to find her. I hoped that once I found someone who knew her, everything would become clearer.'

'Do you always do what your father tells you?'

Scott nodded. 'It's a … It's how we are. It's hard to explain.'

'Sounds like you've never properly grown up. Never flown the nest.'

'Harsh. But there may be some truth in that. I don't like to upset him. He can be … unpleasant when he's upset.'

'Listen,' I said, moving on to the next item on my agenda. 'This Diane is an old friend of your father's, from his school days. She was also known to Richard and Stephen. In which case, I'm pretty sure I know the Diane you're looking for. In which case, I can tell you. Diane is dead.'

## -71-

I'd planned it to be a dramatic announcement and it had the expected effect: Scott was shaken, rocked on his heels, eyes even wider than usual.

'What? Are you sure? Who told you?'

I didn't answer, waiting for my revelation to take firmer root.

'So you do know her, did know her? How did she die? Was she murdered like Stephen Wright?'

I waited some more. I was enjoying this.

'For fuck's sake. Tell me what you know, Frankie. Dad will demand details.'

'She died many years ago.' I spoke with careful deliberations. 'How she died is not important. But there's something else. It will help explain a few things. Diane was my grandmother.'

I felt good. My double whammy had finally put me ahead in the game: I was in the ascendancy, calling the shots. As I expected, Scott was full of questions, about my relationship with my grandmother, what I knew about her life (and death) and her connection with his father. I made up most of my answers. Including saying I'd no idea whether she'd ever known Scott's father. I'd given him the two key facts I wanted him to know. There was no reason to tell him anything else, not anything that was true, anyway. I was building towards telling him my own story, the story that I was hoping would draw him in, persuade him to help me get to his father. More truth would merely get in the way.

I waited until his thought processes brought him back to the questions I wanted to answer. 'So was I right?' he asked. 'Did you go to Hunstanton? Did you speak to Richard Wright? I mean, were you there before he died?'

I nodded.

'You got information about Di, your grandmother?'

'Yes. I tackled him about Diane. He remembered her, but only vaguely, couldn't give me anything useful. He suggested I try Stephen Greene, that he'd be a better bet. He was right, Stephen also remembered her. As did his wife, Caroline. They both helped a lot.'

Caroline was a confusing element in this story, both the real one and the one I was inventing. According to her, she had an affair with Grahame DeFreitas, Scott's father, that lasted off and on for many years. He was the father of her two daughters. But Scott said that when he talked to her, she was unhelpful. It sounded like he'd spoken to her as a stranger, rather than as his father's former lover. Did he know nothing about their history? Did Caroline not let on? Had she been playing games, for some reason that escaped me? Or had Scott lied to me? Too many questions and no answers.

So when I brought Caroline back into the conversation, I watched him carefully, checking for any reaction: there was none. Either she meant nothing to him or he was a better actor than I'd given him credit for.

I continued: 'You're probably wondering why I've been touring the country, searching out these people who used to know my grandmother.' Scott gave a non-committal shrug. 'You see, my family.' I waved a hand in the air. 'It's a mess. I won't bore you with the details, but there's always been a lot of rumour and deceit – misdirection, smoke and mirrors, muddy waters, pick your favourite metaphor. I was told virtually nothing about my past that I could make sense of. And that's not a good thing, is it? Not where you want to be? You need to know, don't you, who you are and where you've come from? So a year or so back I set out to find the details of my ancestry. I'm not talking about research on a grand scale, looking back through multiple generations of historic documentation, like on that TV programme; no, it was only my mother and my grandmother I was interested in. Who were they and what did they contribute to me becoming me? My grandmother's name was Diane Johnson and she was the key. Her daughter, my mother, was called Emily, but apart from their names I knew little about either of them. I had one or two fragments from grandma's life, where she was born, where she grew up, and I used those snippets of information as starting points. The trail took me all over the country. Hunstanton and Richard Wright were the focus for grandma's early life, then on to Hounslow and the Greenes. Next on my list is Grahame DeFreitas, your father. I didn't know for certain that Diane and Grahame were friends, but they were in the same circle as school kids, went to nearby schools. And now you've told me your father was looking for Diane, so they must have known each other.

'What else have you discovered?'

'Oh, nothing interesting. Both Mum and Grandma led very ordinary lives. Just died rather young.'

'How did they die?'

'Like I said, nothing interesting. The main thing is the picture still isn't complete and I think your father could help. Help with the beginning, who Diane was and where she was heading in the early years. Stephen had a feeling that Deffo, as he called him, Grahame DeFreitas, your father, could be the key. He was the kingpin of their little group. I need to talk to him.'

I'd wanted to mention Caroline again, say how useful she'd been, but once I'd said I hadn't got much information, that wouldn't have worked. I was proud of the bit about Scott's father. I always find flattery such a powerful weapon: suggesting Scott's father was important would edge Scott towards being more sympathetic to my needs.

'I need to talk to Dad. Fill him in on all this.' He stood up and began to walk down the hill, taking his phone out of his pocket.

I followed him. 'Ask him if I can come and see him.' He stopped and turned round. 'Tell him who I am.' I waved my hand as I realised that he might misconstrue this. 'Leave out, you know, what's been going on between us, that means nothing anymore, water under the bridge. Just tell him I'm Diane's granddaughter. He may not be able to speak to Diane herself, but perhaps he'll see me as the next best thing.'

Scott walked back up and stood in front of me. My comment had registered with him. 'Frankie. Can we still be friends?'

I was astounded. 'What? You really don't get it, do you? You're acting like we had some sort of teenage romance and then we broke up. Now "Let's be friends," you say. But that's not it, that's not how it was. You used me.' I pointed vigorously at his chest. 'That's the crucial fact. I was a means to an end for you. You thought you could swan into my life and take from it whatever you wanted. So no, we can't be friends. We are not friends. I do not like you, not one little bit.'

## -72-

I think he got the message. I couldn't have been clearer. *But men! What are they like? Arrogant pigs!*

Yet back home, I began to wonder if I'd gone too far. If Scott walked out on me, I'd be back to square one. I needed him to at least give me his father's address. Ideally, he'd introduce me to his father. That way I'd have easy access and a chance of a casual conversation without Grahame DeFreitas being on his guard. During such a relaxed chat, he might tell me the truth about what happened at that party, or at least what he remembered of that night, perhaps how guilty he felt. It had occurred to me that might be why he wanted to meet up with Diane after all these years, to apologise to her, to ask for her forgiveness. If that were so, would it change anything? I wasn't sure. Anyway, I needed to remember that was my main objective: to get Graham DeFreitas. A spat with his son Scott was of no consequence against the backdrop of that mission.

I sent Scott a text:

*Sorry. I went a bit OTT. I hope we can continue to cooperate on our shared objective. But I needed to make it clear – colleagues is what we are, only that, so no more talk of anything else.*

I considered a smiley face, or some other appropriate emoji, but decided against.

Scott replied quickly, as he usually did: he always had his phone within easy reach.

*OK Frankie. I'll keep my distance. But there's no reason we shouldn't work together. Scott x.*

I didn't like that 'x' at the end. But I could live with it.

He then wrote a longer message, telling me he'd contacted his dad, told him Diane was dead and that he'd befriended her granddaughter. I mused over that 'befriended'. DeFreitas senior wanted to meet me. (*Yes!*) Scott added that he was planning on driving down to Brighton the next day and suggested we travelled down together, but I wasn't having any of that: I needed to be in the driving seat and not a passive passenger, both figuratively and literally. I told him I'd follow in a couple of days. That would give me time to get my thoughts in order and my bag properly packed before I met up with Grahame DeFreitas, the third rapist, potentially my third victim.

I also wanted to get domestic matters in order, ready for my return. With only one person living in the house, it stays clean and tidy on the whole, but some chores get overlooked. I gave the cooker a good going over; switched my wardrobe into summer mode, carting the winter gear into the wardrobe in the spare room; I cleared some out-of-date items from the back of the fridge. I gave Felix some advice on managing the garden through the summer months. He would ignore my advice, as usual, but I enjoyed feeling as if I was wielding a level of command.

I put in place my preparations for the trip to Brighton. It wasn't so easy. I couldn't picture the scene where I'd confront that man. The problem was, I didn't know him, I'd never met him. What was he like? In particular, how ill was he? Because I was visiting him at his request, and in some sense with his son as companion, that gave me less flexibility. With Richard, I'd known exactly how that crucial evening was going to end. With Stephen, a full plan hadn't materialised, but it hadn't been needed: all had ended well, without any further intervention by me. This was the trickiest of the three. I didn't want anything to go wrong. I had to complete my mission, earn my triple crown.

I needed options, that was the important thing, I needed to be able to think on my feet and respond to any development as it arose. I didn't want to rely on DeFreitas's illness. I checked the website again and it gave no detail. According to Scott he was dying, and he'd sent

Scott on this mission as, in some sense, his dying wish. But the more I thought about it, the less plausible that seemed. Scott had implied that his father was living in his own home. In what sense was that 'sheltered accommodation'? I had to remember I couldn't trust Scott, any more than I could trust what I read on the internet. When Scott had been calling himself James, I'd allowed myself to get close to him, almost, like an idiot, to develop feelings for him. But he wasn't James, he was Scott. He was a proven liar. He was unreliable. Apart from all the rest, I hadn't yet got to the bottom of the Caroline contradictions.

So I prepared myself well.

Then I set off for Brighton. I started on the M4, heading for Bath. Yes, it would be a meandering route. Not predictable, so less traceable.

# -73-

'You have her features, you share the shape of your face around the cheeks, the same chin.' Those were Grahame DeFreitas's first words to me, swiftly followed by: 'But she was a China-doll, you're more a dusky maiden. Not from pure stock I'm guessing.'

*Christ Almighty!*

According to Scott, his father had invited me to stay at his house. There was plenty of room, he said. That drew another swift negative from me: I had no wish to be indebted to my opponent. Scott had then recommended several hotels on the seafront, but I ignored his suggestions and booked into a small B&B to the east of the town, towards Rottingdean. The landlady was rather too effusive in her welcome, treating me as though I was some long-lost daughter, and once she knew I was a stranger to Brighton, gave me a long lecture on the dangers lurking in every corner of the city, and how a 'pretty, young thing' like me needed to keep herself safe. I nodded in all the right places and extracted myself from the conversation as quickly as I could. I'm sure she meant well, but I hate that sort of inappropriate chumminess from total strangers. *Just do your job and leave me alone.*

I was pleased to find that the B&B had off-road parking. I left my car and took a taxi to the vicinity of DeFreitas's address. It was a smart area to the north of the city. I walked the last half-kilometre and Scott met me at the gates. He didn't understand why I hadn't driven there and parked on the expansive drive like he'd suggested. I refused to explain.

Before shepherding me into his family home, he was anxious to apologise. He said there was something he should have told me, but for some reason he hadn't been able to. He still didn't explain, said I'd find out soon enough, leaving me curious and none the wiser. *Strange man!*

The houses in that area were impressively grand, well separated from neighbours and each surrounded by a couple of acres of land, maybe more, I'm not great at estimating areas. Chez-DeFreitas was typical. It had a stretched frontage, with a sweeping drive, a couple of statues, a triple garage and lots of windows, on both floors. Scott had led me into the front room, or perhaps Drawing Room would have been a better description, and somehow capital letters seem appropriate. It was a large space with wood panelling and discrete lighting, plush carpet, adorned with luxurious furnishings, paintings of dark landscapes on the walls, you can imagine the sort of thing. No bookshelves, which was a major omission as far as I was concerned. But on the plus side, there was no wall-mounted TV: I assumed there was a separate television room, and probably a library as well. I had been expecting to find the 'ill-and-nearly dying' DeFreitas in bed, or at least in a wheelchair. But he was ensconced in a large fireside armchair, pointing his feet towards the flames of a spectacular wood fire, something I hadn't expected to find, given the warmth of the season. He stood up as we entered, he and Scott shook hands without speaking (not sure they even made eye contact) and then Scott introduced me, his 'friend' Frankie, granddaughter of Diane. That's when DeFreitas senior came out with that lovely opening remark. I bit my lip. 'Pleased to meet you, Mr DeFreitas. I've heard so much about you.'

'Likewise, Miss Jackson.'

He offered me a chair and I sat down. I must have looked like Alice in a giant's house, perched on the edge of the substantial chair in order to prevent my legs from lifting off the floor. Then I sat back and let my legs hang, but I'm not sure that configuration worked any better. I'd put on a smart white shirt with a knee-length pleated skirt. I crossed my legs and as I did so, I noticed DeFreitas's eyes paying close attention. *They're all the same, aren't they?*

DeFreitas did not look ill.

On the other hand, his son did. Scott had sat down in the window seat. His head was bowed, and what I could see of his face had turned pale; his hands were clutched together on his lap. Father and son were ignoring each other. I wondered if this was their usual behaviour. *Strange family.*

While I was trying to figure out what was the matter with Scott, and also trying to take in this lavish setting, to assimilate it, come to terms with it, I realised the old man had launched into a diatribe, almost as if he was giving a lecture and I was his audience of one. On the other hand, he didn't appear to be concerned as to whether I was interested or not, or indeed whether I was listening: his speech was directed towards the fire rather than to me. Like son, like father, I could see where Scott got his verbosity and garrulous nature from. The father was expounding at length on the history of the town and surrounding area, and how it had developed into the city it was today, without my having indicated interest in any of this. He didn't invite me to ask questions, and left no space for me to intervene or to contribute in any way.

After several minutes of this discourse, he seemed to come to a natural break (or maybe he'd just paused for breath), so I made my interjection: 'How interesting.' I hoped the sarcasm was clear, but I fear it was lost on him. There was no sign he had even heard me.

I turned to Scott, hoping he would take the initiative in moving the conversation into a more productive direction. I hadn't come all this way for a history lesson. But in the presence of his father, Scott had shrunk. He was no longer the confident, erudite conversationalist I'd known earlier in the year. In its place was a picture of passive subservience, an apology for a man.

'Mr DeFreitas,' I said, interrupting the beginning of the next chapter on the history of Brighton and Hove. 'I understood you were unwell. Are you better now?'

He looked bemused, as well as irritated at the intervention. 'Unwell? No, not me. Oh, apart from the usual aches and pains. When you get to my age you have to expect that. Who told you I was ill?' His last sentence was a challenge, clearly intended to intimidate.

'I must have misunderstood.' My apology was as automatic as his belligerence. I turned again to Scott, expecting some explanation from him, or at least some supportive words, but he wouldn't meet my eye. He stared at his hands and said not a word.

'Right,' said the old man, standing up. 'Down to business.'

*At last*, I thought, but his idea of business wasn't the same as mine.

'Would you like some tea?' He looked at the clock-face above the fire. 'Or something stronger? The sun is over the yardarm.'

# -74-

Grahame Defreitas stood in front of the fire with a whisky in one hand, cigar in the other, feet astride, looking every inch some old-fashioned Lord of the Manor. He was dressed in a three-piece suit, striped tie that no doubt indicated membership of some exclusive club, greased-down grey-hair and a neat (also grey) moustache.

I sat with a glass of red wine in my hand; it was time to take charge. Inside DeFreitas's home, very much on his territory, with his wealth dripping off the walls and stifling the air, I couldn't help a feeling of inferiority, and I hated that feeling. Money isn't everything, but even on those terms I couldn't compete. I'm certainly not poor, I've been left comfortably off with the inheritance from the Jacksons, but my level of wealth is several floors below that of DeFreitas. And it mattered. It mattered to Grahame DeFreitas, and I was guessing it mattered also to his son: knowing where he came from threw a different light on his behaviour towards me, and made me dislike him even more. I didn't want wealth to matter, I wanted to be able to assert myself and not be cowed by this man and his grand display. It was my inexperience that was the obstacle: I'd never met anyone like DeFreitas, and reading about them, these egotists who believe they are born to rule, is not the same as meeting them, it gives you no clue as to how to handle them. I hate the cliché, 'outside my comfort zone,' but it seemed an apt way to describe my situation. He, on the other hand, was entirely comfortable in this setting, entirely used to behaving as a superior being, used to underlings fawning at his feet, doing his bidding. This environment imbued him with power, power that he was comfortable wielding, clothed him in superiority that he was comfortable wearing. Another cliché, the phrase 'pricking his pomposity', came to mind, and I dearly wanted to do that. In my own language, I needed to take the initiative.

DeFreitas sat down and gazed again into the heart of the fire. Before he was able to resume his lecture, I took a swig from my glass and stood up. 'Mr DeFreitas.'

'Please, my dear. Call me Grahame.' Even this innocuous phrase seemed designed to demean me.

'Grahame. I understood you wished to talk to me about my grandmother, Diane. That is why I am here. You knew her when she was a girl, I believe.'

Grahame paused before responding. I'm guessing he judged me to be too forthright for his liking, but didn't know how to call me to account without lapsing from what was, in his eyes, polite behaviour. 'Miss Jackson ...'

'Frankie. Please call me Frankie.'

'Frankie then.' Another prolonged pause. 'Yes. I did know her, your grandmother. Di. Such a sweet girl.'

This was another innocent-sounding phrase, but the way he said it sent a shiver down my spine. There was venom in his eyes and a turn to his lips that was something like a sneer. I didn't understand, but something was wrong, something I hadn't expected. I didn't know what was going on here and I needed to find out.

He continued, still with the same expression on his face and the same tone of derision in his voice, striking a contrast to his words. 'She was so lively. A great dancer. And singer. She listened to the radio non-stop, knew all the songs in the Hit Parade.' He looked into the fire for a minute then turned to me, with a different look on his face, almost a smile. 'You remind me of her. Despite your complexion.'

'Scott told me you wanted to find her. Why is that? After all this time?'

'I have something I need to say to her. A secret, you could say. It's been a secret for so long. I don't want it to stay a secret forever. It's as simple as that.'

'You do know she's dead? Diane? She died thirty-odd years ago.'

'Yes. Scott told me. Such a shame.' Why did I get the impression he didn't mean that? 'What did she die of?'

'I don't know,' I said. 'It was before I was born. I never knew her.'

'Don't talk nonsense.' His natural aggression was quick to surface. 'And don't take me for a fool. I do not enjoy people lying to me. Of course you know what she died of. Your mother will have told you.' He wasn't leaving any scope for his assertion to be contradicted.

'Our family ... It's not ... like other families.' I wasn't sure how much to say, nor how to express it. As I said these words, Scott raised his head and looked at his father, but his father's eyes were still on me. The look on Scott's face was unmistakably one of fear. What was he afraid of? Again I felt there were things going on here of which I had no knowledge.

I sipped the wine and tried again: 'I think ...' I'd lost my thread. Forgotten what I was going to say. I sat back down and tried to gather my thoughts.

I felt very warm. There really was no need for that fire.

What was I doing here? *Focus.* It was about holding Grahame DeFreitas to account. Like I had with Richard Wright. Like provoking Stephen Greene to commit suicide. Two successes and now I needed to concentrate on the third part of my mission, I needed to achieve more success. But Grahame DeFreitas was slippery. Now he was off again, talking about some family history, presumably his own, something about an uncle who'd had an illegitimate child. Why was he telling me? The truth was, he wasn't telling me, I might as well not have been there. He was telling himself the tale, merely mulling over the past, sharing it with the flames of the fire.

I looked once again towards Scott, hoping for some connection. Any feeling I'd had for him, when he'd been James, had long since dissipated, but I hoped he might still be on my side, that he might help me negotiate through this encounter with his father, wherever it might be leading. But Scott did not return my gaze. He was nursing his whisky and his eyes were fixed on the pale liquid, as he swirled it around his glass.

# -75-

I didn't want to be in that place anymore. The room was closing in, feeling increasingly claustrophobic; I felt like I was suffocating. The nausea grew as I sat there and suffered, under the domination of DeFreitas and the indifference of Scott. I was sinking under the heat of the fire and the weight of the situation. I didn't want to be there anymore. I didn't want to be in that room, in the presence of either DeFreitas, father or son. They were sucking me dry, each in their own way. I was tired, my eyes now drooping. And DeFreitas senior droned on about money and business and investments and what little concentration I'd been able to muster earlier now seeped away. I didn't want to listen any more. I felt so, so tired. What I wanted to do was to sleep, to sleep for a long, long time.

Then, with my eyes half closed, it was as though an apparition appeared before me. There was the sound of a door opening and when I turned, there she was. I imagined that Caroline Greene, Stephen's widow, was there with us in that stifling room, and Grahame DeFreitas was shouting something ...

## -76-

'He drugged me. He did. Put something in the wine.'

'Nonsense. He wouldn't. Anyway, why would he?'

We were sitting, Scott and I, in a café near the pier. A proper pier, Brighton pier, one that sticks out into the sea. It was busy, both inside the café and outside, far busier than Hunstanton ever was. Mind you, it was a warm, sunny day, as though summer had finally arrived.

I was still feeling groggy, but when I'd woken up in a strange bed at 2pm, my first thought had been to get out of that house. I hadn't felt safe to drive, so I'd persuaded Scott to take me into town. I wanted to get back to the B&B but first I needed to talk to Scott, hopeful that he could give me some answers, help me understand what was going on.

'So if he didn't drug me, what happened? How come I was one moment sitting in the family drawing room in the early evening, then the next was unconscious for …' I did the calculation. '… Something like eighteen hours?'

'You'd had a long day and it was warm in there. After a long drive and meeting my father. He can be rather intimidating.'

'Crap. Short hop down the M23, no distance at all.' Scott didn't know the real route I'd taken and he didn't need to know. 'And your father doesn't intimidate me.' I drained my macchiato. 'I need more coffee.' I went to the counter and brought back two more drinks to our table near the window, together with two pieces of millionaire's shortbread. I stared out across the coast road to the promenade beyond. The sea looked rough. *Like me*, I thought. Dark clouds were hanging heavy over the waves. A few people were beginning to run for shelter. It looked like the wind had got up. *What had happened last night*? I asked Scott for more detail.

'You dropped off to sleep in your chair. We left you for a while, then Dad said I should help get you to bed. He thought you'd be sleeping in my room, but I told him that wasn't going to happen.'

'Thank God for small mercies.'

'You were awake enough to make it upstairs, leaning on me, and I took you to one of the spare rooms. I left your bag with you so you could change into your night-clothes, but once you were lying on the bed, you went back to sleep. I left you there.'

'I don't remember any of that. I didn't have any night-clothes with me, I wasn't planning on staying the night in that house, was I? The first thing I remember is waking up this afternoon. He'd drugged me, he must have. It's the only thing that makes sense. I never fall asleep half-way through the evening, and I never sleep for that long.'

'Well, it happened.'

We continued to argue, but got nowhere. I couldn't come up with a reasonable explanation for why Scott's father would drug me; he couldn't explain why, if not drugged, I'd slept so easily and for so long. I ate the shortbread, surprised at how peckish I felt, but then remembered I hadn't eaten for many hours.

'Here's another thing,' I said, stirring my coffee. 'What was all the nonsense about your father being ill? He seemed fine to me.'

'It's what he told me to say. I don't know why.'

'And you always do what your father says?'

'Pretty much. Yes.'

'Do you know anything about this secret? What he was planning to tell Diane?'

'No, he never told me.'

I finished my drink, still mulling things over, but feeling that my brain-power was less astute than usual. Scott was still sipping his drink.

'I think you're right,' I said, 'partly right.'

'About what?'

'I don't believe he drugged me in order to kill me. He was trying to frighten me off, that's what I think. Why would he do that?'

'No idea.'

'Well it won't work. If he asks you, you can tell him loud and clear, it won't work. I don't frighten-off that easily. If at all.'

Our conversation had run its course.

'You, Scott, are turning out to be as useless as...' I looked out of the window, searching for the appropriate metaphor. 'As a paper hat in a rainstorm.'

He shrugged. 'What can I say?'

'Not a lot. Because you don't know anything. You've introduced me to your father, so thanks for that. Although to be honest, as far as you're concerned, I think it was for his benefit rather than mine. There are two sides here: your father and me. And I'm clear which side you're on. Maybe you even helped him administer the drug.'

I'd liked to have walked away at that point, stormed out, but I remembered he'd given me a lift and it was pouring with rain, so I needed his help to get back. We drove back to his father's house in silence. He made a couple of attempts to speak, presumably trying to defend himself, but I shut him up. Arriving back, with the rain still heavy, I quickly ran to my own car – I had no desire to bump into Grahame DeFreitas – and drove back to the

B&B, despite still feeling a bit woozy. Thank goodness it wasn't far.

Mrs Patterson, the landlady, did the mother-thing again, delighted to see me safe and well but angry with me for having stayed out all night, which meant (she said) she hadn't slept a wink. I apologised profusely. 'But you'd said you lock up at midnight, so I didn't want to disturb you.'

'You could have rung.'

*God Almighty. Let me get to bed.* 'I'm fine, Mrs Patterson, thank you for thinking about me. I'll be staying another couple of nights. I'll try not to stay out late. If I pay you now, will that be alright?' Splashing the cash turned out to be the magic wand that got her off my back.

I went early to bed, slept off the lingering effects of the drug, and woke up the next morning, much refreshed.

# -77-

I'd brought running kit with me, so that morning before breakfast, I went out for an hour or so. The weather was cool and wind-free. There were more hills than I was used to, but less people, more like Hunstanton in that regard. As I ran, I began to feel a strong sense of openness and cleanliness and other good feelings I couldn't put a name to. Happy to be alive: I guess that about sums it up. I had been through danger and survived: a positive life-affirming experience.

Back at the B&B, I would have liked a leisurely bath but had to settle for a shower. The good feeling persisted as I washed off the remains of yesterday. And then I went down to the dining room and allowed myself the further indulgence of Mrs Patterson's famous (according to her) fried breakfast.

Back in my room, I read a couple of chapters of *The End of the Affair*. I was in the midst of a Graham Greene saturation. Perhaps it had something to do with that author's name.

I was trying to keep the clutter of the past two days out of my mind. That resolution wasn't helped by Scott's repeated texting. He sounded solicitous, checking if I'd arrived safely back at the B&B, hoping I was recovered from my 'turn' as he put it. I didn't reply. I didn't trust him. Did he know what his father was up to? He'd come over all innocent in the café but that meant nothing.

After a while, his texts became more pleading: 'Can we talk?' 'Please reply,' that sort of thing. Having never had a relationship that lasted for any length of time, indeed having never been a party to anything at all that could reasonably be termed a 'relationship', I had no experience of the aftermath. 'Let's try again,' 'Let's be friends;' even, 'I'm sorry.' I knew these were the sort of things that were said, but I had no idea how to manoeuvre my way through the hazardous complexities of such comments. It was simpler to just ignore them all.

I read some more of the novel, had a longish afternoon stroll that took me onto the Downs, went for dinner at a cheap and cheerful restaurant nearby. I turned in for another early night.

The next morning I felt ready, ready for anything.

I began to get my thoughts in order.

The meeting with Grahame DeFreitas had not gone according to plan. I was no nearer exacting revenge. I'd been on the back foot throughout the meeting and then it ended with me unconscious. A bit of a failure all round.

Analysis had to begin with the crucial question: had DeFreitas tried to kill me? If so, why? Perhaps what I'd conjectured with Scott was correct, that his father had merely been trying to frighten me off. It's the only thing that made sense, well, more sense than any of the alternatives. If he'd wanted to kill me, he would have made sure he gave me the correct dose of whatever it was he'd put in the wine. He didn't seem the sort of man who would get something like that wrong.

So he must have something to hide, something he doesn't want me finding out about. *What was that?* It could be the rape of Diane, but somehow, that didn't ring true. As far as I was concerned, this gang-rape was the main event in these men's lives, but for them, apparently, not so. All of the people I'd talked to about those times, about the party, about Diane, had pretty much forgotten it all, merely a few remnants remaining. Why would Grahame DeFreitas be any different?

So, if not the rape of Diane, what else? What was this 'secret' that he talked about? I thought back to Stephen and how with him it wasn't, in the end, the rape of Diane that was the most important thing. It was his far more recent crimes, involving his paedophilia tendencies. As confirmed by his widow, Caroline. Then I remembered. What I had seen, or imagined I'd seen, as I was losing consciousness in the DeFreitas's drawing room. I texted Scott. The time for subtlety had passed. There was no-one in all this that I trusted, but perhaps Scott was my best bet. I sent him a text:

*Does Caroline Greene live with your father?*

As usual, Scott responded almost instantly, but the answer was presumably too complicated for a text message: he rang me.

I hadn't imagined her. Scott told me that he wasn't entirely sure what the situation was, but recently Caroline had often stayed at the house, in between returning to her own house in Hounslow.

'Did the relationship begin while Stephen Greene was still alive?

'To be honest,' said Scott, 'she has been around, off-and-on, for years. So yes, I suppose so.'

An affair lasting for forty-five years, not the four or five Caroline had suggested.

'Back when your mother was still alive?'

'I don't know, but I don't think so. That was a lifetime ago. My mother died when I was still young, only nine. I think it was after that when Caroline began to come round.'

'Really interesting. I wonder if Stephen found out about the affair. Was that a contributory factor to his death?' I don't know why I was asking Scott. He was unlikely to be much help with answers to that sort of question. 'And here's another thought. Obviously, Stephen's death was very convenient for Caroline and your father. Makes you think.'

'My father would never kill anyone.'

'I'm not saying they killed him. But maybe they encouraged him to commit suicide.'

'No.' This was the most emphatic Scott had been since our conversation had begun.

'Okay.' I was about to ring off. 'Thanks for telling me about Caroline.' Now I rang off.

I kept coming up with more reasons why the world would be a better place without Grahame DeFreitas. My imagination produced a worst-case scenario in which he first killed his wife and then later killed Stephen Greene, to clear the way for a permanent arrangement with Caroline; and now he had tried to kill me because I was getting close to the truth. Yes, rather fanciful, not enough proof for CDI Stanhope. *But remember, even if he's entirely innocent of all these later crimes, he's still a rapist: he still deserves to die.*

What I'd discovered during that brief encounter with Grahame DeFreitas had not been much; I needed to move my thoughts forward, to the next encounter. Punishment for DeFreitas. How could that be achieved? I wondered again about involving the police, but as usual couldn't see that route producing results. All I had were fanciful speculation and unsubstantiated intuition. The drug that had been put in the wine would be long disposed of by now – along with the remnants of the wine itself and probably the glass as well – so where would I find any evidence?

Therefore, it was down to me. I felt the adrenalin begin to surge as I contemplated killing that man. I'd already experienced confirmation of that adage, 'Revenge is sweet.' But the knife in the back, so successful with Richard, would be hard to replicate: I couldn't imagine any situation where I'd be close enough to DeFreitas to ambush him in the shower. Overpowering him was never going to be possible: he was a big man. I might persuade Scott to help me, if only I could find some leverage, some way of convincing him that his father was no good. He was very protective of his father. After the phone call, I was less convinced that he was entirely on his father's side. But I was still not sure he was on my side.

What other options were there? If I went back to his home and DeFreitas tried the drug-in-the-wine trick again I could switch glasses. That works well in fiction, but I couldn't see it working in real life. For one thing, he drank whisky while I drank wine: if I changed my choice that would soon send alarms bells ringing. In any case, drugging me a second time didn't make much sense, whatever the objective had been the first time.

As had been the case with DeFreitas from the beginning, my plans never seemed to take effective shape. This revenge business was hard. What I needed was more information. I had to go and see him again, that much was clear, and this time (before drinking any wine) I'd get him to talk about Diane. Did he rape her? Is that why he wanted to see her, to apologise? I had to be able to react to whatever answers I got: flexibility was the key. I checked the contents of my bag.

I would be heading back into the lion's den, so to speak. If he was prepared to drug my wine, even if only in an attempt to scare me or drive me away, he was dangerous. I don't mind danger but I need to be ready for it. More alert than last time, more in control.

But first I needed another conversation with Scott.

# -78-

'I really need you to be honest with me. This is serious now.'

'Yes, I get that. You're not the only one who's been giving this some thought. I don't know what it is you're trying to achieve, what you're hoping to find out, but I get that it's important, and I trust you: if it's important to you, that's good enough for me. And I'm not happy with my father's behaviour. I'm not saying he deliberately drugged you, but ... Well, he didn't treat you well.'

Those wide eyes tend to draw a person in. I'd been drawn in before, more than once. And now again: yes, I wanted to trust Scott. Did I have any choice?

We were back in the café, same table as before. Not a great day weather-wise, grey and dreary, less people around as a result. I'd suggested meeting him and he'd quickly agreed. This time I'd picked him up and we'd driven down to the seafront in my car. I was determined to be mistress of my own fate.

'There are many things that have been troubling me. Your father being ill, then not ill. You pretending you don't know Caroline then admitting you do. These lies on top of all the other ones, those you told me before. But let's start with this. What I'd like to know is why you were acting so strangely when we were at your father's house?'

'How do you mean?'

'You. With your father. It was like...I don't know, like you were a different person.'

'Aren't we all like that? Different settings, different behaviour. We adapt.'

'Hmm. Look Scott. I know we're not ... you know, like we were.' I looked into his big eyes. 'And don't make that face. I've told you, it's over. Forget it. But I do think we got to know each other pretty well.'

'Yes, we got close.'

'I wouldn't say close. No, that's not the word I'd use. These last few weeks, after finding out what you were really about, I've re-appraised our relationship, and I'd say we weren't close at all. All I'm saying is that *at some level...*' I emphasised those words to make my point, and paused to make sure it sank in. 'At some level, I got you. And the way you were at your father's, that was not you. Then again, perhaps it was, perhaps the other, what I saw before, was even more fake than I thought.' I shrugged, inviting a response from him.

'No, no. Not fake. You've got me all wrong, Frankie. No listen. Yes, I've not been entirely truthful with you.'

'I like that "entirely". Have you ever considered a career in politics?'

'Frankie. Just let me have my say. Yes, I sought you out for a particular reason, because I thought you could lead me to Di. And I didn't tell you that, so you can reasonably say I deceived you.'

'How kind.'

'But not for the whole six months.'

'Four months.'

'Okay, four months. It wasn't all pretence. When we were … together. You know … intimate.'

'When we fucked, you mean. Yes, I do remember. I wish I could forget.'

'Ouch! Say what you mean, why don't you? Anyway, at those times, and other occasions when we were just hanging out, chatting, sharing things, I was completely honest. That was the real me.'

I shrugged again and wiped him away with a wave of my hand. 'It doesn't make any difference. You can't separate *why* you were with me and *how* you were with me. The one informs the other.'

'No, I get that. I understand what you're saying. It's just when you talk about being "fake", I never faked my feelings towards you.'

'Okay. Some things are not worth arguing about. End of that conversation. Now tell me why you behaved so oddly in your father's house.'

Scott took his time, spooning sugar into his cup, sipping his coffee, munching on a biscuit. I waited. 'You want the truth?' he asked.

'Well that would be a first, wouldn't it? Make a change.'

'I hate him. I detest him. I loathe him. How many more ways do you want me to say it?'

'Wow.' I was genuinely surprised: I wasn't expecting that. 'That's harsh. As you know, I'm not much into families, but to feel like that about your own father.' I couldn't help but think of Joe, my own father. 'It takes a lot.'

'Oh, believe me, there's been a lot. A hell of a lot. You want the truth? Where do I start?'

# -79-

Scott drained his cup and took a deep breath. 'From my earliest memories. As a child. That's where it begins. My father's punishments were always harsh, unjust, painful. To put it plainly, he beat me, like we were living in some sort of Dickensian novel. He was a brute. I lived in dread of his fists and his feet. At school, I was a high-achieving pupil, but it was never enough for Dad. If I came top of the class in a test (and anything less was entirely unacceptable) he still wanted to know why my 90% wasn't 95%, 100%. I could write a book about his cruel parenting. And it didn't stop there: his bullying behaviour continued into adulthood.

'I was indebted to him and he never allowed me to forget it.' Scott must have seen the querulous look on my face. 'You see, he secured me a place at a prestigious American university. He got me my first job, with his company. He got me promoted. None of it was anything to do with my talent, and nothing (so he told me repeatedly) was earned. It was all down to him. I bore the family name, and that was why he was determined I should be successful.'

'Why did you let it all happen? Once you became a grown man you could have rejected his help, gone your own way. Grown some balls, for Christ's sake. Or were you happy to take his help because of the benefits that accrued, the easy life it enabled you to lead?'

'No, no. There was nothing easy about my life, believe me. You don't understand the hold he had over me. If I walked away from the family home, he'd have sacked me. And he'd have made sure I would never get another job in the industry: yes, he has that much influence.'

'There are other careers. A bright lad like you, you could always retrain.'

'If I walked away, I'd be immediately impoverished. You see, he holds the purse-strings. I may have given you a misleading impression of my financial position.'

'Not another lie. There's a surprise.'

'My father allows me to have a comfortable life-style. But he pays for it and makes sure I know it. He monitors all my expenditure. I have no funds of my own, apart from a small monthly allowance. When he sent me to track down his old girlfriend Diane, I had to submit receipts. That tells you all you need to know about our relationship.'

I didn't know how to take this. I was still suspicious of him. This could all be a pack of lies: for lying, he had form. Or it could be partly true, but exaggerated, to gain my sympathy. Or, God forbid, it could even be all true. It would explain the way he was in his father's presence: like a least favourite pet rather than a son.

'There's something else,' he said. 'You might as well know it all. When I was at university, I … well, let's say I had a brush with the law.'

'So when you say "know it all" you mean you'll tell me what you choose to let me know?'

'Oh, the details aren't important. But it was serious. I was drunk, although I admit that was no excuse. It involved an act of violence. The police were talking about a five-to-ten-year sentence. And Dad got me out of it.'

'How?'

'As far as I could tell, he bought me an alibi. All I know for sure is that having spent a night in the cells, the next morning I was sent home and told there would be no further action. The way the copper told me made it plain that he felt I was guilty as hell but couldn't do anything about it.'

'I guess you were grateful to him.'

'I had no choice. I still have no choice. He never allows me to forget it. That's the hold he has over me. If ever I step out of line, if ever I threaten to do anything that might upset his carefully constructed plans, he reminds me that one word in the right ear would send me to prison for a long time. Keeping me out of prison is my reward for total obedience.'

'I can see how you've come to hate him. If what you say is true, he really isn't a very nice man.'

'It is true. All of it.'

My coffee was cold, but I drank the remains anyway. A few loose ends were beginning to get tidied up in my mind. But I still had some questions.

'Did you know he was going to drug me?'

'No. Honestly, Frankie. No.'

'He told you to keep quiet about his affair with Caroline?'

'Yes.'

'In fact I already knew about it, because Caroline had told me. Although she hadn't told me the full story. Presumably he also told you to keep up the pretence about him being ill? Dying?'

'Yes, again. All true. I'm sorry, Frankie. I really didn't want to deceive you. But perhaps you can now see how it is. I have to do what he says.'

'I think it's about time that ended, don't you?'

'But how? Like I said, he has me over a barrel. I dare not step out of line.'

There were some crumbs remaining on the plate that had held the biscuits. I licked my finger and picked them up, popped them in my mouth. Thinking things through. Thinking how two people could each have their own issues to settle and how they could possibly share a solution. 'I don't suppose your father wants to see me again. In which case, I think it will be a good idea to go visit him. See how he manages to explain himself. There are a few things I'd like to hold him to account for. I may need help. Do you want to help?'

He hesitated. He took a deep breath. He looked out of the window.

I played my ace. 'Will you do it for me?'

That worked. 'Yes,' he said, and then more definite. 'Yes, yes, yes.'

'And you're prepared to do whatever it takes?'

'It's not just what he's done to me. He's spent a lifetime bullying and harassing, using cruelty as a weapon to get his own way. Most recently, how he treated you the other day was unforgivable.' He paused. 'Quite frankly, I've had enough.'

That's what I wanted to hear. 'Okay,' I said. 'Let's talk about how we're going to bring this to an end.'

We would go back to the DeFreitas home. And then what? I didn't know precisely what would happen, but we considered some different scenarios. Scott seemed genuinely on board with helping me, or at least protecting me. Maybe he really did have some feelings for me. But I needed to play my own hand. 'I'll start by speaking to him on my own,' I said, 'but you stay close. That house is something of a labyrinth. I'm sure you know a room that's within earshot.'

## -80-

I parked where the taxi had dropped me off two days previously. Scott wanted to know why, but I ignored him. We walked to the house. Scott opened the door and he turned to the left, while I went to the right, into the drawing room. Scott had texted ahead, so his father was expecting me. He stood up.

'Pleased to meet you again, Miss Jackson.' It was as though our previous meeting had been perfectly normal. 'I hope you are recovered.'

'Yes, thank you. I'm fine. Nothing serious.'

'Pleased to hear. Just time of the month, was it? I know what you girls have to go through.'

He offered me a seat and this time I stayed on the edge, leaning forward. He sat back into his opulent chair. I was pleased to note that the fire wasn't lit. I was less pleased to note that Grahame had a cigar on the go: the atmosphere in the room was clouded with pungent grey smoke. *Don't be distracted*.

Without any preliminaries, I made my prepared statement.

'I believe, Mr DeFreitas, that we both have information about my grandmother, about Diane. Also, we both want to learn more, each for our own reasons. Therefore, it seems to me, that we can be of benefit to each other.'

DeFreitas didn't respond immediately. Of course he didn't. Keeping me waiting was part of his natural strategy in dealing with underlings. He took a deep drag on his cigar, and blew smoke up to the ceiling. 'Straightforward. I admire that in a girl. Call a spade a spade. So to speak.' He smiled. His idea of a joke.

'You said you had a secret. A secret you wanted to tell Diane. Since she's long dead, perhaps telling me is the next best thing.'

Another pause. A deep sigh. He flicked the stub of his cigar into the grate. 'Since our last meeting, I've found out a few more things about you, Miss Jackson. I'll be frank. I don't like you. I think you're a meddling nuisance. I agreed to meet you today. But after today, I don't want to see you again. I want you out of my life, our lives. For good. Is that clear?'

Who was this 'our'? Him and Scott? Or him and Caroline? Or all three of them? I was guessing that it was from Caroline that he'd got more information. No matter. He'd let me into his house a second time, so this would have to do. I had to make the most of it. 'Fair enough, Mr DeFreitas. If it's cards-on-the-table time. I don't like you, either. Any more than I like your son. But you may have information about my grandmother that I can't find out any other way. That's why I'm here. Once you've told me what you know, I'll be gone.'

The inevitable pause. He got another cigar out of his pocket and clipped the end. Lit it, taking plenty of time to do so. Blew more smoke at the ceiling. 'Oh yes. The lovely Di.'

I waited. Held my breath. At last, he was going to talk about my grandmother.

# -81-

Grahame did talk about Diane. But first he talked about himself.

'It's not the done thing, you know. Telling tales out of school.' He'd switched from belligerent to philosophical. That was a good sign, it was a mood in which he was more likely to reveal facts about his past. 'But you asked for it, so I'll give it to you. Both barrels. Schooldays. Best days of your life, so they say. Truth is, some were, some weren't.'

I must have looked bemused.

''Days. In school. There were good days and there were bad days. A mixture. And you tried to get through them as best you could, thinking you knew everything, but in fact knowing nothing. Chaotic way to begin your life.'

He needed encouragement to move from the general to the specific. 'So, Diane?'

'I won't lie to you: as a teenager I was a bit of a bastard. I flitted around from girl to girl, couldn't keep it in my trousers. There were lots of girls available and I enjoyed the chase, in fact enjoyed the chase more than the actual conquest if truth be told, and certainly more than I enjoyed the aftermath. All that weeping and wailing. Couldn't cope with that. Got away sharpish once all that started. You'd have all sorts of names for me, I'm sure. But I was simply a jack-the-lad, admired by the boys and mooned over by the girls.'

He grinned. Was he bragging or was he confessing? It was hard to tell, probably a bit of both. My face must have signalled my disapproval.

'Oh yes, I know what you're thinking. If I'd been a girl, they'd have had a string of insults lined up for me – tart, whore, slut. But I wasn't a girl, I was a bloke. And we didn't have feminism in those days, poking its tits into matters that were none of its concern. So everything was as nature intended, boys were boys, girls were girls. The boys chased the girls and the girls pretended to run away, but not too fast. Everyone knew where they were in the grand scheme, no-one complained. It was how things were.'

He paused and stared into the grate. I was guessing nostalgia was his dominant emotion, he was thinking how good those days had been. Not if you were a girl they weren't.

'Yes, there were many, many girls. But there was only one Di.'

He puffed on his cigar, then stood up. 'Where are my manners? Would you like a drink?'

*What a strange man!* A few minutes earlier he'd been abusing me, calling me a meddling nuisance, wanting me gone; now he was piling on the charm. In his eyes, he was a well-mannered man, a gentleman, the perfect host.

This time I was ready with my response to the offered drink. 'No thank you. I'm fine.' I wasn't going to risk it, not a second time.

'Well, excuse me if I take a snifter.' He walked to the sideboard, poured himself a healthy tumbler of whisky and brought it back to his chair. Sank back and looked at the ceiling.

'Di, darling Di. On the face of it, she was no different from all the others. She was obsessed by music – I seem to remember *Herman's Hermits* being her particular favourite. She knew all the chart songs, was always singing snatches of them. And dancing, she was mad keen on dancing, off to the disco every week. Her hairstyle and make-up were always copied from someone she'd spotted on the previous week's *Top of the Pops*. She had long hair that could be put up into … was it called a beehive? Something like that. And her baby-blue eyes always shone through the mascara and the eye-shadow. Dramatic.

'But all that. It wasn't the real Di. There was much more to her than that.' He looked towards me. 'Oh yes.'

'Yes, that's what I thought,' I said, keen to encourage him. 'It's what I heard from my mother, that she was a very special person. You found that too?'

He raised his eyebrows. For a moment, he had a look of Scott about him, an older version. 'Special? Yes, I suppose you could say that. Di was a special person.' He seemed to be trying out that sentence, to see how it sounded. There was a half-smile on his lips that quickly turned into a snarl, a grimace. He paused, to make sure I was listening carefully. 'But you may have misunderstood the sense in which I regarded her as special. It was not in a good way. She was, in fact, the most evil person I've ever met. I thought at the time that she was bad. Now, a lifetime later, I know for sure. She was as bad as it is possible to be.'

It takes a lot to shock me, to knock my equilibrium. I'm good at riding with changes of mood, not letting myself be caught off balance. But this was something else. I had not seen it coming. Not only had I not seen it coming, but it overturned a whole mindset. Diane as an evil monster? Surely not. I thought about her diary, I thought about Mum's letter. No, this didn't ring true at all, this was not the Diane I felt I knew.

DeFreitas had paused again in his narrative, and that gave me a moment to try and assimilate what he'd said.

My first reaction was simple disbelief. I already had DeFreitas down as an unreliable sort: a rapist and an administer of dope. According to Scott, he was a sadistic bully. Why not also a liar? Paint Diane as evil to excuse his behaviour towards her? Maybe. Even if he was telling the truth as he saw it, there was no reason to believe that his view of Diane was correct. No, I couldn't believe Diane was evil, didn't want to believe it. I'd need a lot of evidence to be convinced it was so. 'I don't believe you,' I said. 'Diane was a good person. A good mother. She had a hard life, but she did her best.'

'Crap. Unadulterated five-star crap. You're entitled to your opinion, but you're wrong. There was no goodness in her, she was evil through and through.'

That sentence floated in the air between us.

I closed my eyes and took a couple of deep breaths. Then I asked the obvious question. 'So what did she actually do that was so bad?'

'You name it, she did it.'

'So name it.'

'First off,' he raised a finger, 'she was the biggest prick-teaser out there. You don't hear that expression in these enlightened times, but I wouldn't mind betting it's a type that's still around. She'd flirt with anything in trousers, using all the usual tricks, fluttering eyelashes, easy smiles, suggestive banter. On top of that, there was the way she dressed: provocative is too mild a word. But once she got into a situation where she was expected to deliver – if you get my drift – the barriers came up, the teeth and claws came out. "Keep your hands to yourself," she'd say; "I'm not that sort of girl." All the usual. Balls-busters. That's the other term for them, another one the PC brigade has wiped from the language.'

'Doesn't sound much,' I said. 'Standard teenage confusion.'

'If that's all there was, then fair enough. She wasn't the only one, merely the worst. But there were plenty of other things.'

'Such as?'

# -82-

'Gossiping, on an industrial scale. Rumour-mongering, muck-raking, shit-spreading. It was well-known that you never told Di anything you didn't want the world to know. She couldn't keep a secret to save her life. It wasn't as if she let it slip. No, it was deliberate. Anything salacious that she had knowledge of, she couldn't wait to tell all and sundry. And if she had no juicy tales to tell, she simply made something up. Never mind the damage it would cause, the friendships she broke up, the humiliation kids suffered. That's the part she enjoyed, seeing the pain she caused.'

'If all that's true, why didn't everyone cotton on to what she was like? Once you get someone like that in a group, people soon stop believing anything they say.'

'Oh, some of us were wise to her. But others...' He shrugged. 'She had a clique, you see, a posse of adoring followers who would hang on her every word. Lap it up.

And spread it further. It was like a virus, circling insidiously through everyone she had any contact with.'

I still felt defensive. This was my grandmother he was talking about. 'Every group of teenagers includes people like that. They don't mean real harm. They like the attention and feed off it. It's not their fault.'

'There speaks the modern do-gooder, the liberal head-patter. Poor things. It's not their fault. Blame the parents, blame society, blame the weather. Blame the crime on everyone but the criminal himself. Or herself.'

'It's hardly criminal to be a bit of a gossip. Especially at that age.'

'I haven't told you yet about the violence.'

Then he told me about the violence. According to DeFreitas, anyone Di took a dislike to was subjected to some sort of physical bullying. He mentioned hitting, pushing and shoving, Chinese burns. She had a particularly painful punch that she delivered with a fist in which the third finger was pushed forward, and she regularly inflicted this blow on the upper arm of her victims. It hurt, it hurt a lot.

'The worst,' Grahame continued, 'was that all this pain was delivered in such an underhand way. She'd be smiling to your face while she kneed you in the bollocks. She'd be laughing and joking until the adults turned away, and then the punishment would be delivered with cruel venom. She was sneaky, devious, snide.'

This still didn't sound so bad. He'd clearly got on the wrong side of her, and so was exaggerating: she probably didn't do half of the things he said. Anyway, these are the type of shenanigans that go on in any school playground. Even with my limited personal knowledge of school, I'd met people like that, seen bullying like that. Was there more?

'She broke Phil's arm. We never found out the true story, and Di claimed it was entirely accidental. But when Phil came back from hospital with his shoulder in plaster, he blamed Di. She'd pushed him against the wall and then twisted his arm as he fell. Deliberately.'

'Not very conclusive. Despite him saying that, it could still have been an accident. Accidents happen.'

'Yes, yes. If you choose not to believe me, that's your prerogative. I understand why you'd be on her side. What if I tell you the probable cause of that fight with Phil, if I tell you what it was actually all about?'

I assumed he was about to hit me with what he regarded as the clincher. Perhaps I should have guessed.

'Drugs,' he said. 'Di sold drugs, in the playground at the girls' school, and after school at the boys' gate. No idea how she got into it, but it suited her personality entirely. All that mattered to Di was Di herself. She didn't care that she could be damaging other kids' lives, by telling lies about them, by hurting them, by getting them hooked on drugs. She got a kick out of all that, and getting kicks was what her life was all about.'

# -83-

If Grahame was telling the truth, even if he was laying it on a bit thick, only some of what he'd said had to be true to conclude that my grandmother was not a nice person. When she was a child, that is. Perhaps 'evil' was overstating it; after all, she was only fifteen, sixteen. I knew how hard her parents had been on her when she told them she was pregnant. From that, I could presume that they were always strict, and it didn't take much imagination to believe her home life could have been traumatic enough to lead to behavioural difficulties. I was still defending her, apologising for her. Was this just liberal head-patting, as Grahame had called it?

Again, I had to remind myself of my objective here. Grahame had told me how wicked he thought Diane was. But how wicked, how 'evil' was Grahame himself?

The father who hit his son, tormented him, blackmailed him? According to Scott.

The man who made a married woman pregnant, twice. According to Caroline.

The man who was associated with two convenient deaths. According to me.

And according to my grandmother, the man who raped her.

If all that was true, if only some of it was true, he was a dangerous man. I placed my hand on my bag, reassured by my knowledge of what it contained.

Grahame helped himself to another drink, this time without offering me. 'How close were the two of you?' I asked, as he sat back down. 'I'm guessing that all you've told me doesn't only come from observation at a distance. Did she do anything to you personally? Hurt you? Get you addicted to drugs?'

'Not that. Thank God. Young and stupid I might have been, but still with sense enough to avoid that. But yes, we had some ...' He hesitated. 'Personal conflict.'

The personal was what I wanted to hear about. We'd finished with the preliminaries, the hors d'oeuvre, and I could feel the main course was on its way. 'Tell me about it,' I said, then wished I hadn't: I sounded too keen.

'Haven't you heard enough? I've told you what your lovely grandmother was really like. You said that's what you came here for, for information about Di. After which, you said you'd leave. So why aren't you leaving?'

'You're right, I should go. But there's more, isn't there. Don't you want to get it all off your chest? You can't talk to Diane herself, you're too late for that, but aren't I the next best thing? This may be your only chance to make sure I get the whole picture.'

DeFreitas weighed things up. I could tell that he'd half a mind to throw me out, but I could also tell he was enjoying seeing the pain on my face as he hit me with his revelations about Diane. He decided to continue.

'I liked her. When I first met her. She was such a pretty girl and that's the first thing a boy of that age goes for, indeed the only thing. She wore short skirts, tight jumpers, she had a dazzling smile and could give plenty of chat. Blue eyes, blonde hair. She was the perfect package. I knew what people said about her, but I thought she'd be different with me. Like I said, I was a very arrogant young man. So I asked her out and we went dancing. It went well, I enjoyed it and she gave the impression she was enjoying it too. During the slow numbers, she held on tight around my neck, pushed her body against mine. I took her home on the bus and we kissed and cuddled on the back seat. Then when she invited me in, I found we had the front room to ourselves. I presumed her parents were in bed. Immediately, she was all over me, kissing me fiercely, tongue darting into my mouth, her fingers pulling at my clothes. You get the picture. But as soon as my hand went up her jumper, she drew back. Then she laid into me.

"What are you playing at?", "What sort of girl do you think I am?", I mumbled an apology and headed for home.'

'You misread the signals. It happens.'

'Oh no. The signals were crystal clear. That girl knew exactly what she was playing at. Yes, playing is the word. It was all a game to her. She enjoyed making fun of the boys. All the boys. Including me. Perhaps especially me, given my reputation.'

'Was that it?'

'Not by a long shot. After that night, she started spreading rumours about me, how puny my private parts were, how I couldn't get it up, that sort of thing. Kids these days complain about the trolling they get on social media. But really, that's nothing new. Fifty years ago, I was routinely humiliated by the lovely Di and her friends. At school, I was a figure of fun for weeks, the whole lot of them on at me. There was nothing I could do about it. Some of them knew what Di was like, but it didn't stop them believing her lies. I was that term's prime whipping boy.

'Eventually, I decided to retaliate, started spreading rumours about her. It felt like the only defence I had, but it was a mistake. If I'd kept quiet, the whole business would probably have rapidly run its course, and everyone would have moved on to focus their attention on some other poor bastard. But after I'd sounded off about her, she wouldn't let it lie. She started sending me hate mail. It was anonymous, but she didn't even bother to disguise her writing. She made all sorts of threats. Someone in her fan-club had a brother that went to our school and she got him to play tricks on me. Oh, you don't want to hear all the details, there was plenty of nonsense – messing with my books, stealing things, getting me in trouble with teachers. There was a whole year when friends turned against me; I was all the time getting shouted at by teachers and ignored by class-mates; every week I was in detention for things I hadn't done. My life was hell and that bitch was the sole cause.'

I didn't know what to say. He was clearly still angry after all these years.

'So have I convinced you?'

'I guess so.'

'It was a whole year, near enough, before I got anything like my old life back, before I was back in favour with old friends.'

We sat in silence for a while. His anger was genuine enough. I needed to take advantage of this. In this frame of mind he was likely to tell me what I needed to know, to confess, but I couldn't see how I could turn the conversation in that direction.

'So why did you want to see her again? After all this time. What was this secret you wanted to tell her?'

'Oh, not really a secret.' He was suddenly calmer, back to his musing style. 'I just said that to whet your appetite. My little joke. But I do wish that I could have met her one more time. Once we left school, our paths never crossed again. I'm sure she soon forgot all about me, quickly moved on to her next victim. But I never forgot her. And I wanted to have a conversation with her, an adult conversation. Okay, she may have been a troubled girl, I wouldn't know anything about that, her mental health, you know, the sort of excuses they come up with these days. But to me, she was plain evil.' He looked directly at me. 'Have I made that clear enough?'

I nodded.

He turned back to the grate. 'If I could have spoken to her, face-to-face, I thought I might get her to confront the person she'd been. If I could tell her the effect she'd had on me, what would she think? I wondered what the grown-up version of Di would think about the child version.'

'You were too late. Too late by thirty-odd years. If it's any comfort, her life was short but pretty lousy, so I've been led to believe.'

# -84-

There was a prolonged silence. I was thinking about strategy. I don't know what he was thinking about: his mood kept changing so it was hard to read his thoughts. I broke the silence. 'Well, thank you Mr DeFreitas. Thank you for being so frank. You've given me plenty to think about.'

I felt this was a good ploy, acting as the grateful recipient of the morsels he'd given me so far, in the hope it might encourage him to give me more. I still couldn't work him out. He'd wanted to see me, presumably as some sort of second-hand revenge, dishing the dirt on Diane in place of haranguing her directly. But he also didn't want me to be there: he wanted to be rid of me.

He smiled at my pathetic attempt to get on his side. More a smirk, really. 'Maybe. But then again, maybe not. I don't know what you're about and I've heard nothing from you that has helped me figure that out. Like I said before, you remind me of her, of your grandmother. But exactly how similar to her are you? That's the question. How much of her evil has passed down to you? Quite a lot, would be my guess. You've certainly inherited her sneakiness.'

'What do you mean by that?'

'Scott told me. You've been sneaking around the country.' He waved his hand around, to depict my movements. 'Meeting up with Dicky Wright, with Caroline's husband, little Robbo. What was that all about? And now you've come to me in your underhand ways. What do you expect to get from me? Both the men you sought out previously are now dead. That worries me.'

'Coincidences,' I said. 'Coincidences happen. I had nothing to do with their deaths. They were both old men. Old men die.'

'I don't believe you. But okay, let's run with it. If you didn't kill them, what were you after? Did they give you what you wanted before they died? Or do you expect me to give you what they didn't?'

'I'm writing a novel. Well, not so much a novel as a memoir, I think that's what it's called. I'm intending to add fictional elements, to make it more commercial. But at heart, it's a family history. I've never known anything, only the dribs and drabs my mother told me. But she's dead, so I can't ask for explanations from her. Diane seems to have been the focus of our family, the pivot, everything spreads out from her. So I need to find out more about her, and that led me to the people you mentioned, those unfortunate gentlemen who have regrettably passed away. And now it's brought me to you.'

'Hmm. Have you written much before?'

'Oh, you know. Some things at school. A few short stories that won small prizes. But I've always wanted to write something on a grand scale. And, "Write what you know," that's what they say.'

I felt I was making a fair job of making this up as I went along. Perhaps I could be a fiction writer after all. I didn't expect DeFreitas to believe me, but it was plausible enough, so he could hardly call me a liar.

'Not sure I buy that. You don't strike me as the type to be a successful author. But, if it's so, have I given you enough? Do you now have a better idea of what your grandmother was like? You should, although I expect your 'fictionalising' of the story will paint her in a better light.'

'No, that's not my intention. I'd like my story to be true to the facts. I'll only make up things to fill gaps where I don't have the knowledge.'

'You now know everything I know. So you can leave now.'

'Sure. Don't want to outstay my welcome.' That was my idea of a joke, but I'm sure he didn't get it. 'But, before I go, I wonder if I could ask you, what happened the last time you saw Diane? I got the feeling from what you said just now that the competitive name-calling wasn't the end of things.'

'How astute you are. Although I can already see how you're watering down my version – I thought I made it clear, there was rather more to it than "competitive name-calling".'

'Sorry. Just shorthand. I heard everything you said and I understand how bad it was. But after that?'

'There is one more tale to tell.' He hesitated. 'It's a minor thing, not important. But perhaps it will satisfy you. Give you a little more material for your so-called memoir. Again, it doesn't show Di in a good light.'

Another drink, another cigar. He may not have been enjoying having me there, but he enjoyed telling his tales.

'Andy and Dicky had this idea for a party, to celebrate the World Cup.'

I tried not to react, but inside I was leaping up and punching the air. I hadn't even had to lead him to it. I was going to hear about the party. His version. *Yes!*

## -85-

'So it must have been 1966, late summer. I wasn't that keen on the idea. I thought it would be a booze up, reliving the goals, all very blokey. Not really my thing, I wasn't big into football. But I went along with it, they were my mates, after all. Then I found out Andy had invited some girls so it began to sound more promising. He told me one of them was Caroline and he knew I was keen on her, so after that I began to look forward to the party. I only found out when I got there that he'd also invited Di and some of her cronies. I was less happy about that.

'Anyway, the party went okay, plenty of drinking, music, Dicky telling his dirty jokes – he had an endless supply of them. And as the evening wore on, I began to make good progress with Caroline, if you get my meaning. But she was knocking back the booze like there was no tomorrow, and around midnight, she fell asleep. Di spotted me on my own and came over. This shows what she was like. It was as if none of the bitchiness had happened, the spreading of gossip, the poison-pen letters. She suggested we should carry on from where we'd left off on our date. And I bought it. Of course, I know I should have run a mile. How could I have been so gullible? It's bad enough being taken for a ride one time, but to then go back for more. My only excuse is that I was young. I was naïve, despite my "womaniser" reputation, and I was also super-randy, always up for it. Di was a stunning girl, as I said before, and it was easy for her to tempt a bloke, and I was up for being tempted.'

'So your girl-friend, Caroline …'

'Not my girl-friend. Not then. Let's be clear about that. She was just…' He didn't seem to know what to call her.

'Your partner for the evening? Up until that point. Then this partner falls asleep. And you take off with the next girl who takes your fancy.'

'That's not entirely fair.'

'This tale isn't exactly showing you in a great light, is it? Never mind Diane.'

'I told you. I was a swirling mass of libido, hormone level at maximum. I was up for it whenever it was on offer. Sex-mad, you might say.'

'Hmm.'

'So Di, Diane as you call her, she suggests going down onto the beach, under the pier, and she doesn't have to ask me twice. Everything's going fine, we're laid down on the beach, wrapped in each other's arms and fumbling hands are finding buttons and zips to undo. Then she pulls her trick again. "What do you think you're doing. I'm not that sort of girl."

'So once again you mumbled your apologies and slunk off.' This was meant rhetorically: I was pretty sure that wasn't what had happened.

'Not this time. Oh no. I wasn't going to be had again. You have to remember, in those days a girl saying "No" wasn't such a red flag. Not like it's supposed to be in this modern world. Back then, it was accepted that once a man had got worked up, it wasn't his fault if things carried on. Nature took over, if you get my meaning. So carry on I did.'

'You raped her?'

He gave me a look. 'That's putting a modern interpretation on an event that took place fifty years ago. Like I said, in those days such matters weren't as black-and-white as they are now. She'd allowed herself to get into a compromising position. I couldn't be blamed for taking advantage of that. It was her own fault.'

'You raped her. Fact. Never mind your excuses.'

I was overjoyed that I'd managed to get him to confess. But what I really wanted him to do was admit he was in the wrong, but he wouldn't. Kept insisting I was too young to understand, from the wrong generation and soaked in political correctness. That in those days, girls knew the risks. If she hadn't wanted it, she shouldn't have put herself in that position. *Yeah, right.*

There was no point in arguing with him. But there was still a possibility I might be able to find out more about that night.

'Okay. You had sexual intercourse. What then?'

He hesitated. 'We straightened our clothes and went back to the party.'

'There was no-one else on the beach?'

Another hesitation. It felt like there was something else to say, but he didn't know how much I knew. 'No, of course not. It was the middle of the night.'

'Richard Wright didn't join you? Stephen Greene?'

'No, definitely not.' He didn't look at me when he said that.

I thought he was lying. Not that it mattered now. Those two gentlemen were dead.

He tried a different tone. 'Look, it was a long time ago. Memories, they get blurred. If those two told you different, then they were mis-remembering. It was me and Di, just the two of us.'

I didn't press him, although I didn't understand. Was he lying, for reasons I couldn't fathom? Was it he who was mis-remembering? Or was his version the true version?

'So the reason you wanted to speak to Diane again after all this time... I'm guessing it was to apologise.' I didn't really think that was it, but I was looking forward to his reaction.

'You're fucking joking.' Now he was surer of himself, back submerged in his blustering self-confidence. 'Apologise to that woman. No fucking way. Pardon my French, but I thought I'd made it clear. That woman was evil. Anything I may or may not have done to her was nothing more than she deserved. In fact, look here's the thing. She actually enjoyed it. Oh yes. That's what all the "yes/no" malarkey was all about. She wanted to be forced.'

He saw the look on my face, but chose to ignore it.

'I never saw her again after that night, and when I thought about all the mischief she'd caused, I realised how much I wanted to confront her. About what she'd done to me. Tell her what a prize pile of shit she was and how many lives she had ruined with her gossiping, her poisonous tongue, her wicked pen. She needed to be told the truth. I'm really sorry she died before I had a chance to confront her.'

I'd always known Diane had been raped. Three times. But this was the first time anyone had used the word 'forced'. To me, it felt like the final justification: what I was doing was definitely the right thing, the right thing for Diane.

## -86-

'Do you feel better for telling me all that? I know it's not the same as telling Diane herself, but still quite therapeutic I'm guessing.'

'Oh. I don't know. Water under the bridge. Perhaps none of it matters anymore.'

This wistful, mulling-over version of DeFreitas had surfaced again. I knew it wouldn't last. Normal service was soon resumed.

'Anyway, that's it. Game over.' He stood up and threw the remains of his cigar into the grate. He took his empty glass back to the sideboard and turned towards me. 'You've got what you came for. So now you can piss off. Crawl back into whatever rat-hole you emerged from and write your maybe-novel. Good luck with that.' His last sentence dripped with sarcasm.

I didn't get up.

'What are you waiting for?'

I couldn't resist it, even though I knew it might be a mistake. I had not thought beyond this point, the point where I'd somehow managed to get a confession out of him, so I had no plan for moving matters through to any sort of conclusion. I hadn't had this moment with either of the other two, so I wanted to make the most of it. He'd admitted to the rape, but having got that, I now wasn't satisfied: I wanted to see him squirm. He hadn't expressed any guilt, any remorse. Perhaps I could squeeze some sort of apology out of him. Diane deserved at least that.

'Why don't you sit back down?' I said, trying to sound authoritative, as though I was the one in control of the situation, the person in charge.

'This is my home, Miss Jackson. No-one tells me what to do in my own home, certainly not some little ...' I wondered what term of abuse he'd use. I had a feeling my complexion would come into it, probably my age and gender as well. But he couldn't be bothered. He waved his hand. 'Oh, just fuck off, will you.' He had, apparently, got beyond apologising for his language.

'I wasn't *telling* you,' I said, trying to find my sweetest voice. 'There's no need to get on your high horse. It was a polite request. I have something to show you.' I smiled and gestured, and he gave me his blackest look in return. Then, with a small shrug, he sat back down, perching on the edge of the chair, ready to get up again at any moment. I reached into my bag and brought out my phone. I touched the screen and then held it up, waved it.

'Here in my hand,' I said, 'I have a recording of you confessing to raping my grandmother. This is what I came for.'

He smiled. I should have known that would be his reaction. No panic, no fear that he'd been caught out. He simply didn't care, it meant nothing to him. 'So what?' he said. 'It means nothing. That little episode occurred a lifetime ago. And as I tried to explain, in quite careful detail, despite the fact that somehow your tiny brain seemed unable to grasp it, it was a different era back then, with different conventions, different rules.'

'But the law was the same, that hasn't changed. Having sex with someone who doesn't want you to: that's rape. It is now, it was then. You committed a crime. You are a criminal.'

He shrugged. He didn't care. He really didn't.

'So, I'll pass this recording on to the police and I'm sure …'

Just as I'd started speaking, I'd heard a sound behind me, but didn't recognise it as the sound of a door opening. So I was taken by surprise when my phone was snatched from my hand.

Caroline Greene took the phone away from me and handed it to DeFreitas. She sat down on the arm of his chair. 'Thank you, dear. Nice timing.' He placed a hand on her elbow. The word 'proprietorial' came into my mind.

'So now you don't even have this paltry piece of evidence.' He waved the phone back at me in a sarcastic imitation of my earlier action. 'Evidence of this so-called crime. So good luck with talking to the police.'

## -87-

Having my phone snatched out of my hand had shaken me, left me floundering. I wanted to get back in control as quickly as possible. 'They'll still investigate,' I said. 'It's a serious crime, rape. And I have other evidence. Don't you worry about that. I have documentation they'll find very interesting.' It was gratifying to see the shadow of a frown cross DeFreitas's face. It didn't stay there long, he was so sure of himself, but for a moment I'd pierced that outer layer: despite his assured demeanour, he'd allowed himself, momentarily, to show vulnerability.

'And on top of the rape, there are a couple of deaths of people who you were close to, people whose demise was very convenient for you. Deaths that helped clear the way for you and Caroline to be together.' I nodded towards the woman perched on the arm of his chair. 'I've spoken to a few people who had interesting stories to tell me. Stephen in particular. He told me about conversations with you, interesting conversations. About your late wife. I'm sure the police will also be keen to look into all that if it's drawn to their attention.'

'Shut your fucking mouth!' DeFreitas stood up and bellowed in my face. My mention of Stephen had been speculative but seemed to have hit a spot. 'Enough! I've had enough of your bullshit. So you can stop right there, you pathetic, dark-skinned whore. Button up your fat lip and cease your pitiful scandal-mongering, your slanderous, fatuous accusations. They are not true. They are lies. They have no basis in fact, no evidence to support them, and they stop right now. Let me be quite clear: you are not going to the police. Absolutely not. I will not permit it. Are you listening to me?'

I do not like being bullied. 'Why not? How are you going to stop me? Knock me out with drugs, like you did before? Oh yes, that's another incident I'm sure the police will be interested to hear about, it will help them see you for the crook that you are.'

He shook his head, but he had regained control of his emotions. He sat back down, leant into the armchair, crossed his legs. 'What a nasty piece of work you are. Very much your grandmother's granddaughter, stirred with a splash of Afro-Caribbean to add even more bitterness.' He was sure he was holding the better hand, so he had no need to overplay it. But the absurdity he came out with next took me by surprise. Made me think Stephen really did have knowledge that DeFreitas was afraid he'd shared with me.

'Look, I'm a reasonable man. I have no fear of anything you think you might have on me, but fending off the police could be tiresome. Yes, I accept, you have the power to annoy me. So what do you make of this? You have all these stupid notions that you think you'll be able to trot out to the police and they'll take seriously. Actually, it's more likely they'll throw you out on your ear. But okay, let's just say they did listen to you, and came to question me. Well, I'd rather they didn't. It would, as I say, be irritating. So here's my question: how much would it cost? Shall we say a hundred grand? Two hundred. Okay, half a million quid. Would that persuade you not to go to the police?'

It was my turn for a sarcastic smile, a derisive smirk. I even laughed. 'No chance. I don't need your money.'

'You could buy yourself a nice house. A yacht if you prefer. There's a lot you can do with that amount of money.

'I have a house and I don't need a yacht. So now we can add bribery to the charge sheet. Perverting the course of justice. What else do you have in your criminal's tool-kit?'

'You are a very foolish young woman.' He paused for thought. I noticed that Caroline was saying nothing. She was chewing her fingernails, and, from time-to-time, raking her hand through her hair. I wondered what she thought about all this.

'Okay. If the cash doesn't do it for you, here's something you might find more interesting. A sort of *quid pro quo*. You tell the police your suspicions about me, your *unfounded* suspicions, I might add. And I tell them about you. Your trips to Hunstanton. To Hounslow. The deaths, those so-called coincidences.'

'Fine. Go ahead. I've got nothing to hide. I've committed no crime.' I couldn't help thinking about old Mum's suitcase in the attic at home. Some items in there I would rather the police didn't see. But DeFreitas knew nothing of that. 'Let's do it.' I stood up.

'Sit. Stay.' He leaned forward and shook his head. 'Yes, a very foolish woman indeed. You seem intent on not listening to sense. So that leaves us no choice. This you just might pay attention to.'

'So following bribery and blackmail, you've got some other pathetic little wheeze.'

'Shut up! Stop your foolish mumbling and sit down.' He was back into angry-man mode.

I sat down. DeFreitas nodded to Caroline and she went across to the sideboard. I thought perhaps I was in for another attempt to drug me, but it wasn't that. She came back, carrying a heavy object, and placed it in DeFreitas's outstretched hand. He held it up and pointed it at me.

It was a gun.

# -88-

There are some moments that stay with you all your life, scenes that become permanent memories. A night in a hotel. A soft bed in a hospital. Richard Wright in the shower, gasping as the knife slides between his ribs; Stephen Greene's body slowly rotating in that shed, with the fragments from the broken train-track crunching under my feet; James earning his score of nine.

And then there was that time when a gun was pointing at me. Another memorable moment.

In the suspension of time that occurs as I stare at the gun, the comment by Anton Chekhov comes into my mind, what he wrote about when a gun appears in a scene, what he said has to happen next. It's a bizarre thought and not even relevant. Chekhov was talking about fiction and this is very much not fiction, this is real life. Anyway, someone – Hemingway I think it was – contradicted him. It doesn't have to happen, he said. A gun can appear in a scene and never be fired. There's nothing wrong with that.

The pause in time continues, stretches, hangs suspended.

Nothing is happening; nobody is moving.

Grahame DeFreitas is not moving; Caroline Greene is not moving; the gun is not moving.

I am barely breathing.

I start to shake. I try to stop, but don't know how. I don't think I've ever seen a gun before. And this one is pointed at me. What should I do? Am I supposed to raise my hands above my head? Am I supposed to scream? To call for help? When should I have learned how to behave in this situation? Who should have taught me? Then I realise it doesn't matter what I'm supposed to do, I can't do anything: I'm paralysed. Fear does that, I suppose.

DeFreitas puts the gun down on the coffee table. 'You look scared.' So he's noticed. He smiles. Of course he does, that smile, so humourless, is becoming a permanent feature on that old man's wrinkled face. 'There's no need to be frightened, Frankie. We're not going to hurt you, are we Caroline?' Caroline says nothing. She has the look of someone who wants to distance themselves from current events. Yet it was she who snatched my phone, she who produced the gun: she's involved whether she likes it or not.

De Freitas continues in his calm-yet-threatening voice. 'We're not going to hurt you because you're going to do what I tell you. You're going to forget all that nonsense about the police. The gun is just to show you we're serious. Do you understand?'

I nod. I couldn't speak if I tried. My mouth is dry, my tongue's stuck to the roof of my mouth, my throat's constricted.

'So. No police. No accusations of rape. No spreading of malicious, unfounded rumours. Nothing on *Twitter*, *Instagram,* all those other silly games. You go away from here and you get on with your life, scribbling your pointless words, and forget all about me. And in return, I forget about you. The gun stays unfired. Everybody stays safe and sound. Everybody's happy.'

This time I do hear the door opening behind me.

'Ah,' says DeFreitas. 'Welcome. The other weasel has arrived. Glad you could join us.'

Scott stands next to my chair, puts his hand on my shoulder, and for the first time I'm confident that he really is on my side. And I stop shaking. It's what I needed, support. I trust him. I don't know why, perhaps because there is no other choice, perhaps, after what he said to me in the café, I now properly get him. It's not because he's a man and I'm a weak and insignificant woman. Definitely not that, I'm stronger than him in every way that matters. But as a team, we may be a match for the evil man sitting opposite us.

Time gets back up to speed, normal speed. I'm ready for action. I know now what's going to happen next.

I know what I'm going to do. I know what Scott is going to do. Soon, DeFreitas will no longer be in charge. Soon (maybe) he'll even stop smiling.

For now, he's still talking, DeFreitas senior, but I'm no longer paying much attention. He's drizzling scorn all over his son, disparaging, belittling words, saving some for me. He's so sure of himself.

But I'm sure of myself too.

I reach into my bag, find what I'm searching for and press the button.

The piercing shriek explodes at a satisfyingly ear-splitting pitch. It was advertised as at the limit of the human pain threshold: that sounds about right. I knew it was coming, was able to prepare myself, so although it's a deafening screech, it doesn't disable me. It does disable DeFreitas and Caroline. They were not expecting it, don't know what it is, and they both duck down, holding hands over their ears, letting out screams that add to the cacophony. I'm pleased with the effect: the alarm is doing its job.

I'd discussed with Scott several possible scenarios. I hadn't anticipated a gun, but I knew I might be placed on the back foot and would need to wrest back control, so this situation had been broadly considered. The main point: Scott knew about the rape alarm. He was prepared. He is not disabled.

Scott snatches up the gun from the table.

Two minutes duration was advertised, but it's somewhat less than that when the shrieking stops. It sounds like it's still going, echoing around the room, the walls, the ceiling, but it's not. It's over. Caroline and DeFreitas cautiously sit back up. Caroline stands and lets out a small gasp. Scott is aiming the gun at his father. I do believe there's fear in Grahame DeFreitas's eyes, and the sight of that makes me glad. It doesn't last.

DeFreitas gives us his sardonic smile. He gives three slow, ironic claps of his hands. 'Well done, you two. What a performance! Such team-work. So what happens now? What will you do for an encore?'

Caroline continues to look scared. She's staring at Scott, at the gun. Is she disassociating herself from DeFreitas? They no longer seem to be a team. Her fingernail is lodged in her mouth.

Nobody says anything. It's like a taut string, ready to snap. Or maybe ready to be let loose, to hang limp: it could go either way.

DeFreitas thinks he knows how it will go. He speaks in a lazy drawl. 'Are you going to shoot your old man, Scott? Do you really think you're up to it? You know, from my knowledge of you, having got to know you pretty well over the years, I really do not think you'd have the bottle to do that. It's not in your nature, is it?'

'Shut up,' says Scott. 'I've listened to you for far too long. All my life. I don't want to hear your voice anymore.'

He doesn't sound like he usually does. There are two version I know. The garrulous James I met earlier in the year. The taciturn Scott I'd recently had largely pointless café-conversations with. This version doesn't sound like either of them. And yet it sounds familiar. Then I get it. The register, the tone, the steeliness: Scott's voice matches that of his father. Like father, like son. There must be something in the genes.

'Oh,' says the father. 'Grown a pair, have we? Now there's a surprise! After all this time.' He makes a move as if he's about to stand up.

'I said shut up, and don't even think about moving. I'll tell you when to move. I'm in charge now.'

'Fair enough.' DeFreitas holds his hands up in a parody of surrender. 'Just thought you might like to hear one thing. You may consider it important.'

Again there's a pause. What's he going to say? He certainly knows how to raise the tension, to aim for the maximum dramatic effect.

'You see. There is a problem with the idea of you shooting me. That gun isn't loaded.'

# -89-

I'm proud of myself, of how I've been handling this encounter so far. It's not been easy, so many unpredictable twists and turns. But most of the time, I've kept ahead of the game. Some of the deviations I'd prepared for, discussed them with Scott in advance, others not so much. Either way, I haven't let Grahame DeFreitas dominate, at least only temporarily, not as he likes to do, not as he's used to doing. I've been a match for him. When he produced the gun, that was a heart-stopping moment and it put him in charge. But it was only a pause, my heart soon got going again and I turned things around. The game seemed to be won.

But now. He no longer has the gun, which is good. We have the gun, which is even better. But the gun is not loaded, it is useless. This is not good.

Where do we go from here? Who's winning now?

DeFreitas is smirking, so assured, always so assured. He thinks he's got us beaten. Perhaps he has it all planned out, knows how it will end.

But there is another dimension. I had not prepared for it; perhaps I should have. All year, I have been impressed by the breadth and depth of Scott's knowledge, especially when he was still James, when he was trying to impress me. There seemed to be no topic he didn't know something about, and most topics he knew a lot about. And that knowledge, so I'm finding out now, extends to knowing about guns, and knowing about bullets in guns, recognising when a gun is loaded and when it is not. That knowledge also extends, and this is the less predictable part, to him finally understanding his father, understanding his relationship to his father, understanding how he needs to manage that relationship so that he can break free. And he has arrived at a decision as to what to do about his father, after many years of subservience, of passivity, many years of indecision.

Scott DeFreitas fires the gun.

A neat circular hole appears in the middle of Grahame DeFreitas's forehead. A less neat spatter appears on the wall behind him, a spatter consisting of blood and flesh, bone fragments and particles of brain.

Caroline Greene screams.

The body of Grahame DeFreitas slips down in the chair.

Scott DeFreitas smiles, looking more like his father than ever.

I pick up my phone which has fallen from DeFreitas's hand and I grab my bag. I take one final look at the body, the hole, the blood-spatter. To Caroline and Scott I offer a parting observation: 'I think that gun was loaded.'

I leave.

# -90-

Back home, my first action was to run a bath, warm and deep, with bubbles and scented candles. I was in the mood for a new experience, so I opted for a piano concerto on the player, *Rachmaninov*. It wasn't so bad. It lacked the energy and vitality of my usual choice of rock music. Or rather, it had a different sort of vitality, a subtler, calmer version. I was okay with that, peace and tranquillity were the order of the day. I needed to breathe, deeply and slowly.

My journey home had been trouble-free: all I'd had to do was reverse my steps from four days earlier. From DeFreitas's house, I drove to the B&B, stopping just long enough to throw my things into the holdall. Mrs Johnson was nowhere to be seen, thank goodness. I was already fully paid up, but I left two extra £50 notes on the hall stand with a swiftly written 'Thank you.'

I drove down to the seafront and then headed west on the coast road. It's an old route, used to be a main road, but isn't anymore. It's been replaced by a motorway which takes all the through traffic. This route meanders through several towns and villages, lots of traffic lights, pedestrian crossings, speed restrictions. It was slow, but I was in no rush.

Past Southampton, I stopped in a quiet lay-by and took off the fake number plates, then drove up to the hotel on the outskirts of Bath. It was one of those anonymous hotels, part of a nationwide chain, where the staff at the desk is forever changing and they never know who comes and who goes and when. I felt in need of alcohol, so went to the pub next door for a few pints of lager. Then I soaked up the beer with their pie and chips and home-cooked veg, which was passably palatable. I was absolutely whacked, so had no trouble sleeping, despite the lumpy mattress and the even lumpier images infesting my brain.

Next morning, I had breakfast in the same pub. I was impressed by how they managed to transform the bar overnight from a venue for beer and crisps into an appropriate setting for toast and coffee. Regular hotel visitors must get used to this. Back at the hotel, I had a long chat with the current lady at the desk, 'Fiona' was her name (according to her badge), discussing my (fictional) sight-seeing excursions into Bath since I'd picked up my key at the beginning of the week. It was apparent she had no idea that I'd not been there. My absence hadn't been reported by any cleaner. I wasn't surprised. Why would they report it? It makes their life simpler if the bed-linen and towels are unused.

I drove back up the M4, stopping for lunch at a service station. Burger and fries. *Why not?* It occurred to me that all the subterfuge, the misdirection, the fake number plates and the tortuous route, all that was somewhat of a waste. As it turned out, I had no need of an alibi. But then, four days ago I hadn't known that.

The bath was soothing, as was the music. I began to believe I could develop a taste for classical piano music. I made a mental note to try some other composers. The scent from the candles added to the mood.

I closed my eyes and tried not to think about anything.

I failed: the thoughts came, unbidden.

# -91-

I thought about Scott. When I stopped off at the B&B I'd phoned the emergency services, suggesting they might care to visit the DeFreitas address. That was my last call before I destroyed the phone and discarded the remains. Scott would have had a few minutes to construct a story. I wondered what it would be. He might try and claim self-defence, although I wasn't sure how well that would hold up. It all depended on what Caroline said. Whose side would she be on? She'd screamed when the shot was fired, but I hadn't waited around long enough to witness her reaction afterwards.

I was fairly sure Scott wouldn't involve me. We hadn't discussed it, but then I'd left in such a rush, there had been no time. But what would be the point in him giving my name to the police? It wouldn't help him any. I was in the clear as far as any suspicion of murder was concerned: I had no apparent grievance against the deceased, I didn't fire the bullet and I hadn't even handled the gun. All I had done in that room was to have a conversation with Grahame DeFreitas and set off a rape alarm. Hardly evidence of a crime, certainly not of murder.

Various thoughts, accumulated through the recent months, continued to crowd through my brain. There were too many.

James as my lover, changing into Scott, the bullied son of my third victim.

Caroline, the widow of victim two and the lover of victim three.

Grahame DeFreitas, the rapist, with a collection of further crimes as long as your arm, some I was sure about, others less so.

The gun, pointing at me.

The gun, snatched by Scott.

The hole in Grahame's forehead and the spatter on the wall.

I wrapped myself in a soft fluffy bath-robe and opened a bottle of Chablis. My preference is generally for red wine, especially Italian, but the label suggested this was a quality white and I was looking forward to it. I scanned the bookshelves. *Ah yes, Ulysses.* I stretched out full length on the large sofa, a cushion under my head. I sipped the wine, which lived up to the promise of its label. I read. People say that *Ulysses* is hard to read. They're wrong. It's easy, you simply have to let the words roll over you, lap around you, you have to submerge yourself in that

Dublin day. It's relaxing. The wine contributed by relaxing me from within.

Around midnight, I went to bed, pleased that I'd put on clean sheets before I left for Brighton. Cool, clean sheets. A remedy for anything. Well, almost anything.

# -92-

My first task the next morning was to walk down to the tattooist on the corner. His name's Kyle, or at least that's the name over the door. Before he started, he wanted to check that he didn't need to leave space for any more numbers.

'You're okay,' I said. 'Just add a "3".' Joe didn't figure in my reckoning.

As he was working, curiosity got the better of him. 'So what we counting here? Boyfriends? One, two, three? No more?'

I didn't answer.

'None of my business,' he said. *Too right!*

Number three, another death, another slice of revenge to mull over. Of the three of them, Grahame was the most unpleasant: using his own word, 'evil' did not seem unduly harsh. He was the only one who had admitted to raping Diane, but without any hint of apology or remorse. Quite the opposite: he was proud of his actions, believed that Diane, of 'Di' as he called her, got what she had coming to her. Then there was his son's report of the years of abuse he'd suffered at the hands of his father. I was dubious at first, but now I believed he'd been telling the truth. That squeeze of the trigger had set the seal on it: Scott hated his father as much as it is possible for one man to hate another. Beyond that, I had my suspicions about Grahame's involvement in Stephen's suicide, and maybe the death of his wife as well. I had no evidence, so this was nothing but speculation on my part, but his reaction when I hinted at it was not the response of an innocent man. Not that it mattered now, it was all done and dusted. That evil man was dead and I was pleased.

How truthful had he been? I was sceptical from the beginning about his stories of Diane, of how wicked she had been when at school, and the more I thought about it the less plausible those tales appeared. I never knew my grandmother, and Mum hadn't talked about her much, except to say that despite her problems she'd been a good mother to her, in her own way. So most of my knowledge about Diane came from her diary. Although it was no sort of proof, the tone of her diary entries never gave any hint of the viciousness DeFreitas had described. As far as I could tell, when Diane disliked someone, she simply avoided them; there was no indication that she bullied them or hurt them. Perhaps all that so-called evil behaviour was an invention on DeFreitas's part, because he needed to justify his own abuse of her. Yes, that made sense. I could live with that version.

In the days that followed, I gradually began to emerge from the claustrophobia of Brighton and DeFreitas and the rest, to feel released from the burden of constant analysis of those events. It was a familiar process. After Hunstanton it had been the same; ditto after Hounslow. Freedom slowly seeped back into my life. I resumed my usual activities, first as distraction from the incessant internal dialogue, but then as purposeful activities in their own right. I relaxed into normal life: this was who I was. I returned to how I had been, plus I had grown in ways that I had yet to explore fully. Life changes you, that's simply a fact. My version of life had perhaps changed me more than I realised, given me layers of maturity I had yet to explore.

My first 10k was slow and I staggered at the end, my legs and lungs complaining as though I'd run a marathon. But I wasn't too bothered: my speed and stamina would soon pick up as the training resumed, as the sessions became more regular.

I resolved to be more experimental, more expansive in my habits and hobbies. I was twenty-one now, adult by most definitions.

I considered training for a triathlon. Running and swimming would be okay, but I'd need to buy a decent bike and get stuck into some serious cycle training. I could do that.

I searched the internet for popular classical composers and set up my player to shuffle through them. I skipped the opera, but apart from that, most of the other pieces were tolerable, some more so than others. Bach and Chopin were emerging as particular favourites.

I explored a few different cooking techniques. Thai cuisine particularly appealed to me, but also Japanese and Mexican seemed worth a try.

I found a set of language tutorials online and began to learn Spanish.

The piano in the downstairs study had remained unused since new Mum tried to teach me, a lifetime ago (so it seemed). I could acquire some simple sheet music and give it another go. Leave out all those scales and finger exercises and the other boring bits; concentrate on learning tunes and playing them.

Other ideas that were alive but for the moment were relegated to the back-burner included learning to knit, acquiring a cat and taking up smoking.

You could say that now I'd completed my mission, my life had an emptiness that I was trying to fill. I knew I should have felt contented: I'd set myself a challenge, the hard challenge of avenging Diane for the crimes committed against her all those years ago. And, one way or another I'd been successful. But it didn't feel as though it were enough. What I craved, I suppose, was some sign of gratitude, some thanks for a job well done. Diane couldn't thank me. But the men, those ageing criminals, what I'd wanted from them was some recognition of what I'd done. Not thanks, clearly not that. But if I could have found a way to make them realise the crime they had committed, the significance of it. Any remorse or apology would have been a bonus. But a simple recognition that I'd found them out: that was what was lacking. And it was too late now. In that sense, I felt I'd failed.

I wasn't clear what I now wanted for my life, for the rest of my life. But of one thing I was sure: I did not want to feel again that sense of failure. My future life would be filled with success.

# -93-

It was three months after my return from Brighton, early in October when there was still some warmth in the autumn sun, that Caroline rang my front-door bell. To say I was surprised would be an understatement. I had wondered about Scott, wondered if he might get in touch although I very much hoped he wouldn't. But as far as Caroline went, my only thoughts had been to wonder how she'd go about reconstructing her life after the loss of both husband and lover. I never in a million years thought it might involve me.

As was her way, there were no preliminaries, no phone call, no text; she simply arrived.

She had changed, or rather, she'd changed back. She had that superior, confident air that I remembered from when I first met her and she had told me about her husband's obsession with trains. I was struck now by how upright she seemed to carry herself, her head slightly tilted back so her chin stuck out. Radiating confidence, she'd lost the tentative, apologetic air of her last visit to my house. She was dressed smartly, like a businesswoman. Hadn't she once mentioned that she used to be in business? I could see how that could have been so.

'Sorry to call like this,' she said, standing tall in the doorway. 'I won't stay long.'

Inside, I offered her tea and after a moment's hesitation she accepted. The situation mimicked that of her last visit, but her demeanour was so changed. She stirred her tea, helped herself to a biscuit, and even with these simple actions she radiated her restored composure.

She wanted to reassure me, that's why she said she'd come. She was confident that Scott hadn't mentioned my name to the police. I was in the clear.

'Of course, I can't be certain what he told them once they took him away, but from what he said to me before the police arrived, he regarded the whole affair as concerning him and his father and no-one else. Not me, not you. He was aware that what he'd done was wrong but he felt justified because of all he'd suffered at the hands of that man. He was prepared to accept whatever punishment was coming his way. So, I thought you'd be pleased to hear that. That's the main reason why I came.' She spread her hands. I wondered about that "main reason".

'Thank you, Mrs Greene. That's very kind of you.'

'Caroline, please. I presume you've had no contact from the police.'

'No. I did wonder at first. But no, nothing.'

'Only, you know what they're like.'

'Sorry?'

'Well, you hear things. I know they're supposed to be entirely unbiased and all that, and they'll have had the diversity training, but there's no accounting for human nature.'

'You're talking about the colour of my skin?'

'Well yes. You know. It must cause you problems. Sometimes.'

There's no point in fighting it. 'Yes, sometimes,' I said. 'Sometimes.'

On the last occasion she'd been in this room she'd just lost her husband to suicide and hadn't seemed very upset. This time, she'd lost her long-time lover and father of her two daughters, even witnessed his dramatic death at the hands of his son, but if anything she was even less upset. Heart-broken she was not. Or if she was, she was making a grand job of hiding it.

I decided to be blunt: Caroline's bringing my skin-colour into the conversation made bluntness on my part feel appropriate. 'You're not sorry he's dead, are you?'

'Absolutely not. He was a bastard.' She sipped her tea. My face must have given away my surprise at her stark words. She shook her head. 'Back in the day. All different, of course. I'd fallen for him when I was a kid, and fallen for him again on more than one occasion as an adult when I should have known better. There's no fool like a plain girl who's relentlessly wooed by a handsome fellow. Not a very modern view, but I'm sure it's as true as it ever was. He was hard to resist, you know, when he was younger. It may not have seemed like it when you saw him, but he used to be everything you'd want in a man. Handsome, charming, humorous. He had a way with words, very seductive. I was readily seduced.' She smiled. I thought about Scott, or rather 'James', son of Grahame, and his many words, and I thought again about genetics. 'But it was not something that stood the test of time. When he came back to me a couple of years ago, I didn't want to know. I'd managed to develop an immunity. Finally grown out of him, I suppose.'

I was confused. 'But you were at his house. A regular visitor, even if not living there. Sharing his life. That's what it looked like, and Scott confirmed it. It surprised me, I struggled to make sense of it, because you'd told me you hadn't seen him since your daughter was born.'

'Yes, I wasn't entirely honest with you last time. Sorry. But you say things, don't you? To avoid awkward questions. The truth is, the facts were too complicated for easy answers. I'd turned him down, but you see he wouldn't accept that, wouldn't leave me alone.'

# -94-

'I'm sure you don't want to hear the ins-and-outs of some stranger's love-life.' She sipped her tea and helped herself to another biscuit. I kept my expression non-committal. 'On the other hand, perhaps "strangers"' (she did the quotation-marks-thing with her fingers) 'isn't quite the word, given what we've been through together.'

I nodded a little encouragement.

'Perhaps you'd welcome some background detail, it might help to explain a few things. I'm sure you're curious.' I nodded again, smiled. She took another sip of tea, presumably deciding how much to tell me. 'You see, once the charm had failed to work, Grahame quickly moved on to Plan B. He always had a Plan B, as I'd realised by then. He was manipulative, expected to get his own way, and the charm offensive was just one of the tools in his extensive armoury. Of course, you know that, you've seen what he's like.'

I nodded yet again.

'He threatened to tell the girls that he was their father. That didn't bother me so much, it was ancient history and with them both now grown up, it wouldn't cause much harm. I wasn't even sure it would have come as a complete surprise, they might well have had suspicions, although the subject has never been openly discussed. But you see.' She leaned forward. 'What worried me more was *how* he'd tell them, the lies he'd build around the simple truth. He would paint me as the evil one, the scarlet woman, the adulterer. Him as the meek and mild victim. That could well have split the family permanently, even though they were not great fans of Robbo, and I was not prepared to risk that. A mother and her daughters ...' She leant back again. 'Of course, you're too young ...'

I interrupted. 'I may not have children of my own, but I understand the bond that exists. I do get it, that you'd do everything you could to keep the love of your children.' I said the words. Not sure I believed them, at least not as deeply as others might.

'Anyway, soon after that Robbo died, as you know, and that added a further complication.' She put her cup back on its saucer and took the last biscuit.

I was still in the mood to be blunt: 'Here's what I wondered: did Grahame have anything to do with Stephen's death?'

I was expecting a flat denial: that isn't what I got. 'I think so,' she said. 'I know they spoke together a couple of times in the weeks before the suicide, on the phone, in private. Robbo wouldn't tell me what they talked about. They didn't have the sort of friendship where they'd have simply chatted, caught up on the latest news, or even recapped some nostalgic episode from their schooldays. When they were young, Grahame had treated Robbo with disdain, always running him down, calling him weak and pathetic. I've more than once heard versions of that. From both sides. So I know that was how things were between them and, as far as I was aware, nothing had happened in their adult lives to change that.

'So perhaps he did plant ideas in Robbo's head. Whether he did or not, once Robbo was gone, Grahame came on to me even more strongly, saying I should sell up and move in with him. Even hinted at marriage. And that's when he started talking about Di. He seemed to become quite obsessed with her. Robbo must have said something to him, made him remember the girl and so he decided he wanted to see her again. At one point I remember asking him if it was me he wanted or Di? He laughed at that. Definitely you, he said.'

'That's interesting. I had wondered what had caused him to start searching for Diane after all these years. Everything you say ... he sounds like a strange man to be close to.'

'It's hard to explain, what it was like, having him so insistent, badgering me. To tell the truth, I was scared, not just scared what he would say, but what he would do. What he would do to me.'

'Did he ever physically harm you?'

Caroline hesitated and that told me a lot. But she answered in the negative. 'No. Not really. Not in any important way. But I suppose I feared that he might. So I tried to appease him.'

'You pretended you were still attracted to him? You faked your feelings?'

She nodded. 'It wasn't difficult. I was used to it. I'd had years of faking. All my married life. My idea was that if I could see it through, keep him sweet for maybe a year or so, then I might find a way of breaking free of him without there being any repercussions. I never thought it would happen so quickly, or so ... well, completely. With him dying. It's hard to believe. Scott killing him gave me a perfect solution.' She let out a short, humourless laugh. 'What a heartless cow I am!'

I offered her more tea, but she said she really should be going. She hadn't meant to stay so long.

'But there's one more thing I should say, and this is the most important. Thank you. I know it's Scott I should really thank, but you played a part, a big part. You came to Grahame to find the truth about your grandmother, and that's why ... what happened, happened. So thank you.

Really, honestly. Now I can finally move on to the rest of my life, as a merry widow! It's as though the shackles have come off. I cannot wait to begin my life free of that man.'

# -95-

It's six months now since Caroline's visit and I've just found Diane's letter.

A lot has happened in the past half-year. After Christmas, I sold the house in town, the Jackson's old house, and bought a cottage in Scotland, in the borders. I felt it was time for a change of scenery and the DeFreitas affair made my mind up for me. It worried me that Caroline and Scott both knew my address and though I couldn't imagine either of them posing a threat, I didn't know who they might talk to. I'd learned my lesson from the business with Danny and Joe. So I thought it would be a good idea to put plenty of miles between myself and any connection with Brighton. It was time for a fresh start. In any case, there was no-one in my old neighbourhood that would miss me for long, if at all. I think they call it 'putting down roots': that was something I hadn't done. There was no-one I felt compelled to give a forwarding address to. I also sold my old *Ford Focus*, another dimension to my new beginning. I bought a *Suzuki Vitara*. Only two years old, but definitely 'as new'. When I moved in, there was a stack of snow on the ground and I realised that getting around in this part of the country could require a more robust vehicle.

I've not been here long, but I'm beginning to think village life will suit me. The locals are friendly enough, but only as in 'passing-the-time-of-day', no-one seems anxious to get to know me, or to burrow into my past. I'm content with that.

I've been true to my pledge to expand my horizons. I entered a spring marathon, so the last couple of months has seen a big increase in my weekly mileage with the accompanying warm glow/ache that comes from weary limbs and black toenails. All the routes round here involve stiff hills, so that makes for tough running, but in the end it's a good thing: should make running on the flat a breeze. I've brought the piano up with me, and begun to work my way through some simple pieces. It's so much more enjoyable now I'm not playing in the shadow of Mrs Jackson's critical eyes and ears. Not sure about the quality of my performance, but no neighbours have complained as yet, so that's all good.

I've thought a lot about Caroline and what she told me. The police never did contact me, so she must have been right about Scott keeping me out of his statement. He was charged with murder, but I don't believe his trial has come to court yet. Mostly, when I think of Caroline, I think about how much she suffered at the hands of DeFreitas. And the same with Scott: both of them were victims of that evil man, we're all well shot of him. I know he's not the only one, there are plenty more men like him around. And plenty of suffering women. I wish I could save them all.

When out on a long run, I need some idle thoughts to pass away the miles, and I've been playing a game with myself. Mulling over those three men, those three rapists who escaped for so long but have now got what they deserved, I ponder which of the three of them might actually have been my grandfather. Is there any way of telling? It's just a game, I'll never know for certain. But there are features that I can imagine might have travelled down the generations. Despite all three of them being such unpleasant characters, I can find attributes of each of them that I share, at least in part, attributes which I'm not entirely ashamed to share.

Richard Greene, for instance. Looking underneath his old-fashioned bigotry, he was something of a free spirit with his love of water-sports and his multi-faceted, busy life. I like to think of myself as similarly untied to convention, that I relish freedom. When out on a run, for instance, away from civilisation, with only the ground beneath my feet and the air in my lungs, it can feel as though I've shaken off all constraints, as if I'm floating, even flying: free as a bird. So maybe I could have inherited that desire for liberty from Richard. It's not such a bad thing.

Stephen was surely the least like me, with his geekiness and his dry, academic obsessions. And yet, I do recognise that there is a love of learning within me, lying dormant at the moment, but who knows, one day it might break out. I do believe, for instance, that there is more to literature than the simple joy of reading. I can imagine taking a degree in English Literature, learning to read more closely, to study, analyse and criticise. Also, my interest in music is developing, as is a desire to know more about the art world. Yes, it isn't beyond the realms of probability that I might develop into an intellectual, a woman of culture. Not that I'd ever again want anything to do with maths: I've had enough of that hideous subject to last a lifetime!

It's most difficult to find some attribute in DeFreitas's character that I wouldn't mind inheriting. Who would want that monster as a grandfather? Such a hateful individual. And yet, having had some responsibility in the deaths of three men, perhaps 'ruthlessness' is an adjective some might apply to me. Even 'evil'? I wouldn't own up to those adjectives myself, because I regard all my actions as justified, but some people consider killing to be wrong, whatever the circumstances.

It's only a game. I'll never know for sure whose genes I carry. It's just a bit of speculative fun.

But now I've found the letter, and such speculation has become entirely pointless.

# -96-

I wish I'd found the letter earlier, but I can understand why I didn't. I'd always assumed Diane's entries in her diary had stopped in August, at the time of the party, apart from the single 'PREGNANT' entry in October. I'd flipped through the later pages, but they were obviously empty. What I had never scrutinised was the back cover. Tucked into it was an envelope. It only came to light when I unpacked, so it must have got dislodged during the move.

The envelope wasn't sealed, and inside was an old-fashioned hand-written letter, with an address in the top right-hand corner, date underneath; it began with '*Dear Andy.*'

That name rang a bell, but the context didn't feel right. Surely he wasn't a friend of Diane? Why was she writing to him. I read on. The letter was written in a tidier version of what was unmistakably Diane's handwriting, the writing I'd got used to from studying her diary.

*Mrs Falkner, our English teacher, says you should always begin a story with a dramatic sentence. When she hands an essay back, there's always a red line through my first paragraph and she scrawls 'throat-clearing!' in the margin. Not sure if the same thing applies to letters, but here goes.*

*I'm pregnant!!!*

*That's a dramatic enough statement, isn't it?!!*

*Quite a shock, I'm sure, but don't panic!! I'm not going to insist you do the right thing, whatever that's supposed to mean. I'm not expecting us to get married or any of that nonsense. I won't even tell anyone that you're the father, because I wouldn't want to upset your plans, your place at Oxford and all that. So you won't have my dad coming after you with a shotgun!! I just thought you should know.*

*I know what you said afterwards.*

*I promise I won't try and talk to you, or anything, I won't come between you and her. It will be difficult. I'll try not to let you see me cry!!*

*Oh, ignore me. Being a silly-dilly as usual! None of that's important now. I just wanted to say. If some time in the future you wanted to*

And that's where the letter finished, in mid-sentence. I read it again, more slowly, and then a third time. It was clear enough what it was saying, but hard to interpret the implications.

Obviously, the letter hadn't actually been sent. But was this a draft? Had Diane rewritten it, finished it off properly, and then sent it to Andy? Now I had the context, I realised who it was: this must have been the Andy who hosted the World Cup party. Had she kept her promise and steered clear of him afterwards? Lots of unanswered questions, unanswerable questions. Perhaps the letter was simply a fake, some pretend game Diane was playing, for her own amusement, or to share with friends. No, that didn't seem likely. If that were the case, she'd have thrown the letter away after they'd laughed about it, not saved it in her diary, like some precious memento.

So I turned back to Diane's diary, looking for an explanation, seeking relevant evidence. Now that I saw her words through the lens of the letter to Andy, I could find meanings I hadn't seen before. There were some ambiguous phrases in her description of the party that I could now interpret as references to Andy. Diane used initials whenever she named people, and I could tell that A seemed to have a girlfriend called 'J': there were some negative, quite bitchy, comments about 'J'. Another sentence struck me: 'Revolver is a fab LP and I love Paul.' An ordinary diary entry, except that the four letter 'a's were written in capital with a double circle around them: that sentence was really about her feelings for Andy.

I tried to imagine Diane at the party, mooning over Andy, maybe thinking he could be the love of her life. I couldn't construct a narrative that would lead from that image to one in which she allowed herself to be enticed onto the beach in the early hours by three sex-hungry lads. There had never been any suggestion, either from what Diane told Mum, as reported to me by Mum's letter, or from anything else, that she'd gone to the beach other than willingly. It wasn't until they got under the pier that the aggression – the 'forcing' – had taken place.

No, I could not believe it, it was too much of a leap, a total mismatch between character and action. I was as certain as I could be: Diane would not have gone down to the beach, in the middle of the night, with Richard, Stephen and Grahame. Not with all of them together, not with any of them individually. The only plausible explanation was that Diane had lied in her diary when she wrote those three names. Of course, there was nothing in her diary entry that actually accused those three boys of a crime, the assertion that they were rapists came from Mum's letter, her relaying of a conversation with Diane that occurred much later. In the diary, they were merely presented as a list, surrounded by stars, although that in itself was incongruous when no other name was spelled out in full in the whole diary.

Here's what I decided: when she wrote in her diary, Diane must have already identified these three lads as candidates for accusation. The actual accusation came years later, when (I'm guessing) her daughter, my mother, pressed her for information about who her father was. So Diane had pointed the finger at those three in order to protect the reputation of the real father of her child, this Andy.

Andy. My grandfather.

# -97-

This is the obvious conclusion to come to, now I have Diane's letter to Andy; it's the only explanation that makes sense. Diane lied about what happened that night, and I have been wrong about those men all along, they did not rape her. But that still leaves a problem. This version doesn't fit with what Stephen and Grahame told me. Stephen claimed he had sex with Diane, on Brighton beach, that night. Grahame went as far as admitting that he raped her, also on the beach, that same night.

If those statements were not true, what possible reason did those men have to lie to me?

## -98-

No, they didn't lie.

The penny drops by accident. Not so much the penny as the final piece of a jigsaw, the final archway in the maze which leads to escape into the light. Vera Stanhope never needs any chance element to enable her to solve a mystery because she has an author and script-writers to look after her. I don't, so I just had to get lucky.

I no longer pore over the contents of old Mum's suitcase on a regular basis, not like I had back in the day. But I still turn to it from time to time, driven by nostalgia, not for the items themselves, or the moments and events they reflect, but more for the memories of the times when I scrutinised those objects, the occasions when I wondered about them, discovering aspects of them for the first time. I've never paid much attention to the photographs. There is one of me as a baby, looking like a baby. They're all the same, aren't they, baby photos, bland and uninteresting. There's one of Mum and Joe's wedding, the two of them not looking particularly happy, but with the required fixed smiles. Then there is one of a young girl wearing old-fashioned clothes. The name on the back is Diane: it is a picture of my grandmother when she was a young girl. I must have seen the photo before, but never took much notice of it.

If I'd given the matter more thorough analysis (in the way Vera would have done) I'd have come to the solution much earlier. I have always had an impression in my mind of what Diane was like, based in part, I suppose, on that photo, vaguely remembered. I picture her as a pretty girl, full of energy, with a dazzling smile. But beyond that, the image has always been blurred, distorted, ill-defined. But now I study that photo, and for the first time register what Diane really looked like.

Stephen spoke about her blue eyes and her blonde hair.

Grahame talked of her baby-blue eyes and her long blonde hair.

Now in front of me is the photo from Mum's suitcase and I see Diane, Diane when she was a young teen, smiling back at me. She has short dark hair and dark eyes. This girl, this Diane, my grandmother, is not the girl that Stephen and Grahame talked about. And therefore, she is not the girl either of them had sex with on that Brighton beach in 1966.

So, finally I have it: there was another Diane. There must have been two girls called Diane in that friendship circle – not surprising, as it was a popular name - there were two Diane's at the party. One was the 'evil' girl Grahame told me about, the bully, the drug-dealer, the one the boys seemed to call 'Di'. It was she who had sex with Stephen and was raped by Grahame. The other one was chasing after Andy; she was my grandmother and that night she went nowhere near the beach, nowhere near those three men.

Once again, I look back at Diane's diary with a different perspective and eventually I find it. There are references, not many, but a few, to a girl called 'D'. And 'D's gang' gets a mention. It's clear that this 'D' is not a close friend of Diane, in fact Diane seems to go out of her way to avoid her. One telling reference, written in Diane's usual enigmatic style. *D is for despicable. D is for disgusting. D is for depraved.*

And in the party entry, just one reference. *'D's gang have arrived. What a Drag!*

# -99-

Twenty-two miles. My longest run yet, and I finished feeling good, tired but not struggling, not exhausted. It's given me a healthy charge of confidence for the marathon next month. It helped that it was a fine day, not cold but also not too warm, and most importantly, no wind. I remember running into the wind on Hunstanton prom: what a nightmare that was!

My new house has a back garden with a well-tended lawn, mature shrubs and a number of small trees. That sounds like I'm reading from an estate agent's brochure, which I suppose I sort of am: the house still feels like a house-for-sale rather than the house I've bought. It will take me a while to settle in, and accept that this house is really mine. Perhaps I'll become a more active gardener here, I'm sure I could cope with this garden. I could even do something creative with it, develop some landscaping skills.

The third start to my life. Or is it the fourth? I've lost count.

The lawn slopes down to a small stream. The previous owner told me that there are fish in it, although she may have made that up to entice me. Not that I needed much enticing: I fell in love with this cottage at first viewing. I haven't seen any fish yet, but I'll keep looking. There's a wooden bench near the stream, under a willow tree. From there you can hear the rippling of the water and watch the sunlight flicker across the surface. It's a delightful spot.

Freshly showered, I take my copy of *The Wind in the Willows* down to the bench. I don't read it often, but sometimes, between more serious books, I like to dip back into it.

I admire good writing. I think back to Richard Wright's short career as an author. I wonder if his publisher went ahead with releasing the novel, isn't it a fact that posthumously published books generally sell well? I should look it up. I do believe I could write a novel. Perhaps I could rewrite *The Wind in the Willows*. They say you should always write what you know, so I would need to populate it with characters from my life. I'd be Moley, the main protagonist. DeFreitas would have to be Toad, because he's the poshest person I've ever met, plus he had criminal tendencies (and how!), so he's a shoo-in. Richard would be Ratty because of his love of water sports, and that would leave Stephen as the wise and elusive Badger. The plot would need reworking somewhat. For one thing, a happy ending would be hard to manage with three of the main characters dying.

The sun's rays are gaining power now we're approaching the middle of the day.

I lean back. I feel content.

Yes, I am content.

I put the book down and take a walk around the garden, keeping the legs moving in order to shift that lactic acid. I wonder about the various plants. I need James/Scott to tell me their names and some useful facts about them. Perhaps I could study botany, become a botanist. Probably that's not as boring as you'd imagine.

Once this marathon's done, I must plan properly for the future. So many options, so many paths I might follow. I still haven't given up hope of being a second Vera, a real-life version, solving crimes and bringing criminals to justice.

I still think of my grandmother a lot, still feel sorry for her. Maybe she didn't suffer the fate I thought she had, that gang rape, when she was a teenager, but she still had a hard time. A single mum, shunned by her family, determined to continue to protect the identity of the father of her child. Bringing up that child on her own, the best she could. Despite the direction her life took, I'm proud of her, proud that I carry her genes.

I also think about that party and wonder what really happened there. I have many versions, told to me by people who probably had unreliable memories alongside their ulterior motives. There are things that I still cannot make sense of, but have no means by which to resolve those discrepancies. Maybe my grandmother knew about those men raping the other Di, and that is why she listed them in her diary. Who knows? Mostly the events of that night are a mystery and will forever remain a mystery.

I sometimes wonder if I should try and track down that Andy. He may be interested to know that he has a grand-daughter, although I believe men don't always welcome surprise news of previously unknown progeny. But I'd like to know what he's like and whether I've inherited any characteristics from him. I could add his version of the party to all the others.

Of one thing I'm fairly certain, and that's that he'd be an improvement on those other three, any one of whom I thought might have been my grandfather; although in the end – thank God - none of them was.

Three men the world is better off without.

Three men who, each in their turn, were the focus of my life for near enough a year.

Three men who caused me a lot of pain.

And yet, I can't help but smile. They might have brought me pain but they also brought me pleasure.

I enjoyed the chase. I enjoyed tracking them down. I enjoyed planning my revenge. I relished their deaths.

Yes, I may feel content now. But when I was dealing with those vermin, that's when I felt really alive.

Thank you for reading 'Three Cold Dishes'.

I hope you enjoyed it.

If you have any comments about the story, whether positive or negative, I'd be pleased to read them.

Email me: bill140347@btinternet.com

Printed in Great Britain
by Amazon